Mrs. Odboddy: And Then There Was a Tiger

A WWII tale of conflict and carnivals, turmoil and tigers.

An Elaine Faber Mystery

Elk Grove Publications

Mrs. Odboddy
And Then There Was a Tiger

Published by Elk Grove Publications

© 2018 by Elaine Faber

ISBN-13:978-1-940781-21-1

This novel is a work of fiction. Though based on actual WWII historical events, involvement of the novel's characters are purely fiction and the product of the author's imagination. Any resemblance to actual events, locales, organizations,or persons, living or dead, is entirely coincidental and beyond the intent of either the author or publisher.

Cover photos: *Can we talk?* © Everett Collection, Shutterstock.com ID:227271556; *Wesołe miasteczko retro* © Chorazin, Fotolia.com ID: 37889778

Scene Break Circus Tiger © anttohoho, iStock.com ID: 470710808

Cover layout and book formatting: JulieDeWilliams@gmail.com
Printed in the United States of America

Acknowledgments

This book is dedicated to the following very special people, without whom, this story would never be told.

Thank you, beta readers: Lois Parrish, Ruth Powers, and Londa Faber for your corrections, punctuation suggestions, and plot line tweaks. Wish we could catch all the boo-boos. Any mistakes are entirely my own.

Thank you, writer's critique group, for helping me write a more compelling story: Sharon Darrow, Margaret Duarte, Judy Pierce, Judy Vaughan, and Gini Grossenbacher. Your insight and enthusiasm have made this an easy journey.

Thank you, Julie Williams, for your invaluable help formatting, creating the cover design, and encouraging words when I call and whine.

Thank you, Leland Faber, my long-suffering husband, for advice with technical terms and descriptions related to WWII guns and cars. Also, for your willingness to stop and listen, whenever I need to sort out the wording of a particular phrase or paragraph.

Thanks to Mrs. Yeager, whoever she may be, for her Rhubarb-Apple pie recipe found on an old recipe card on the internet.

Thank you, Michael Faber at Elk Grove Publications for providing assistance with all my publishing needs and for putting your law practice on hold whenever my publishing needs be met. Thanks also for legal advice regarding issues that arise in my storyline.

Thank you, devoted readers, small in number, but large in loyalty, without whom I'd have given up writing long ago. Your kind words of encouragement keep me working on the next story. I hope you all enjoy another Agnes adventure. This one is for all of you.

Glossary of Characters in Order of Their Appearance

Agnes Agatha Odboddy: Elderly, eccentric woman, who fights WWII from the home front.

Ling-Ling Odboddy: Agnes's cross-eyed Siamese cat.

Katherine Odboddy: Agnes's granddaughter, who works at Curls to Dye For, and moonlights at the local mortuary, doing hair and make-up for the 'dearly departed.'

Chief Waddlemucker: Newbury's Chief of Police. Despite appearances, he really likes Agnes.

Mildred Higgenbottom: Agnes's best friend. They served together during WWI, doing covert activities.

Maddie: Katherine's young ward, recently added to the Odboddy household.

George Wilkey: A teenage boy denied military service due to Agnes's advice to the Military Admissions Council.

Mrs. Wilkey: Judgmental grocery store owner whose nose tends to defy gravity.

Godfrey Baumgarten: Agnes's boyfriend, who often pops in and out of her life.

Dr. Don Dew-Right: Katherine's fiancé, who loves Katherine, but wants nothing to do with little Maddie.

Sally and Joe Hawkins: Waitress and owner of the local railroad diner.

Vincent Buckwalder: A rival for Katherine's affections; he drives Dr. Don to distraction.

Homer Blenkinsop: Newbury Dailey Gazette's editor, an upstanding Newbury citizen.

Edith Braithwaite: Member of The First Church of the Evening Star and Everlasting Light.

Jackson Jackson: "A friend to the Newbury widda' ladies that needs his help."

Mrs. Lickleiter: Pastor Lickleiter's wife, who dutifully attends every church activity.

Shere Khan: A tiger who, despite his fierce appearance, is as meek as a kitten.

Mr. Higgenbottom: Mildred's brother provides Agnes's chickens a home on his farm.

Mrs. Higgenbottom: The farmer's wife with an exceptional pitching arm.

Juanita Blenkinsop: Manager of Gently Used Clothing and Shoes a charitable organization.

Mrs. Odboddy –
And Then There Was a Tiger

A true account as it occurred in the fall of 1943. Only the facts were made up...

Chapter One

"That'll give them something to pray about." Agnes

Whard in tarnation is all that mess on the front porch?" A tattered shoebox leaned against the newel post beside the front step. Clumps of string lay amidst more shredded paper on the porch.

Agnes switched off the motor of her 1930 Model A Ford. She pulled on the hand brake, jammed her silver chopsticks firmly into the bun on the back of her hennaed hair, and stepped out of the car.

Shreds of brown paper skittered across the lawn. Her frown deepened as she picked up pieces of cardboard and string.

Agnes Agatha Odboddy, in big bold letters, was scribbled across the middle of the brown wrapping paper. She flipped the shoebox over. An offensive odor wafted up from inside. "What the devil…"

Agnes glanced toward the porch and noticed the front door standing ajar. "Jumping Jehoshaphat." Her granddaughter, Katherine, must have forgotten to lock it when she took their ward, Maddie, to school this morning.

She pushed open the front door, and peeked inside. "Good gravy!" Pillows–askew on the sofa. Magazines–scattered across the rug. Remnants of her grandmother's vase speckled the hearth.

"Oh, my stars. We've been burgled." Agnes rushed through the living room and into the kitchen. Breakfast coffee puddled in the middle of the table. A cup lay shattered in the sink. A kitchen chair lay sideways on the linoleum floor.

A scuffling sound came from the back bedroom. Agnes spun around. Was someone in there, ransacking her jewelry box? Should she run back out the front door? Agnes Odboddy, self-appointed scourge of the underworld–run for cover? *Not on your tintype!*

She grabbed a rolling pin from the drawer, the weapon of choice for a woman of a certain age, planning to sneak up on the thief, crack his head, and bring him to his cowardly knees.

Before she had taken three steps, a rat barreled out of her bedroom and down the hall. Agnes jumped back. "Yikes!"

The spindly-tailed rodent raced into the living room and scrambled up the flowered drapes to the top of the curtain rod. Ling-Ling, a feline nemesis in camo-gray, followed.

Merciful Heavens. A measly rodent? Agnes sent the rolling pin flying. It hit the wall, barely missing the front window, and clattered to the floor.

Rrowww! Ling-Ling clawed her way up the curtain, knocking a table lamp to the floor. *Thud!* The fringed shade spun off the lamp and rolled toward the front door. Down came the rod with a crash, as the rat dropped to the floor and raced out the front door with Ling-Ling, the Siamese avenger three leaps behind.

Agnes shook her finger. "Ling-Ling. Bad girl. No! No..." What was she saying? "Go get her, girl."

Agnes stepped onto the porch and put her hand to her eyes in time to see the pair racing up the street, headed toward The First Church of the Evening Star and Everlasting Light. She checked her watch. *Yep, folks should just about be arriving for the afternoon prayer meeting. That'll give them something to pray about.* She stepped back into the house to assess the damage.

Never in her seventy-plus years had she seen such destruction. What unknown scoundrel hated her enough to leave a rat-filled shoebox addressed to her on the porch?

Agnes pondered the situation. Ling-Ling must come upon the shoebox and smelled the rodent through the wrapping paper. She could almost see her determined Siamese killing-machine scratching and kicking the box until she had shredded a hole big enough for the rat to escape, dash through the open door, and into the house. The image sent shivers up Agnes's spine.

Ling-Ling would have followed with murder in her crossed blue eyes and the chase ensued. Not even an air raid from the Flying Tigers could have left her living room and kitchen in such a mess. No telling how the rest of the house would have suffered if Agnes hadn't returned just at that moment.

What if Ling-Ling hadn't found the box and taken matters into her own paws? Why, she might have cut the string herself, opened the box, and the rat would have leaped into her face. Maybe that was exactly the sender's intention.

Katherine pulled into the driveway, shoved the gear shift into neutral and pulled on the hand brake. As she reached for the key to turn off her dark blue Buick, a hairpin tumbled into her lap. She retrieved the pin, bit it open and refastened her hair behind her ear. Checking her image in the rear view mirror, she patted her victory roll coiffure back into place. She thanked the father she never knew, a victim of WWI when she was a baby, for her thick auburn hair and the freckles on her nose so admired by her fiancé, Dr. Don Dew-Right.

Katherine leaned forward to peer through the windshield at the shreds of paper blowing through the leaves on the lawn. Had Maddie been cutting paper dolls on the front porch again? It might explain the shreds of paper blowing about the yard. Getting her to clean up her own messes was a daily challenge.

Perhaps the decision to bring a nine-year-old child home from Washington D.C. several months ago wasn't as well thought out as it should have been, considering her earlier life. Although the child added youthful enthusiasm to the household, she also added a fair amount of frustration and concern. But, what nine-year-old didn't need guidance and training? Hopefully, foster-mothering such a precocious child would be possible. That is, if she even got the chance.

Katherine fingered her engagement ring. Whether her fiancé, Dr. Don, would get on board with the plan to adopt Maddie was another story. Grandmother had rightfully warned that it was unwise to bring the child into their life without discussing the matter with Dr. Don, and sure as kittens in springtime, he had resisted the plan. Now, with the wedding date fast approaching, Maddie's future was at the center of contentious conversations, casting a pall on their relationship.

Katherine sighed and gathered her belongings. She stepped through the front door and stopped short at the sight of Grandmother, crouched on her hands and knees, scrubbing the carpet. "What are you doing?" Katherine laid her sweater and lunch box on the sofa, knelt, and took the scrub brush from Grandma's hand. "Here. Let me do that. What happened? Did Maddie spill her milk, again?" She glanced around the room. "Why isn't she–?"

Grandma sat back on her knees. "Nothing like that. She just got home a few minutes ago. I told her to play in her room." Grandma clambered off the floor, perspiration dotting her forehead. She rubbed her back, and flopped into the sofa chair beside the fireplace. "Oh, my aching back. I've already scrubbed the kitchen floor, the table and the counters with Lysol." She gestured toward the bathroom. "My bedspread is soaking in the bathtub as we speak."

"Whatever for?" Katherine gave the rug a few more swipes and stood. She set the bucket and cleaning rag on the coffee table. "That should do it. So, if it's not Maddie's milk, what am I cleaning up here?"

"Rat pee."

Katherine's hand flew to her cheek. "Rat… What? I don't understand."

"Wait here." Grandma stood and went to the kitchen. She returned with the tattered shoebox. "This was on the porch when I got home. Ling-Ling was in the house, engaged in WWIII with a huge rat. Everything was topsy-turvy." She pushed a strand of hair off her forehead and pointed at the damp spot on the carpet. "I suspect that's rat pee."

"Ling-Ling carried it inside?" Katherine raised an eyebrow. "How did she get in the house? We don't have a cat door."

"That's the odd part. The front door was ajar when I came home and the darlings were racing the Indy-500 through the back of the house and–"

"I'm sure I locked it this morning when I left. How did–?"

"I suspect the lock was picked and someone broke in. I don't know, maybe they were looking for something to steal. As for the rat… smell this." She shoved the shoebox toward Katherine.

Katherine leaned forward, wrinkled her nose and pushed it away. "*Ewww!* Grandma! It smells like *rat*. Why would someone leave a rat on the porch and then break into the house?"

"That's a good question. When you come up with a good answer, let me know."

Katherine's brow furrowed. "*Humm.* If they went to all the trouble to break in anyway, why not leave the rat inside the house? None of this makes sense. Is anything missing?"

"Hard to say. Nothing obvious that I can see. I'll call Chief Waddlemucker and report the break-in. What does it mean when someone gift-wraps a rat and leaves it on your porch?"

Katherine stared around the room, observing the window drape hanging askew. "It sounds like the workings of an irrational mind. Although, it is nearly Halloween. Do you suppose a group of the high school boys were playing a horrible prank?"

"Humph!" Grandmother turned back to the kitchen. "If the rat on the front porch was a high school prank, then why pick the lock on the front door?" She tossed her head. "Why don't you keep Maddie busy while I call the chief? She doesn't need to hear about this. Who knows what this nutcase might do next? We'll need to keep a close eye on her for a while."

"I'll drive her to school if you'll pick her up. She shouldn't walk home alone anymore."

"I'll try." Grandmother's forehead wrinkled. "Some days I'm too busy at three o'clock." She opened the kitchen door and tossed the shredded box onto the back porch.

Katherine found Maddie sitting on her bed, fitting two pieces of broken ceramic together. "Hi, sweetheart. How was your day?" She ran her hand through Maddie's curls and kissed her cheek.

"I got *a hundred* on my spelling test. But, when I got home, my little tiger was on the floor." She held up the pieces. "See? It's broken. What happened?"

"Oh, I'm sorry. I'll bet Ling-Ling jumped up on your dresser and accidentally knocked it off. Let's take it to the garage and glue it back together." *I'm surprised there's not more broken than the tiger.* A shiver ran down Katherine's neck. Was there a fall chill in the air, or was the broken tiger a forewarning of things to come?

Chapter Two

Having memorized the telephone number at the police station, Agnes let her fingers do the walking around the telephone dial. She tapped her foot as the phone rang. Surely, this time, Chief Wadddlemucker would get off his high horse and pay attention to her concerns.

After a brief exchange with the dispatch operator, she was connected to the chief's office.

"Mrs. Odboddy? What's on your mind this fine day? The operator said you're calling about a hatbox?"

"That's not what I said at all. I said a rat in a box. A shoebox! Some thug left a rodent on my front porch and then broke into the house. If Ling-Ling hadn't made a direct assault on the shoebox, the rat would have jumped right into my face." She ran her hand across her face as the image of such a thing popped into her mind.

"My dear Mrs. Odboddy... Well now, are we sure we aren't creating another imaginary conspiracy? Really? A rat in a shoebox? Balderdash! Perhaps it was a toy rat, one of your little girl's toys or—"

"Toy rat, my Aunt Fannie. If you think, at my age I can't tell a toy rat from the one my cat chased around this house, leaving it in shambles, I might add, just come over and smell the box yourself. *Humph!*" Every time she reported a legitimate conspiracy or a Nazi spy to the chief, he snorted and as much as called her a lunatic. Had he already forgotten her solving the ration book fiasco last summer when

Godfrey came to town?

A pain shot through her chest at the thought of Godfrey. She hadn't heard from him for months. She hoped he was well, wherever the old scoundrel was… *When an old love unexpectedly re-enters your life after twenty-five years and then leaves again almost as quickly…* She pushed away unwelcome thoughts of Godfrey. "Hello?"

The chief hadn't spoken for a while. Had he hung up on her? Not that it mattered much whether the chief believed her or not. She was used to that. Being a self-appointed scourge of the underworld often gave the townsfolk fodder for derision and gossip. Most of them wavered between thinking she was a crackpot, versus just a bit eccentric. At present, the majority leaned toward eccentric, but that could change at any moment. Reporting a rat in a shoebox wrapped in brown paper, tied up with a bow, and left on the front porch could easily tip the scales.

Her wobbly reputation had improved a bit after she and Katherine's recent Washington, D.C. trip and their hasty decision to bring Maddie back to Newbury. "Hello? Hello? Are you still there, Chief?"

"I'm here. I was just thinking. So, the house was broken into? Is anything missing? What do you suppose they were looking for?" Did his raspy voice have an edge of irritation, or was he still smoking those ten-cent cigars?

"Couldn't say." Agnes's mouth tightened. "I haven't noticed anything obvious. Katherine thought I should call and let you know, but it appears you're not interested–"

"Wait. I didn't say I wasn't interested. There have been a number of small businesses reporting *break-ins* recently. I was just wondering if it might be the same person, but I can't see a connection between breaking into businesses and breaking into a private residence. Leaving a rat on the porch is not their *modus operandi*. I'll send an officer over to take a report, but about the rat …" He sighed. "Sounds more like high school hijinks to me. I'll talk to the Newbury High School coach and see if he's heard any scuttlebutt from the football team. I wouldn't worry about it if I were you."

"You're probably right. It could be kids up to pre-Halloween tricks. Don't bother sending an officer. If I find anything missing, I'll let you know." *I'll just have to investigate myself. He's obviously too busy to give a rat's aaa–*

"Take care, Mrs. O. I'll probably see you at the carnival this weekend."

"We'll be there. Mildred and I are hosting a pumpkin carving booth for the Ladies' Society at The First Church of the Evening Star and Everlasting Light. Katherine is hosting a dessert booth."

"How is it that the church ladies and the carnival have joined forces?"

"The carnival consortium wanted to use the church parking lot to set up their rides. The deacons agreed, providing we could add a few of our own booths as fundraisers to benefit next year's Bible School. And, of course, there will be a war-bond booth. How could they say no?"

Chief Waddlemucker chuckled. "Makes sense. Then I'll see you later. Good-bye for now."

Agnes peeked out the kitchen window just as the gathering clouds overhead gave way to rain. A bolt of lightning flashed. "We're in for it now. It's coming down cats and frogs."

The rain progressed to a steady downpour by late that night. The living room curtain rod was finally re-hung and the last bit of broken glass in the kitchen swept away. Maddie and Ling-Ling were in bed and Katherine was lollygagging in a bubble bath.

Agnes glanced up as thunder clapped. Rain streaked down the kitchen window and puddled on the sill.

Ring! Ring!

Agnes pulled the receiver from the kitchen wall phone. "Agnes, here."

"Agnes?" The line crackled. The caller's voice sounded hollow and far away. "Agnes? Can you hear me? It's Mildred."

"Mildred? You sound funny. What's wrong?"

The line crackled again. "…need your help. Car… Wilkey's…. Can't…start..." The connection went dead.

"Hello? Hello? Mildred?" *Oh my stars and little fishes!* What was her dear friend, Mildred, doing out at Wilkey's Market on a night like this? Did she say her car wouldn't start?

Agnes rapped on the bathroom door. "Katherine. Mildred's having car trouble. I have to go to Wilkey's Market and pick her up."

"Grandma? You can't go out now. It's storming out there." A splash from the tub accompanied Katherine's logic. "Can't she call her brother or the police department?" More splashes. "They could send an officer to check on her." *Thud.* She must have dropped the soap. "I don't think you should…" *Splash.*

"No time. I'll just run down to the market and give her a ride home. I won't be long. We can deal with her car tomorrow." Wouldn't you know, on a night like this, she'd have to weather the storm to help a friend in need. This day had just gone from bad, to worse, to a real stinker.

Now, what coat should she wear? Not her new blue serge coat. She hurried to the back porch. An echo of mothballs wafted up from her deceased husband's old raincoat hanging on the peg on the back porch. Better this ratty old thing should get soaked than her new coat. She donned the coat and tied the belt under her ample bosom. *I really should donate this old thing to one of the agencies collecting for the refugees.* She grabbed her purse and an umbrella and hurried to her car.

Agnes drove the twelve blocks across town through the pelting rain and turned into the Wilkey's Market parking lot. Empty. Now, where was Mildred's car? The rain sluiced down in sheets across the concrete and swished across the windshield.

A man on a bicycle trundled by, steering with one hand and holding an open umbrella over his head with the other. His overcoat pulled up to his neck, and his hat pulled low on his forehead, obscured his face. Agnes chuckled. His appearance was almost comical, peddling through the rain like that with an umbrella.

Where was Mildred? Had she parked behind the store for some reason? Agnes drove around the back of the store. Come to think of it, where had she called from? Inside the store? She did say Wilkey's Market... *Or did I misunderstand?*

Agnes jerked on the brake. Rain slashed against the dark window in the back of the store. Soaked, cardboard boxes lay limp, stacked beside the back door. The windshield wipers whooshed back and forth, barely clearing the sheets of rain streaking across her car window. Rain seeped through the crack at the top of the car door and splattered on her hand. A chill wiggled its way up her spine and onto her neck. Where was Mildred? Uneasiness swept through her chest. It *was* Mildred, wasn't it?

How could she possibly be inside the market if her car wasn't here? Agnes released the brake and eased the car as close as possible to the back entrance. She sprang up her umbrella, dashed to the back door and grasped the black ceramic door knob. Locked! She rubbed a circular spot on the window and peered into the dark interior. Dark as the inside of a cow. She knocked on the door. If there was anyone inside, they were sitting in the dark with the door locked. That certainly didn't make any sense.

Agnes hurried back to her car, shook the umbrella and ducked inside. She had either misunderstood Mildred's message or someone had helped her get the car started. *Maybe she didn't realize I was coming down and went on home.*

Agnes drove slowly across town to Mildred's street. How odd. Her house was dark. If she got a ride home, how could she have gone to bed already? Dismay tickled the back of her neck as she pulled into Mildred's driveway. *Something's wrong here.* She hurried up the sidewalk, huddled on the front porch and pounded on the door. Rain dripped from her umbrella onto her sensible orthopedic brown shoes.

A light flicked on inside.

Footsteps shuffled across the hardwood floors.

The front door lock clicked. The door swung open and Mildred stood in the light, clutching her bathrobe to her neck. She shaded her eyes. "Agnes? What's wrong?" She grabbed Agnes's arm. "Come in out of the rain. You'll catch your death out there."

"What do you mean, *what's wrong?* You called me. Said you were in trouble. I came as soon as I could but…" Agnes shook her umbrella out on the porch and shoved it into Mildred's umbrella stand. She closed the front door. "What's going on?"

"I don't understand. I…I didn't call you, Agnes. I've been in bed for half an hour."

Agnes put her hand to her chilled cheek. "Then, who called?" Why had they pretended to be Mildred? Was it a ruse to get her out of the house and leave Katherine and Maddie alone? "I need to use your phone!" She rushed into Mildred's kitchen, grabbed the phone and dialed her house. "Pick up, Katherine. Pick up." *Please don't still be in the bathtub.*

"Hello? Odboddy residence."

"Katherine. It's me. Are you all right? Run and lock the front and back doors. Make sure Maddie's okay."

"Whatever are you talking about? Where are you?"

"The phone call! It wasn't Mildred. It was a ruse. Someone wanted me out of the house. I'm worried about you girls."

"Oh, Grandma, what's happening?"

"I don't know, dear, but I'll be home as soon as I can. Now, run lock the doors."

Mildred turned her pale face toward Agnes. "I'm so sorry, Agnes. Why would someone use my name and say–"

"I better go, Mildred." Agnes grabbed her umbrella. Her mouth turned up into a wobbly smile. "Someone's got it in for me this week. First, the rat on the front porch, and now this."

"A…a rat?"

Agnes closed her eyes and shook her head. "Don't have time to explain. I'll call you in the morning and tell you all about it. It was probably just another prank. Don't worry."

"If this was a prank, they've got a pretty disturbed sense of humor." Mildred gripped Agnes's arm. "Hurry on home, now. Call me first thing tomorrow."

"I will. I'm glad you're okay. See you soon." Agnes dashed through the rain to her car and rocketed home at the breakneck speed of thirty miles per hour.

Chapter Three

Agnes woke early Wednesday morning. Though the girls had come to no harm last night, the frightening possibilities had rocked her fitful dreams, and a poor night's sleep left her with a headache. At least she'd have a quiet house today. Since it was a school holiday, Katherine had taken the day off from work at the Curls to Dye For Beauty Salon to take Maddie to the Crest Theater to see the latest Disney movie, *Bambi*.

After breakfast and seeing the girls off, she called Mildred and poured out her frustration and fears. By the time her tea was cold, she'd developed a cramp in her hand from holding the receiver to her ear. "Goodness gracious, Mildred. Look at the time. I should let you get about your day. Thanks for being such a good listener."

"If there's anything I can do, just say the word." Mildred's reassuring tone warmed Agnes's heart. She hung the receiver back onto the black wall phone, and glanced around the kitchen. Everything was clean and back in its place. The excitement of last night was over, and the girls were safe, the floor scrubbed, and the bedspread back on her bed. Agnes tucked a letter from her friend, Lilly, into her pocket.

The letter reminded her of the scarf she was knitting for her friend, Jackson Jackson, who ran the elevator at the court house. She dug in the closet and found her knitting bag where it lay ignored for months behind a pair of rubber galoshes. She settled on the sofa, pulled the knitted piece from the bag, with needles still attached, and spread it across her lap. *I don't recall it taking on such a peculiar shape.*

Ling-Ling jumped up alongside, her tail curled around her nose, the picture of innocence after yesterday's wild adventure. She now wore the *red scratch of courage* on her nose, a memento of her rat-battle. Thank goodness, that was the worst of it.

Agnes chuckled, remembering the previous evening when Ling-Ling slunk into the house. "Hold her still, Katherine," Agnes had advised as she applied Methylate on the bridge of Ling-Ling's nose. "No telling where that rat has been."

"Probably just around and about its customary rat affairs." Katherine had grinned.

Agnes picked up the knitting needles. Now, what was it that Lilly used to say while teaching knitting for the troops at the Red Cross class? 'Over and around, knit one, purl two… Knit one, purl two…'

Lilly's letter crinkled in her pocket. *Lilly!* Agnes laid the knitted conglomeration on the coffee table, leaned back and closed her eyes. *Why am I doing this? I hate to knit.*

Almost two years had passed since Pearl Harbor, and over a year since President Roosevelt sent the Japanese-American citizens to internment camps. "Please take care of my pets," Lilly had pleaded, before she was hauled away like a common criminal.

Agnes stroked Ling-Ling's soft dark ears. "That's how you came to live with me." She hoped it wouldn't be long before Lilly returned to Newbury and to the flower nursery founded by her grandfather thirty years before. Whether Ling-Ling would return to Lilly's home was unlikely.

President Roosevelt's decision had shaken Agnes's devotion and unwavering loyalty during those dark days. But, it hadn't altered her resolve to do whatever possible to fight the war from the home front.

The sound of the door opening jerked Agnes from her reverie.

Katherine and Maddie closed the front door and hung their coats on the coat rack.

"How was the movie?" Agnes said.

"It was fun. We had popcorn, didn't we, sweetheart." Katherine gave Maddie's hair a tumble.

"We saw Bambi," Maddie said. "I cried when Bambi's mama died. Why did they make her die, Grandma? Couldn't they make a happy ending? I didn't like it when they made the mama die." Tears puddled in her eyes. "Like my mama…" Maddie dashed the tears from her cheeks and ran sobbing into her room.

"She's been weepy ever since we left the theater."

"Oh, dear. I'd hoped they hadn't put that part in the movie. Guess it wasn't such a good choice, was it?" Agnes followed Katherine to the kitchen. She set the tea kettle on the stove, struck a match, held it to the burner, and turned on the gas. "Tea?"

Katherine shook her head. "Later. I'd better go and see to her. We're likely in for another nightmare tonight. I didn't even think…" She hurried down the hall toward her room. Sharing her bedroom with Maddie was somewhat of an inconvenience, but it did make it easier to respond to Maddie's frequent nightmares.

By the time the tea kettle boiled, Katherine returned. "She cried herself to sleep. Best let her nap for a while." She shook her auburn curls and reached for the teapot. "Let's open that nice box of lemon-orange tea Myrtle gave me for my birthday. Want to give it a try?" She pulled another mug from the cupboard.

"That would be lovely." Agnes drew Lilly's letter from her pocket. "I got a letter from Lilly this morning. I wish there was something more I could do for her."

"How's she doing? Where is she now?"

"Her family is at the Crystal City internment camp in Texas." Agnes opened the envelope. "Here, I'll read it to you."

Dear Agnes:

A quick note to thank you for the shampoo, tea, and art supplies for the children. Sarah loves to draw. We can only get the bare necessities here at this camp. The kids are in school, but classes are large and they have limited supplies.

The weather was terribly hot this summer, but it's cooler now. Thankfully, we have a little house of our own and don't have to share space, though it is a long way from the bath house. Some of the men ran a water pipe closer to the cabins so I don't have to walk so far for water.

We got a letter from our son, Milton, last month. He's somewhere in the Pacific and says he is well.

I try not to complain, Agnes. I understand why President Roosevelt made the decision, but some nights I can't keep from weeping, thinking of our home in Newbury. We are so thankful that Mr. and Mrs. Haverstaff moved into our house. They are making the loan payment, so when the war is over, I'll have a home to return to.

How are Ling-Ling and Piffles? Hope he is happy at your friend's farm.

It's nearly midnight and I should get some sleep. Thank you for all you do for us.

Lilly

Agnes laid the letter on the table.

"She tries to sound cheerful," Katherine said, "but it must be horrible. At least they let her send and receive mail. I feel so guilty. Even with all the shortages and rationing, we have so much to be thankful for."

Agnes smoothed the wrinkles from the paper, folded it and put it back into her pocket. "Lilly can send out a few letters each month. I'm sending her stamps and stationery, but I think the authorities open and censure everything. I'm not sure she gets everything I send."

"Grandma. You do so much for her. You're a saint."

"No, I'm not." Agnes stood and paced the kitchen floor. "Lilly's son is somewhere in the Pacific fighting for our country and his parents and little sister are basically in jail. Where is the justice?" Agnes slumped into a kitchen chair and picked up a pencil. "Now that we're friends with Mrs. Roosevelt, maybe I should write to her. The president's wife should have influence in Washington. I wonder if she could help Lilly and her family."

Ling-Ling hopped into Agnes's lap. She stroked the cat's back. "You know we're talking about your former mama, don't you?"

Katherine sipped the last of her tea, stood, and placed her cup in the sink. "The president's executive order sent all the Japanese-Americans into internment camps for the duration of the war. There's nothing Mrs. Roosevelt can do to change that, but, who knows, go ahead and write to her.

"Listen, I've got to run to the library and spend some time in the research area," This American History class is killing me, so I'll see you later. If Maddie wakes up, tell her I'll read her a story later this evening." Katherine pulled her purse and jacket from the coat rack and opened the front door.

"Okay. See you later." *Bless her heart, working at the beauty shop all day and taking night school classes.* It was no surprise that Katherine looked so tired lately.

Agnes twirled the pencil, stroked the cat and gazed out the kitchen window where her chickens used to peek at her from the top of their coop. *Wish I could get some advice from Chicken Mildred.* Thinking of her former feathered pets made her smile. They should be happy at the Higgenbottom farm. She bent her head and began to write…

Dear Mrs. Roosevelt,

Thank you for your kindness when we recently met in Washington. I'm sure sorry that our planned trip together didn't work out.

In three succinct paragraphs, Agnes laid out her opinion of President Roosevelt's decision to inter all the Japanese-Americans in general, and Lilly's family in particular. She licked the end of her pencil and continued…

Here is my plan. Lilly could move back to her house here in Newbury, and our Chief Waddlemucker will watch over her, if that's what everyone is worried about.

I don't know if there's anything you can do to change President Roosevelt's mind about all the Japanese-Americans in camps, but,

thank you for whatever you can do to help Lilly.
   Sincerely yours,
   Agnes Agatha Odboddy
   P.S. We all got home safely and Maddie is very happy living with
us.

Agnes laid down her pencil and read through the letter. She wrinkled her brow and nodded. "Yes, that sounds good, if I do say so myself." She addressed an envelope, attached a three-cent postage stamp, inserted the letter and licked the flap.

She stroked Ling-Ling's tan back again. "I wonder if I should have asked if she could do something for the injured veterans coming home. Maybe next time... Mrs. Roosevelt is busy and I want her to concentrate on Lilly. Maybe she can arrange for her family to be released."

Wouldn't it be nice to give Lilly a welcome home party? They would invite the volunteers at the hospital and the ladies from The First Church of the Evening Star and Everlasting Light. She and Mildred would save their sugar ration stamps for a month and bake a chocolate cake covered with boiled Three-Minute Sugar Icing and write *Welcome Home* on the top.

The youth choir would perform their latest medley of show tunes.

Pastor Lickleiter could wax poetic about citizenship, Christian service, and patriotism.

Lilly would be so grateful, maybe she would have her nursery deliver a huge Philodendron to Agnes's home to replace the one Ling-Ling destroyed yesterday, chasing the rat.

Possibly sensing that her aberrant behavior had become part Agnes's daydream, Ling-Ling slipped off her lap with a chirp and slunk into the living room.

Once again reminded of the rat on the porch, Agnes's thoughts turned back to yesterday's break-in. She stood and scanned the kitchen, the living room, and then headed for the bedrooms. What could the thief have been looking for? Nothing seemed to be missing.

Halfway down the hall, the phone rang. She hurried back to the kitchen and grabbed the receiver. "Hello. Agnes Odboddy here…"

"It's Chief Waddlemucker. Will you be home for a while?"

"Sure," Agnes said. "I'm here the rest of the day. What do you need?"

"Something serious has come up. I'd rather discuss it in person, if you don't mind. I'll be right over." The phone clicked.

"Well of all things. He didn't even say 'good-bye!'"

Chapter Four

Agnes had just hung up the phone with Chief Waddlemucker, and Maddie wandered into the kitchen, rubbing her eyes. Her rumpled hair tumbled over her forehead. "Can I have a glass of milk?"

Agnes's heart wrenched with love for the child. "First, let's fix your hair, and then I'll get your milk. You want to look nice for Chief Waddlemucker when he comes by in a few minutes."

"Is that the fat man with the funny nose?" Maddie scratched her nose.

"Maddie! That's impolite. Don't say that in front of him." She chuckled. "He's very sensitive about his funny nose. Now, run and bring me your brush."

Several minutes later, Maddie's hair was brushed and freshly braided with little red ribbons on each braid. She sat at the kitchen table with a glass of milk.

Bing...Bong...

"That must be the chief, Maddie. Take your milk to your room, okay?"

Agnes hurried to open the door. "That was quick. Come on in, Chief. Can I fix you a cup of coffee? Left over from breakfast, of course, but I can heat it up. Have a seat." She waved toward the sofa.

"No coffee, Agnes...er...Mrs. Odboddy. This is more or less an official visit. If you'll sit down, I have a few questions for you." Chief

Waddlemucker laid papers on the coffee table and sat on the sofa.

What's going on? Agnes settled in the sofa chair beside the fireplace. "That was quick. I suppose you've figured out who left the rat on my porch? What did the high school principal say?" She leaned forward. "I appreciate that you got to the bottom of things so quickly"

The chief pulled at his collar. "*Ahem*" His cheeks flushed. "Mrs. Odboddy, can you tell me your whereabouts last night from approximately nine o'clock through midnight?"

"Why, of course. I was home all…" Agnes's head snapped up. "No. Wait. That's not true. I got a call from my friend, Mildred." She raised a finger. "Well, come to think of it, I guess it wasn't from Mildred. The caller *claimed* to be Mildred and that she was in trouble down at Wilkey's Market."

"So, you admit that you were at Wilkey's Market last night?"

"Yeesss… It was raining cats and frogs. I got the call, so I went to give Mildred a ride home. I was under the impression she couldn't start her car. When I couldn't find her at the market, I drove to her house. Mildred said she hadn't called. We talked for a minute and then I came straight home. Why do you ask?" Agnes clasped her hands to keep them from trembling.

"There was a break-in at Wilkey's Market last night. We have reason to believe that you were involved."

"Me? That's absurd. What makes you think that? I'm a…a… decent, hard-working citizen, and hometown patriot. You know I would never do such a thing."

Chief Waddlemucker nodded–his face now almost the same shade as the flowers in Agnes's maroon drapes. "You're a fine lady, Mrs. Odboddy, and that's a fact. I never would have thought… But, here's what we know…" He pulled his handkerchief from his pocket and mopped his brow. "We have evidence that implicates you in the Wilkey Market break-in. That also makes you a suspect for all the recent break-ins around town. Your patriotism would be a good cover. Who would suspect a nice old lady like you?" He tucked the handkerchief back into his pocket.

Agnes threw back her shoulders. "What evidence could you possibly have when I wasn't anywhere near… Well, that is to say, I was *near*, but I didn't…"

Chief Waddlemucker's forehead speckled with perspiration again. "We found a partial fingerprint on the back doorknob and your handkerchief lying on the floor beside the cash register. We have a witness who described your car. He saw you pull into the parking lot about ten o'clock."

The man on the bicycle! "That's ridiculous. I washed and ironed my handkerchiefs last Tuesday and I know for a fact that every hankie was—"

"I'm sorry, Agnes, but the evidence suggests the contrary." The chief removed an envelope from his pocket and shook a hankie onto the coffee table. "Do you deny this is yours?" He held up a handkerchief with the initials AAO stitched in bright red embroidery thread in the corner.

Agnes's stomach did a flip-flop as heat rose through her chest into her face. It was undeniably the hankie Katherine embroidered for her last Christmas, but how it got to the scene of a crime was anyone's guess. *Maybe I dropped it?*

Agnes grabbed a sofa pillow and hugged it to her chest. "I've already told you why I went down there last night. You can ask Katherine. She knew where I was going. Why would I go out in a hellacious storm if I hadn't received a call from Mildred saying she was in trouble?"

"Maybe you spoke to Katherine to create an alibi. Going to Mildred's house afterwards would be another clever way to cover your escapade last night." Chief Waddlemucker's large nose looked even more red than usual. "I suppose I'm open to a reasonable explanation of how your handkerchief got into the market and your fingerprint on the door, if you have something to say about this."

"I guess I touched the doorknob last night, but it was locked. I thought maybe Mildred was inside. Maybe I dropped my handkerchief the last time I shopped there or maybe…"

A chill crept up Agnes's neck. There was another possibility. "Maybe the thief who broke in yesterday took it from my bedroom." She snapped her fingers. "That's got to be it. That's why he broke in. So he could steal something of mine to leave at the scene of the crime. Can't you see? It's as plain as the nose on your… *Umm*… I'm being framed." She jumped up and paced the living room, tapping her finger on her lips. "It all makes sense, now. Someone is trying to ruin my reputation, but why?"

The chief sat on the sofa, shaking his head. "So, you completely deny the charges in spite of the evidence we found? Your only defense is that someone is framing you?"

Agnes stopped and turned. "I assure you I had nothing to do with this. I'll stand on my good name. It's my only defense." She bent close and whispered. "If you're going to arrest me, can you please wait until Katherine comes home? I can't leave Maddie here alone."

Chief Waddlemucker stood, scooped up the hankie and dropped it back into the envelope. "I don't think we have to go that far. At present, you're still classified as a *person of interest*. We'll keep the investigation quiet around town. I don't want to ruin your reputation… such as it is." His smile implied there wasn't much reputation left to ruin, which was probably true. "Please don't leave town, in case we have further questions."

"I had no intention of leaving town."

"If it makes any difference, Agnes, I never believed you were guilty, but I had to ask. I have to tell you, it doesn't look good. If we don't get a break to suggest another suspect…" He shook his head and opened the front door. "Sure sorry to bring such bad news. Call me if you can think of anything that would clear up this mess."

Agnes closed the door and leaned against it. Whoever was behind this skullduggery was doing a bang-up job of dishing up a passel of grief. There was only one person she could think of who might want to cause her so much trouble, but how was that possible? The last time she saw that miscreant, was heading out the back door of the police station in Washington, D.C. With the authorities not two steps behind, why would the crook risk returning to Newbury? *Just to cause me trouble?* Wouldn't it make more sense to head the opposite direction…say, to Mexico or Ubangi?

Agnes was up against a ruthless, but anonymous adversary. What if someone tried to take this a step further and break into the house some dark night? Maddie and Katherine could be in danger. She'd best hunt up her World War I pistol from her undercover agent days.

Didn't she and Mildred have some adventures back in the day? Particularly that weekend in Paris with Godfrey Baumgarten; even though he was responsible for her fall from grace. *Don't think about him, Agnes.* She had enough problems in the present without dwelling on the mistakes and consequences of a mid-life crisis.

On the way to her bedroom, Agnes stopped briefly to peek into Maddie's room. Her books and crayons lay scattered across her dresser. A large bride doll with a voluminous skirt lay across the child's pillow; a gift from Mildred upon her arrival in Newbury.

There sat Maddie in the middle of the floor, cutting out evening gowns from the old Sears and Roebuck catalogue, ready to fit onto the bodies of her paper dolls. Snippets of the magazine littered the floor. For once, the child was appropriately occupied, employing her imagination.

On the other side of the room was Katherine's wrinkle-free bed, and on her dresser, a mirror, comb, and brush lined up at exactly forty-five degree angles. Slippers lay side by side beneath the bed, and her bathrobe lay carefully across the chair against the wall.

Sharing her room with Maddie was inconvenient for Katherine, but necessary until she and Dr. Don were married.

Agnes gave Maddie a smile and hurried down the hall to her bedroom. She closed her bedroom door, pulled a box from the closet's top shelf, and sat on the bed with the box on her lap.

Carefully lifting the lid, she drew out a .32 caliber Colt pistol, closed one eye and pointed the gun at her reflection in the mirror. "Bang!" Now, all she had to do was load the dang thing and hide it in a safe place, ready to challenge any intruder who might try to threaten her family. Now, where would it be safe from an inquisitive child?

How about the fireplace mantle in the living room? No, Maddie could still reach it up there.

She could put it in her purse, like when they traveled to Washington D.C. this summer. Too risky with a curious child in the house.

She snapped her fingers. She could empty the flour bin on the kitchen counter and hide it there. Just the thing. Close at hand in case of an emergency, but a place Maddie would never think to look.

Agnes tiptoed down the hall past Maddie's room. She poured the flour into a cloth bag used for making boiled puddings, loaded the gun and tucked it into the flour bin. Perfect. Out of sight from inquiring minds but close enough to grab if needed.

"What are you doing, Grandma? Are you baking a cake?"

Agnes whirled around. *Rats!* Maddie stood in the doorway with scissors in one hand and a paper doll in the other. How long had she been there? Had she seen her slip the gun inside the flour bin? Maybe that wasn't such a good hiding place after all. Warmth crept up Agnes's neck "I...I...*um*... Nothing. Nothing. Run along now. Grandma is busy thinking."

"But, what are you doing? I saw you getting flour from the bin."

Double rats! "Oh, that." Agnes's heart raced. What could she say that would get Maddie's mind off the flour bin? "I was just...just... checking to see if I needed to buy more flour. Yes. That's what I was doing. I'm baking cupcakes for the Harvest Festival this weekend, you see, and I had to be sure I had enough flour." *Sounds good. God forgive me for lying to a child.*

Maddie's eyes gleamed. "Can we make chocolate cupcakes? I like chocolate."

"We'll see. Maybe I can get come cocoa powder at Wilkey's

Market." *That is, if I dare show my face in there again, now that I'm a suspected criminal.* She shook her head. What was she thinking? Mrs. Wilkey didn't know anything about her being a burglary suspect.

"Okay." Maddie turned back to her room.

As the front door opened, a whoosh of cool air and a few leaves accompanied Katherine inside. "*Brrr!* It's getting chilly out there. It sure feels like fall is in the air."

Agnes walked into the living room, her shoulders hunched and her head down. She flopped into a chair and put her hands over her face.

"Grandma? What's wrong? You look positively peaked. I'll make some tea."

"Never mind the tea, *punkin.* I have some rather disturbing news." Here was the moment of truth, sharing Chief Waddlemucker's disastrous news with Katherine. She was already upset, with the rat on the doorstep and conjuring up perverse reasons for the call that took Agnes into the storm last night. "Before I go into details, remember, no matter what happens, we'll get through this together. So, don't worry."

"Whatever are you talking about? You're scaring me. What have you done this time?" Katherine's lips trembled. "Tell me what's wrong."

Agnes shared Chief Waddlemucker's accusations, the primary evidence against her and her possible arrest. Not surprisingly, Katherine collapsed in a puddle of frustration and tears.

What more could go wrong? Shivers raced a marathon up Agnes's spine, careened up her neck, turned and collided with more shivers on their way back down.

Chapter Five

Agnes paused just inside Wilkey's Market, her fishnet shopping bag hanging on her arm. The aroma of freshly ground coffee and spices filled the store. She sighed. *I love coming in here.* She pulled a little shopping cart from the corner and started down the vegetable aisle. A stack of corn from a nearby farm caught her eye. On a table nearby, neatly stacked tomatoes and carrots looked fresh, and the price was right, especially since her victory garden had finished bearing.

Off to the left, Mrs. Wilkey's young son, George, wearing an oversized apron, knelt beside an end display table, pulling cans of pinto beans from a cardboard box. He marked the price on the end of each can with a wax crayon and stacked them with other canned vegetables.

George glanced up at Agnes. His face paled, and then his eyes narrowed. His hostile glare almost bordered on hatred.

What on earth was wrong with that boy? *Teenage hormones, no doubt.* Agnes gazed around the store. Where would she find cocoa? Most likely near the coffee and tea. As she pushed her cart around the corner, eyeing the rows of breakfast cereal, she heard Mrs. Wilkey's voice. "And, how are you today, Mrs. Snodgrass?"

Hearing her neighbor's name, Agnes looked down the aisle toward the check-out stand where Mrs. Wilkey stood placing items into Mrs. Snodgrass's shopping bag.

Agnes wheeled her cart toward the ladies. Before she could greet them, Mrs. Snodgrass spotted Agnes, lifted her nose and sniffed as though she smelled an unpleasant odor.

That's odd. Must be her indigestion acting up. Agnes nodded, "Good morning, Mrs. Wilkey, Mrs. Snodgrass. Nice to get a bit of rain, isn't it, though I must say, last night's…"

Mrs. Wilkey's head went up. Her jaw twitched and her mouth turned down. "Mrs. Odboddy. How thoughtful of you to drop by this morning." The tone of her voice suggested just the opposite. She glanced at her son, still marking cans nearby, and frowned as she put a bunch of carrots into Mrs. Snodgrass's shopping bag. "There you go, my dear. Have a nice day."

Agnes turned toward the elderly woman. "How have you been, Mrs. Snodgrass? Give my regards to your husband. I heard he had surgery. Is he recuperating well?"

Mrs. Snodgrass glared at Agnes. Without a word, she scurried out the door and dashed across the parking lot like she'd been shot out of a cannon.

Uh-oh! Did her husband die? Surely, Katherine would have mentioned if he'd come into the Whistlemeyer Mortuary where she fixed the hair and make-up on the *dearly departed.*

Prickles crept across Agnes's chest. The kind you get with the flu, not the kind you get when someone compliments your blueberry muffins at a potluck supper. "Well, I never. What's gotten into her, Mrs. Wilkey? What did I say? Did her husband pass away?"

Mrs. Wilkey twisted her hands. "What do you expect? Word gets around pretty quickly, you know. Breaking in and robbing my store! How could you betray me like that? There must have been at least $87.00 in that cash register. How am I supposed to pay the electric bill? You have some nerve showing up here this morning." Her eyebrows danced over her eyes like hot grease on a skillet.

Agnes sputtered. Her stomach flipped. How could Mrs. Wilkey know that Chief Waddlemucker considered her a person of interest? "How could you think such a thing? We've been friends for years.

Didn't I speak up and keep George out of the military, so you wouldn't have to lose another son?" Her heart felt as if it would burst. Tears stung her eyes. Talk about being betrayed. What about her loyalty as a customer, much less their friendship? *She might think I'm a crackpot, but she knows I'm not a criminal.*

Was this how it was going to be? Friends and neighbors turning against her, even before she was charged, much less convicted of a crime? What about Mildred and the ladies at The First Church of the Evening Star and Everlasting Light? Would they turn against her, too?

"Mrs. Odboddy. You're right. They haven't arrested you yet, but from what I hear, it's just a matter of time. After all, your handkerchief was right by the cash register. How do you explain that?"

Agnes sucked in her breath. *My handkerchief...* "Where did you hear all these details, Mrs. Wilkey? Chief Waddlemucker only told *me* about the handkerchief yesterday. What scallywag have you talked to?"

"Don't smart talk me and make excuses." Mrs. Wilkey's face reddened. "It just so happens I received a phone call saying that it was your handkerchief."

"Who called you?" Agnes swallowed the dust bunny in her mouth. Her fingers tightened around the handle of the shopping cart. No one at the police station would have spread the news around town. *The real burglar? The one framing me for the crime?*

"I don't know. The caller wouldn't leave a name, but she seemed to have all the information. I assumed she was from the police department or the newspaper." Mrs. Wilkey fiddled with a towel, wiping down the counter. Her lips trembled. Likely, she realized that the call came from an unauthorized source.

"You said 'she'? It was a woman?"

"Maybe. I don't know. It sounded like a woman. What difference does it make?"

Only the thief would know the specific evidence that incriminated Agnes. "You have to believe me, Mrs. Wilkey; I didn't break into your store. I'm being framed. Someone is trying to destroy my reputation.

First, they left a live rat in a shoebox on my doorstep and now—"

"Really, Mrs. Odboddy. A rat, indeed! Who would go to such lengths as that?" Mrs. Wilkey's nose raised several degrees. *"Humph!"*

"It has to be the…" Agnes gasped. She wasn't prepared to share her concerns that might convince Mrs. Wilkey of her innocence. The events at Agnes's house and the subsequent burglary were likely planned and executed with one goal in mind—destroy Agnes Agatha Odboddy, hometown patriot and scourge of the underworld.

At the moment, Agnes didn't feel much like the scourge of old kitchen grease, much less the underworld. Clearly, the perpetrator of the ensuing scandal had the upper hand. Agnes would have to be very clever or very lucky to get out of this predicament.

Mrs. Wilkey's nose elevated another notch, threatening to end up on the top of her head if she raised it any higher. "Until this situation is settled, Mrs. Odboddy, I would prefer that you shop elsewhere."

Agnes lowered her head. At the moment, unable to change this quandary until her name was cleared, she would have to endure the slings and arrows of injustice…again. "At least, may I buy a box of cocoa before I go? I promised Maddie we'd bake chocolate cupcakes for the church Harvest Festival this weekend. Must I disappoint her?"

"Do you really think they'll let you participate in the church festival after what you've done?"

Agnes pulled her shoulders back. "I'm hoping that *my true friends* will believe in my innocence, Mrs. Wilkey. I expect *my true friends* will allow me to manage the pumpkin carving booth, as planned. I don't think there's much that my presence can do to contaminate a few pumpkins. Now, about that cocoa? Are you going to sell it to me or must I drive eleven miles to the Boyles Springs Market, just to make a little girl happy?"

Mrs. Wilkey stammered. "Well, seeing as you're baking for the church fund raiser, I'll sell you the cocoa, but this is the last time until this business is settled."

"By the way, if I was a thief like you suggest, I would have just snitched the cocoa."

Where to purchase groceries in the future could be a problem. With the current gas rationing program, driving twenty-two miles round trip to the Boyles Springs Market would prove even more problematic this winter. Maybe she could get Mildred to do her shopping. The matter of ration stamps made that impractical, however. *Oh dear!* Would Mrs. Wilkey allow Katherine to shop here?

Agnes stomped to the back of the store, grabbed the cocoa and three juicy tomatoes from the vegetable display and returned to the counter. She passed by the dairy box. Hopefully, the milkman wouldn't hear the gossip and refuse to deliver milk and eggs to her front door.

"I thought you said you wanted to buy cocoa. What's this?" Mrs. Wilkey said, pointing to the tomatoes.

"Perhaps with your nose so high in the air, you couldn't see clearly. This would be three tomatoes for the child's supper. Katherine is out of luck this trip," Agnes snapped, "Do you mind? For old time's sake?"

"Humph! Mrs. Wilkey's cheeks flushed. "I suppose. Just this time! That will be $1.36," she said, punching in the numbers on her cash register.

"Highway robbery," Agnes muttered. She dug through her purse and handed Mrs. Wilkey a ten-dollar bill. "Here you go."

"Is that the smallest bill you have? We don't have much change this early in the day."

Agnes shrugged. "That's all I've got." *Serves you right for accusing me of thievery, you old hen.*

Mrs. Wilkey drew a five-dollar bill, three ones and some coins from the register and counted the change into Agnes's hand. She slammed the cash register door. "Remember what I said. Don't let me see your face in here again."

Agnes shoved the items into her shopping bag, stomped away from the counter, and opened the door. "You have a lovely day, too, ya' hear?"

Chapter Six

Agnes pulled the covers over her head as her bedroom door squeaked open.

"Are you getting up sometime today, or not?"

Agnes cringed at Katherine's muffled voice. She moaned and pulled the pillow tighter around her ears. "No. I'm never getting out of bed again. Everyone hates me. Nobody believes me, and—"

"I'm going out and eat worms," Katherine sang. "Really, Grandma, you know that's not true. You haven't even talked to Mildred or the ladies at the church. They'll stand by you."

Agnes tossed the pillow off her head. "They haven't called me either, you'll notice."

"I doubt they've even heard about anything yet. Chief Waddlemucker wouldn't have said anything that would get into the paper. Listen," Katherine glanced at her watch. "I'm late. I'll drive Maddie to school. You should get up. Isn't this your day to roll bandages at the hospital?"

"Yes…but…I might skip it today." Agnes sat up and pulled the sheet up to her neck. "Really, Katherine, I don't feel very well. I think I'll just laze in bed for a while."

"Suit yourself. I have to go. Dr. Don and I are going out to a movie tonight. We'll get something to eat downtown. You'll have to pick Maddie up after school and the two of you are on your own for dinner."

Agnes sighed. "Okay. Have a good day. Did Maddie finish her

homework last night?"

"Got it handled. See you." Katherine stepped into the hall. "Come on Maddie, let's go."

Agnes called, "Has Dr. Don said anything more about Maddie and whether—"

"Bye, Grandma!" The front door slammed and within minutes, Katherine's car rumbled down the street.

"Guess not." Agnes stroked Ling-Ling, who leaned against the side of her hip. "I can't imagine how this is going to work. Katherine wants to adopt Maddie, and if Dr. Don doesn't agree, that's no way to start a marriage."

Ling-Ling lifted her head. She blinked, a look of pure adoration on her face as her crossed eyes stared more or less in Agnes's direction.

She smiled at the cat and stroked her back. "Don't worry. Your situation is safe. You're not going anywhere." Agnes glanced around the bedroom. Should she put her head back under the pillow, or get up and get dressed? Or, she could call Chief Waddlemucker and see if there was any progress in finding the thief. *I could let him know that I know that Mrs. Wilkey knows…whatever!*

Agnes closed her eyes and bowed her head. "Lord, listen, it's me again. This is important. You and I have an understanding. You know I'm the biggest sinner in Newbury, but aren't I always sorry the next day and ask for forgiveness? Lord, this time, you know I'm innocent. I didn't rob the grocery store. If You could see Your way clear to make this go away, I promise that I'll… This time I really promise that…"

Agnes paused. *Careful, Agnes.* She'd gotten into trouble with the Big Guy before; making crazy promises she had no intention of keeping. *Better think this through before you commit yourself—*

She shuddered, recalling a time when she actually promised God she would stop *freshening* the henna color on her hair if He would save her from a harrowing situation. She'd vowed to stop calling Chief Waddlemucker an idiot, and wasn't that impossible since he was one? She even swore she would stop telling lies…*er*…fibs. Even God knew that wasn't likely to happen. So, what promises were safe when you negotiated with God? Making unreasonable promises you couldn't keep was just setting yourself up for a reservation in H.E. double hockey sticks. Where was the advantage in that?

"If You'll just give me a minute, God, I'll be right with You…" She reached up and scratched her head, peeked open one eye and glanced around the bedroom.

Her red flannel bathrobe hung on the end of her four-poster bed. One slipper lay beside the bedroom chair and the other beside the closet door. On the dresser, her diamond earrings glittered in a shaft of sunlight streaming through the window. *Aha! That's it!*

She could promise to give up wearing her diamond earrings until the matter at Wilkey's Market was resolved. The fact that she only wore the earrings when she was going someplace special might factor into the value her commitment carried with God. Perhaps He wouldn't judge her any harsher than He did last year when she gave up eating Brussel sprouts for Lent. He must have known she didn't particularly like Brussel sprouts. That's what God was good at, wasn't it? He'd always come through in the past, even when she was a big disappointment to Him.

Chill bumps pricked her arms. Guilt, pure and simple. Agnes shook her head. On the other hand, she really needed God to intervene this time, since she was in a peck of trouble. Perhaps it was to her advantage to come up with a bigger sacrifice than her diamond earrings. "Okay, God, if You will just get me out of this mess, I promise to…to…go to church every Sunday, rain or shine, for the next three months."

As an almost regular church goer, she only cut church when the weather was particularly bad…or particularly good. Promising regular church attendance without regard to the weather for three months straight seemed like a fair exchange for the beneficent intervention from the Most High.

She refolded her hands and bowed her head. "Here's the deal, Lord, three straight months and no excuses. Of course, if they put me in jail, I won't be able to keep my promise, so You can see why it's so important that You help me with this." *Hey, that's a pretty good angle I hadn't even thought of.*

Feeling more confident in her vindication than she had several minutes before, Agnes tossed back the covers, tumbling Ling-Ling off the bed. "Sorry!" Agnes reached for her robe.

The doorbell sounded as she thrust her arms into her red flannel robe and tied the sash. Who could be here at this hour? She glanced at the bedroom clock. Not quite eight-thirty. Much too early for the Fuller Brush man or the Jewel Tea distributor. Even the Avon lady had the decency to wait until after ten o'clock.

Agnes hurried to the door, flung it open and came face to face with Godfrey Baumgarten, her old lover from the distant past. *Great Caesar's Ghost!* Her hand flew to her cheek as a wave of dizziness crashed through her head. She grabbed the door jamb. "My stars! What…? What are you doing here? I thought you were in—"

"Australia? Nope. Right here in Newbury." He put his foot inside the door. "Surprise!"

Tears leaped to Agnes's eyes. "Godfrey." She hadn't seen him since last spring when he turned up unexpectedly to reignite old passions after his first twenty-four-year absence. Unfortunately, fate and Godfrey's poor judgment had intervened, resulting in her heart being smashed to smithereens. How many nights since he left town had she lain awake, worrying about his scrawny *aa*…him, wondering where he was and why she hadn't heard from him?

Who would expect to find him on her doorstep this morning, of all mornings, his sky blue eyes piercing her soul, and his wicked smile awakening emotions that made her weak in the knees?

Memories of their short torrid affair in Paris in 1918 were the kind you never quite forget, no matter how many years pass or how many regrets they generate. She glanced at her late husband's picture on the mantle, a wave of guilt stabbing her heart yet again.

She staggered. Godfrey stepped through the door, caught her in his arms and half-carried, half-steered her to the sofa. "Here, dear-heart, you look as if you're going to take a header." He lowered her to the sofa. Even through her flannel bathrobe, her shoulder burned at his touch.

Tears pricked her eyes. On the one hand, hadn't he returned just when she desperately needed a friend? On the other hand, how could she explain her reaction to his touch after his behavior last year? *For crying out loud, what's wrong with me?* She should be knocking his ears together! She touched her flyaway hair and then clutched the neck of her robe. Reeling between shock, confusing emotions, and self-consciousness, Agnes tried to blink back tears. No luck. She put her head against the back of the sofa and sobbed.

"Here," Godfrey held out a thin white cotton square smelling of Old Spice with the initials FBI stitched in the corner. "Take my handkerchief. You never have a handkerchief when you need one," he chuckled. His lopsided grin ground into her heart and the scent of his after-shave swirled around her head.

"Oh, my Lord above. I never thought I'd see your face again. Where have you been all these months?"

Godfrey blushed. "I…I… Really, Agnes. The least said about my absence, the better. It's difficult to explain—"

"Difficult, my Aunt Fanny." Agnes reared up, snatched Godfrey's handkerchief and swiped the tears from her face. "I haven't heard from you for all this time and you tell me *it's difficult?* I'll *difficult* you right into the outhouse if you don't explain. Just where exactly—"

"Let's just say I had a spot of trouble at the U.S. border." Godfrey's blush deepened. "The FBI took exception to my plans to travel and confiscated all the—"

"I should think so. Didn't I tell you that was a bad idea?" Agnes shook her finger in Godfrey's face. "You never listened to me twenty-four years ago, and you haven't changed a bit in your wretched old age. So, what's the story? Please explain why you never contacted me again after you left town so unexpectedly last year." Her arms crossed over her ample bosom as she glared into Godfrey's blue eyes. Those eyes that with just one glance could melt the ears off a chocolate Easter bunny. Those eyes that, with one come hither glance, had turned a WWI undercover assignment in Paris into a steaming assignation, and a loyal wife and mother into a fallen woman with multiple regrets.

Agnes's head swirled as she looked into Godfrey's face. A shock of hair fell over his forehead, no longer black as it so often appeared in her dreams, but now burnished with silver.

Agnes touched her own hair, still bright auburn, aided by the application of a monthly henna rinse to *freshen* it. But not to worry, since his visit last year, Godfrey knew that she was fifty pounds heavier than in Paris, and time had left its mark on her as well, and he hadn't given a whit. Hadn't he declared his undying love last year, and even asked her to share his life?

Galloping goose feathers! She'd let her mind wander. *What did he just say?* Something about the FBI? "I'm sorry. I missed that. Where exactly did you say you were for the past eighteen months?"

"I didn't say. Oh, Agnes, do we have to talk about this now? Can't you just offer me a cup of coffee and we can sit and chat about old times? Tell me all about Katherine." He glanced around the living room. "Nothing much has changed in here. How's Ling-Ling? And, Mrs. Whistlemeyer? Is Chicken Mildred still giving you advice? What about—"

Agnes held up her hand. "Stop! I'll make you some coffee, but we aren't going to talk about anything else until you tell me why I haven't heard diddly-squat from you for over a year. What kind of nincompoop do you take me for? As for Mrs. Whistlemeyer and the other roosters, I took them out to the Higgenbottom farm. They're in seventh heaven out there, romancing Mr. Higgenbottom's flock of hens."

Godfrey lowered his head. "I see. Can't tell you how many times I've thought of Mrs. Whistlemeyer and the crew." The corner of his mouth twitched, as though the mention of the chickens had brought back pleasant memories. His boyish grin was the same one that got her into trouble so long ago.

Agnes gripped his handkerchief in a death grip. "I suppose we could drive out to the farm one of these days to check up on them. That is, if you plan to stay long enough this time. What exactly are your plans?"

Did she dare hope to have a third chance at romance? Maybe he just came by to say hello. Agnes's ears itched. Was Godfrey back for good? Or would he get another wild hair up his…his…posterior region…at a moment's notice, sending him flying somewhere across the world again? How many seventy-something-year-old women get second and third chances at love with the same man? Or would he break her heart…yet again?

Cold prickles raced up her spine. She could not let this happen again. She hardened her heart. At her age, she could not risk the pain. If he wasn't ready to settle down, she would send him packing. In any event, he hadn't explained his reason for not contacting her for over a year, and it had better be a good one.

"Well, dear, if you insist on an explanation, it's like this. As I said, I had a spot of trouble at the border. The FBI gave me a choice. A dangerous undercover assignment they'd cooked up in South America with a drug cartel," he ran his finger around the back of his collar, "or jail. Difficult choice… I chose South America."

Agnes gasped, her fist pressed against her mouth. "South America?" *Golden sunsets, steamy guitar music, dark-eyed beauties with clicking castanets. Get a grip, Agnes.*

Godfrey nodded. "The FBI contrived a false identity for me as a crook named Frank Bernard Ingraham. I was supposed to infiltrate a smuggling cartel. We concocted a convincing background story about me breaking out of jail. I had to promise that under no circumstances would I contact anyone in the States, for fear it would blow my cover. The cartel wouldn't think twice about chopping me into little pieces and feeding me to the fishes if they discovered I was FBI, or for that matter, they might come after my loved ones. So…that's where I've been."

Agnes glanced at the initials on the handkerchief wadded in her hand. FBI? *Frank Bernard Ingraham?* She smiled. Wasn't it just like Godfrey and his cohorts to come up with a moniker like that? Pretty brazen, and oh, so Godfrey!

A muscle twitched beside Agnes's eye. She scooted further away from him. She had to put some space between them if she was to think clearly. Was Godfrey capable of creating such a fantastic story? It sounded more like something *she* might have come up with, given the circumstances. But, how much was true and how much a lie? Had he really spent the last year and a half living with a drug cartel, with his life hanging by a thread?

She shook her head to erase the image of dancing senoritas with blood-red lips and slithering hips. "So, considering your previous exhilarating life facing death at every turn, how do you happen to be here today in dull Newbury?"

Godfrey chuckled. "I seem to be at loose odds for a job. My testimony helped bring down the cartel and most of them are either dead or in jail. The few remaining would like to find me and…well, never mind about that. They knew me as Frank Ingraham, escaped convict, number six on the FBI's most-wanted list, not boring old Godfrey Baumgarten, disgraced ex-agent, so I think I can retire here in relative safety.

"In return for my assistance in South America, the government expunged the misdeeds from my record, but the FBI handed me walking papers. 'Conflict of interest…lack of confidence… *blah…blah…blah.* Thanks for the years of service, but don't let the door hit you in the rump on your way out.' So I skedaddled with my retirement check before they changed their mind, and here I am."

"So you are." Agnes frowned. Now, what was she supposed to do with him?

"I thought of you so often, Agnes." He reached for her hand. "I wanted desperately to talk to you so many times. I came back as soon as possible. You were right about that business last year… I made a foolish decision. I should have stayed with you." Godfrey slid off the couch, crouched on one knee and kissed her fingers. "Can you forgive me or is it too late for us?"

Agnes closed her eyes. She couldn't think with him looking at her. "This is all too sudden. Please, Godfrey… You don't have any idea what's going on here now." She pulled her hand away, stood and strode to the fireplace, turning her back to him. "I have to think. Please leave and give me some time to sort out a few things."

"I understand. Can I come back tonight? We can talk more then. I have some business in town to take care of. I'm staying at the Sleepy Time Motel. Here's the phone number." He pulled a card from his wallet and laid it on the coffee table. "Whatever you decide about us, I'm going to retire here in Newbury."

She turned to face him. "What are you going to do? I don't see you as part of the spit and whittle club." Agnes smoothed the wrinkles from her robe and crossed her arms across her chest. She had to get him out of the house. She couldn't think straight with him two feet away, smelling of peppermints and Old Spice. She never could. As much as her heart wanted to throw caution to the wind, it wasn't practical. Too many things had come between them, not once, but twice. What were the odds it would work out a third time? Rash decisions so early in the morning were rarely a good idea.

Agnes took his arm and propelled him toward the door. "Go. Go now!" She opened the door and shoved him onto the porch.

He turned. The look on his face reminded her of a lost puppy in a pet shop. "I'll go, Agnes, but I'll be back tonight. I'm anxious to tell you about my plans."

"Not tonight. I need more time than that. Come by the church tomorrow. I'll be at the church Harvest Fair, at the pumpkin carving booth with Mildred. Maybe we can talk then."

"Gotcha! Good-bye, honey biscuit." Godfrey turned and grinning like a schoolboy on the first day of summer, blew her kiss and was gone.

Chapter Seven

Agnes paced the living room as Godfrey's car pulled away from the curb. She returned to her bedroom, dressed and made her bed.

As she drew the covers over the pillows, she thought about Godfrey's declaration of love and the excuses for his absence. Truth? Or lies? Did it matter? Hadn't she decided long ago that one's moral judgment and acceptance of another's misdeeds are measured in direct proportion to how much they are loved? Don't we excuse a loved one for a multitude of sins? Was that the answer? Did she still love the old reprobate?

She pounded the pillows and tossed them toward the headboard. Was she willing to forget the anguish of months of silence and five hundred sleepless nights she had suffered, worrying about him? Was she to believe his wild, almost inconceivable story about an undercover assignment with a South American drug cartel? *How stupid does he think I am?*

More likely, some widow he'd shacked up with in Wisconsin had tossed him out. More likely, they caught him at the U.S. border and he'd spent the last year and a half in a holding cell in Leavenworth. She grabbed the garish senorita doll with the voluminous skirt and heaved it toward the pillows.

Either way, did it matter? If she loved him, should she accept his excuses at face value and allow him back into her life? Where could she seek advice? She, alone, knew the real reason for his sudden departure last year from Newbury. At the time, she'd felt it best to allow Katherine and all her friends to think he had returned to Washington, D.C. on business, and had voluntarily chosen to shut her out of his life and break her heart.

Wasn't there enough to explain to friends and neighbors about the Wilkey's Market break-in, without dragging up Godfrey's notorious past escapades? Speaking of friends, a call to her best friend, Mildred, was long overdue.

Agnes put the kettle on the stove, flipped the burner, and held a match to the gas. The blue flame whooshed and circled the prongs under the tea kettle. A nice cup of tea and a chat with Mildred should calm her nerves. Surely, she'd understand if anyone could. Agnes dialed her number on the wall phone.

"Hello? Mildred Higgenbottom."

"Why so formal, Mildred? It's just me."

"Oh, hi, Agnes. I was expecting a call from my insurance man. How are you? I've been thinking about you."

Agnes poured boiling water over the tea ball in her cup, set it on the kitchen table and pulled out a chair.

Ling-Ling jumped into her lap, the stickers in her coat suggesting a recent tromp through the victory garden.

Agnes absently picked stickers from Ling-Ling's fur as she shared the details of Chief Waddlemucker's visit, her run-in with Mrs. Wilkey, and Godfrey's unexpected return.

Mildred listened with rapt devotion. She commiserated and empathized with appropriate gasps of exasperation and disbelief at Mrs. Wilkey's preposterous accusations, Chief Waddlemucker's suspicions, and Godfrey's annoying excuses. By the time thirty minutes had passed, Agnes's tea was cold, Ling-Ling was sticker-free, and Mildred had restored Agnes's faith in their friendship with her utter re-assurance of her belief in Agnes's innocence.

Ling-Ling dropped off Agnes's lap and meowed at the door. Agnes stood, stretched the phone cord to its full length, and opened the screen door. She peeked out the window overlooking the abandoned chicken yard connected to the kitchen wall.

Ling-Ling hopped onto the little chicken coop beneath the kitchen window and peered into the nearby apple tree where a mockingbird sat singing its heart out.

The thought of getting another couple of hens popped into Agnes's head, since she already had the coop and yard. Free eggs every week would be wonderful, particularly now that she couldn't shop at Wilkey's Market. She chuckled at the memories of last year's chicken escapades. And, speaking of memories, just what was she going to do about Godfrey?

"Yoo-Hoo. Over here." Katherine waved as Dr. Don entered Joe's Railroad Diner, hung his coat on the rack and slid onto the stool beside her at the counter.

"Have you waited long?" Don leaned forward and pecked a kiss on Katherine's cheek.

"Not long. I ordered tea. I was reading the menu. What do you want to eat? They have deviled egg and tomato sandwiches. Or would you rather have pancakes? They serve breakfast all day." Katherine handed him the menu.

Don perused the food choices and then tossed the menu on the counter. "Pancakes sound good." He lifted his hand and waved to the waitress. "Sally? We're ready to order."

The stout waitress sidled up to the counter, grinned and laid her pad and pencil on the counter. "What can I get for you, honey?"

Katherine's head snapped around. *Honey? That was pretty chummy. She must know him pretty well.*

Don tapped the menu. "The lady will have the egg and tomato

sandwich and I'll have the pancakes with maple syrup. Could I also get a cup of coffee?"

"Of course, sweetie-pie. You can have anything you want." The waitress winked, dashed off his order on her tablet, fluffed her hair and sidled away from the counter.

Katherine turned to Don, her cheeks warm. "You don't need to encourage that woman. She's already *making eyes* at you."

Dr. Don's face pinked up. "Sally? Don't be silly. She knows I'm single, that's all. With all the eligible men off to war, a single man is a rare treat to some of these gals. They all act that way when I come in here. Besides, she's married."

"They? You mean there's more than one?" Katherine twisted the engagement ring on her left hand. She glanced around the diner. Sure enough, all three waitresses were staring at Don, giggling or inching closer, wiping imaginary spots off the counter or fiddling with the salt and pepper shakers. Had he encouraged them? Jealousy stabbed her chest.

Sally brought the coffee pot and filled Don's cup. "Your order will be here in a jiffy, Dr. Don." She grinned, batted her eyes, and glanced at Katherine. Her smile faded. She turned on her heel and set the coffee pot back on the burner.

Katherine ducked her head. Her cheeks burned. *Get used to it, Katherine.* Women would always throw themselves at a good-looking doctor. Patients, nurses, shop keepers, even other women doctors. Would he be the kind of husband who would stray, or would he stay loyal to his wife? Doubt niggled at her mind. She shook her head.

"Here's your…" Sally slapped Katherine's plate on the counter. The egg sandwich slid precariously toward the counter's edge. As Sally made a grab for the plate, her hand knocked against Katherine's teacup. Tea streamed across the counter, soaked into the napkin, and then dripped off the edge into Katherine's lap.

She jumped off the stool as the tea flowed onto the floor, grabbed a handful of napkin from the dispenser and swiped at the wet spot on her skirt. "Oh, my stars. Look at this."

"Sorry, sorry!" Sally's hand shook as she handed Katherine a towel. "I'm so sorry."

"What's going on here?" Joe, the cook, rushed out of the kitchen, his red face prickled with perspiration. He glared at Don and then at Sally. "Up to your old tricks, are you, Sal? What have you done this time? Flirting, as usual, *huh*?" Joe pulled another towel from his waistband and tossed it toward Katherine.

Dr. Don caught the towel and dabbed at Katherine's skirt. "Don't worry about it. No harm done. Come sit over here on my stool, Katherine," he said as he dried the tea off her stool.

"Get a mop and clean this mess up!" Joe shoved Sally toward the back room. "If you didn't flirt with every man that comes through the door.... Rich doctors, coming in here, turning a decent woman's head..." He disappeared through the swinging door into the back room.

Sally scurried toward the kitchen door. "I...I'm sorry, Joe, honey. I didn't mean nothin.'"

Katherine patted at her wet skirt with a napkin. *The brazen hussy! She did that on purpose.* "Let's go, Don. I can't sit here in a wet skirt. I'm so embarrassed. Everyone is staring."

"Now, Katherine. No one is staring. Accidents happen. You should know. You're no stranger to embarrassing situations, if you'll recall how we met." He chuckled. "Sally didn't spill your tea on purpose."

"Sally? You're on a first name basis? You must know her pretty well. She practically threw the sandwich at me. Let's go. I have to change my clothes. We can make a sandwich at home. It will give you a chance to spend some time with Maddie."

Don shrugged. "Lucky me..."

"That was rude." Katherine reached for her jacket on the coat rack. "Maybe you'd rather just sit there and have supper with your girlfriend." Katherine's fingers shook as she buttoned her coat. Her face warmed. Now, why did she say that? She sounded like a spoiled brat.

Dr. Don raised an eyebrow. "Why are you so mad? You know it

was just a silly accident. Don't act like such a princess."

Katherine reached for the doorknob. "Me? A princess? Maybe you're right. This princess is leaving. Are you coming with me, or not?"

Don's mouth tightened. "I don't think so. Why don't you go on home to your precious Maddie and cool off. I'll call you later."

"*My* precious Maddie? I thought she was *our* precious Maddie. She's going to be our daughter, after all."

Don dropped a couple of dollars on the counter and turned. "That's just the thing. Don't you think it would be nice to consider how I feel before *we* adopt a disturbed child? Now you expect me to be happy about it?"

"Well, of course she's a disturbed child, coming from her background." Katherine blinked back tears. She glanced at the waitresses, hovering nearby, listening to them argue. "Everything will be fixed once we're married and she has a loving home life and caring parents."

Don lowered his voice. "That's just the thing, Katherine. If I have to raise a child that needs fixing, I'd rather it was our own child, not someone else's problem. Why don't you go on home and change your clothes. I don't want to quarrel with you. I could use some time alone right now."

"Fine. I'll just do that." Katherine slammed the diner door and hurried to her car, tears pricking her eyes. Now they'd quarreled again. When was this Maddie thing going to get settled?

Lately, more and more conversations with Don ended in an argument. They were supposed to be married next month. What had gone wrong? They hadn't argued as much over the past year as they had since she came back from Washington, D.C. with Grandma—and Maddie.

Katherine slid into her Buick, poked the key in the slot and punched the starter button. The engine rumbled to life. She pulled a hankie from her purse and dabbed her eyes. Not a good idea to drive with tears streaming. Maybe if she waited a bit, Don would come outside and apologize.

She stared out the car window at the customers entering the silver railroad car diner. Red and green neon lights flashed in the window and a row of red lights gleamed across the roofline. Not the sort of place two lovers should quarrel about something as silly as spilled tea. But, it wasn't really about spilled tea, was it? It was her jealous outburst and Don's unwillingness to accept Maddie.

Katherine remembered his stricken face when he met them at the bus station and she shoved the child into his arms. "This is Maddie. She's going to be part of our family once we're married. Isn't it wonderful?"

Maddie's future was at the heart of one argument after another. How had she so misjudged Don's love of children? That wasn't true. In her heart, she knew she was to blame. Despite Grandmother's warning, Katherine was determined that Maddie should be part of their life, and hadn't paused for a moment to consider Don's opinion, before bringing her home.

"It *is* my fault! I was wrong," she whispered in the cold, dark car. "Now, what am I going to do? If things keep on this way, I may have to choose between them."

Of course, Grandma would keep Maddie, if she could. But, due to Grandma's age, the authorities only approved Maddie's placement, naming Katherine as the foster parent. When they married, if Don didn't agree to accept Maddie, she might be removed from Grandma's home and made a ward of the court.

Katherine put the car into gear and pulled out of the parking lot. She had waited long enough. Don wasn't going to follow her and *make nice*. He must have decided to have supper with Sally, after all. She glanced down at her engagement ring. Should she give back the ring? Maybe this was the final quarrel that ruined any chance of her being the future Mrs. Don Dew-Right.

Chapter Eight

Agnes glanced up from her magazine when Katherine's car door slammed. *Back already?* The Saturday Evening Post slid off her lap as Katherine came through the door and tossed her jacket onto the coat rack.

"I thought you were going for dinner and a movie with Dr. Don."

Katherine scowled and glanced toward the hallway. "Is Maddie in her room?" She dropped onto the sofa and put her hand over her eyes.

"Oh, dear! Did you and Dr. Don have another quarrel?"

"You could say that." Katherine stood and gestured toward her wet skirt. "I have to change my clothes. I'll be back in a minute."

Agnes twisted her hands. What could be the problem this time? Lovebirds shouldn't be fighting *before* the honeymoon. She stood and went to the kitchen, lit the stove burner, and set the tea kettle on to boil. A nice cup of tea always made things better. Agnes opened the ice box, peered inside and then called down the hall. "Did you have dinner?"

"No. I had a cup of tea tossed in my lap before I had a chance to eat." Katherine called from her bedroom.

"Tea?" *I was right. They have quarreled. Gee willikers!*

Ling-Ling lifted her head from her bed beside the stove. She gave a discerning blink, which could only be interpreted as her agreeing with Agnes's thought.

Agnes pulled cheese and a hunk of bologna from the icebox, left over from her and Maddie's sandwiches she had made for dinner.

"Do you want me to fix you a bologna sandwich?" She turned toward Katherine's bedroom. "Oh, there you are."

Katherine stood in the doorway, wrapped in her blue striped flannel robe and slippers. She had pulled her hair back in a ponytail, tied with a ribbon. "Thanks. Sit down. I'll do it."

Observing Katherine's attire, Agnes said, "Well, for a lady who just quarreled with her beau, you apparently don't expect him to come knocking on the door any time soon. It must have been a doozy of a fight this time."

"Oh, it was silly. This dumb waitress down at the diner practically crawled in Don's lap, and then she dumped a cup of tea all over my skirt. You should have seen Don. He rode to her defense like Don Juan on a white charger. I got mad and left. Obviously, he didn't stop me. I know it was stupid. Then we quarreled about…" She glanced down the hallway and continued in a whisper "…Maddie. Don doesn't want to adopt her. That's the whole problem in a nutshell." Tears sparkled in her eyes.

"I seem to remember that I warned you about this."

"You don't need to say, 'I told you so.' Don't you think I feel bad enough already? I love the kid and if Don doesn't, then maybe it would be better if we called it quits."

"Oh, Katherine. You can't mean it. You wouldn't break up with him over this, would you?" Agnes pulled mugs from the cupboard and proceeded to make tea. "Tea?"

"Thanks." Katherine reached for her mug and took a sip. "*Ummm.*"

Agnes sat at the table and wrapped her hands around her cup. "Maybe Maddie should stay with me. Perhaps after you're married a few months, Don will see things differently. When he gets to know her a little better, I'm sure he'll come around. Don't worry about it. Just back off, respect his wishes, and see what happens."

"It's not that easy, Grandma. Quarreling about Maddie is just the tip of the iceberg. We're quarreling about everything. You wouldn't believe that waitress down at the Railroad Diner. Her husband, the fry cook, was also upset with her flirting. I'll admit, I was jealous, but I wonder if he flirts with all the girls behind my back?"

"Now, Katherine. He loves you. He's not going to risk your relationship by messing around with another woman. He's not a complete nincompoop!"

Katherine's lips wavered. "Only half a nincompoop? Maybe not, but you should have seen her, Grandma. She was wiggling her hips, flipping her hair and batting her eyes like she was about to go blind. And, when she deliberately dumped tea in my lap, he defended her."

"Surely not." Agnes chuckled. "I'm sorry. But it does sound funny, the way you tell it. I wish I'd been there."

"If you'd been there, you'd have seen—"

Bing... Bong...

"See?" Agnes stood and headed for the front room. "What did I tell you? There he is now, coming to apologize. Run and get dressed. I'll answer the door."

Ling-Ling bounced along behind Katherine as she scurried down the hall.

Agnes pulled open the door. "Come in, Dr...." Agnes stared into the eyes of a tall man standing in the doorway–not Dr. Don. Her mouth dropped open.

"Mrs. Odboddy? How have you been?"

"Irv... Irving?" What was an FBI agent from Washington, D.C. doing in Newbury?

"Vincent. Vincent Buckwalder. Remember? That's my real name. Irving is the undercover name I use when I'm on a case. If you don't mind, I'd just as soon you didn't use it here in Newbury. I might need that *nom de plume* again, someday." He pulled off his hat and twisted it. "*Umm...* May I come in?" Vincent cleared his throat.

"Of course. What was I thinking? Come in. What brings you to Newbury?"

"I have relatives in Boyles Springs. I had some time off, so I came to spend some time here in Northern California. Being so close,

I thought it only proper to drop by and say hello. Is Katherine home?" Drops of perspiration beaded his forehead as he pulled on his tie.

"She'll be right out. She's changing her clothes. Won't you sit down? Let me take your coat." Agnes directed the tall young man to the sofa. "Can I fix you a cold drink? Or coffee? I think there's some left from breakfast." How many more surprises could today bring? *First Godfrey, and then Irv…er… Vincent.* She hung up his coat and hat on the coat rack.

"No, thanks. I'm fine." As Vincent sat, his gaze moved around the room to the doilies pinned to the arm of the overstuffed chair, the cross-stitched sampler hanging over the fireplace, and the tall, somewhat tattered Philodendron plant in the corner: a result of Ling-Ling's recent battle with the rat. "How's the little girl getting along? What's her name?"

"Maddie? She's great. She started school a few weeks ago. She's doing well, considering."

Vincent's left eye twitched. "I don't suppose you've had any trouble related to that situation we dealt with in Washington…or have you?"

Agnes raised an eyebrow. Was there more to Vincent's innocent question than it implied? Was he really visiting family, or was he here in a more official capacity, following their encounter in Washington D.C.?

Agnes had a hunch that being framed for the Wilkey Market burglary might be connected to the Washington incident, but without proof, she'd been hesitant to bring it up with Chief Waddlemucker. Perhaps Vincent could help. "Actually, we have had some trouble. Let me fill you in on what's going on."

Over the next several minutes, Agnes shared the details of the rat on the porch, the late night phone call that took her into the storm, the Wilkey's Market burglary, and the evidence implicating her as the guilty party.

Vincent listened and nodded from time to time.

"Well, what do you think?" Agnes completed her tale, folded her hands and leaned forward.

Vincent drew a deep breath. "Do you think this could be the work of the Nazi agent we arrested in Washington?"

"You mean the one the police let slip through their fingers?" Agnes blotted a handkerchief across her damp forehead. Just the mention of the incident made her uncomfortable. Hadn't she worried about this very possibility about a hundred times a day? But, having an FBI agent say it out loud was even more unnerving.

"We're currently tracking a number of stolen cars and gas station robberies across four states, all headed toward California. There's a possibility that our escaped Nazi agent is headed for Newbury. Guess it's a good thing I'm here. I'll be on hand if *our friend* shows up and tries anything."

The wrinkles deepened in Agnes's brow. "We've been worried about Maddie. I feel better knowing you're here."

Vincent checked his notes. "We caught several members of the cell operating in Newbury County this summer, but there could be more. As long as I'm here, I'll do a little snooping around and see if I can figure out if there's any connection to your troubles."

Tears pricked Agnes's eyes. "It's been most disconcerting. Because of the gossip, some of the townsfolk have turned against me. I guess I can't blame them. The evidence at the store was pretty damning."

Katherine came around the corner from the hallway and stopped short in the doorway. "I heard voices…Well, I declare." She ran her hand over her hair. "Aren't you the last person I expected to see sitting in my living room?"

Vincent hopped up from the sofa. He reached into his pocket and pulled out a Hershey's chocolate bar. "Miss Katherine, I brought this for you."

"Thank you," Katherine stammered. "Why did you… I can't believe you remembered that I love chocolate. What is this for?"

"Sweets for the sweet," he said with a grin.

Katherine's cheek flushed. "Please. Sit down. "Can we get you anything to drink? What brings you to Newbury?" She laid the chocolate bar on the coffee table.

"I already asked." Agnes said. *Just see the way he's looking at her! Why, his face is redder than Katherine's.* "Come and sit down, both of you. Vincent is visiting family nearby. He just stopped by to say hello. Isn't that nice?"

Vincent's gaze followed Katherine across the room to the easy chair by the fireplace.

"Miss Katherine," Vincent said, his hand trembling. "Before I sit down, I want to lay my cards on the table right from the start so there's no misunderstanding."

Katherine sucked in her breath. "I'm afraid I don't understand. What are we talking about now?" Her hands clutched together.

Vincent swallowed and threw back his shoulders. "I haven't stopped thinking about you since the day we met this summer. I asked for a leave of absence to come to Newbury because I wanted to see your face when I asked you an important question. Would you do me the honor of stepping out with me…with the goal of a relationship, hopefully leading to marriage?"

Chapter Nine

Katherine gulped. Her hand flew to her mouth. Perspiration beaded between her breasts. "Well, I declare. You don't beat around the bush, do you? I'm flabbergasted. I had no idea you felt that way about me. Irv—"

"Please call me Vincent. That's my real name."

"All right…*umm*…Vincent." How do you gracefully turn down a marriage proposal from a man you barely know? "Perhaps you're not aware that I've been dating someone for quite some time now. We're planning to marry…soon, in fact. I hope I never said anything to lead you to think—"

"Oh! I never meant to suggest that you ever said or did anything of the sort. It's just that considering how we met and then everything that happened in Washington D.C., we got to know each other pretty well, and I thought... I mean, I had hoped… Please don't be embarrassed. I'm the one embarrassed. I was unaware of your previous commitment." Vincent's blush had now reached his neck. He ran his finger around his collar.

Before Katherine could say a word, Agnes interrupted. "Katherine is engaged to Dr. Don Dew-Right at the Newbury Hospital. They're planning to be married next month." She shuffled magazines around the coffee table, coughed and cleared her throat. "It's been in all the local papers. I'm surprised you didn't see their engagement announcement."

"I've been in Washington, D.C. for quite some time. I'm so sorry.

Now I've made a fool of myself."

"Don't be silly." Katherine waved her hand. "There's no need to apologize. I'm honored that you would ask." She lowered her gaze, and then looked up. "Actually, I was feeling a little down in the dumps this evening. You've made me feel a hundred percent better." She giggled. "I wonder what Don would say if he knew he had competition for my hand."

Vincent's gaze darted between Agnes and Katherine. "Am I wrong, or did you just imply that I might still have a chance?"

Katherine was quick to shake her head. "Oh, I didn't mean to suggest that." Or maybe she did. The way Don was acting, she wasn't sure what might happen. *And I do like...umm... Vincent. He was a Godsend in Washington.* She stared at the fireplace for a moment and then turned back toward Vincent. "Of course, nothing is in stone until the preacher says the words, 'I now pronounce you man and wife.'

"Why don't you give me a call in a few days? Perhaps we can get together and...and...talk." Her face warmed. "I'd love to hear what's going on in Washington, D.C. Just because we're friends, you understand. You can tell me all the latest news about Mrs. Roosevelt." Katherine gazed around, looking everywhere except at her grandmother.

"I'd like that." Vincent stepped toward the coat rack to retrieve his coat and hat. "In fact, I'd love that. And, I'm looking forward to seeing...what's the child's name, again? I'm so flustered, I can't remember."

"Maddie. We call her Maddie."

"I'd love to see Maddie again. Perhaps she'd like to visit the Newbury Wild Bird Sanctuary near Boyles Springs. I could drive her out there one afternoon... Perhaps you'd accompany us, Miss Katherine. That is, if you think that's appropriate."

"Actually, Maddie is quite an artist. She's always drawing animals and birds. We were planning to take her to the Higgenbottom farm to visit our chickens one of these days. Maybe we could make an afternoon of it." *Just what would Don say about that? Probably have a cat fit. But, Vincent invited Maddie. I'd just go along as a chaperone.*

Agnes stood and opened the door. "Nice to see you again, Vincent. Let me know if you learn anything about…that matter we discussed."

Vincent nodded. "I'll call you tomorrow, Katherine, and we can set a date, or…whatever."

"Not tomorrow. The Harvest Festival down at The First Church of the Evening Star and Everlasting Light is tomorrow. Grandma and I are both managing a booth. It's a fund raiser for next summer's Bible School. Perhaps you'd like to drop by and spend some money. We'll have games, apple dunking, pumpkin carving, and a dessert booth. I've heard that the traveling carnival has a merry-go-round and even a performing tiger. It's all for the kids."

Vincent slid his arms into his coat and stepped onto the porch. "Sounds like fun. I'd love to come. I'm pretty good at apple dunking. I'll see you tomorrow then, for sure." He grinned and winked at Katherine.

Agnes closed the door and exchanged glances with Katherine. "You know," she said, "Vincent didn't look at all like a man whose marriage proposal just got turned down, as unexpected as it was. He looked more like he was thinking, 'It's not over until the fat lady sings.'"

Katherine buried her face in her hands and shook her head. "What am I supposed to say?"

"I'd say he plans to fight for you, engaged or not, and apparently he thinks an FBI agent against a small town doctor might be a battle he can win."

The color faded from Katherine's cheeks. "At this point, I haven't got a clue."

Ring,.. Ring…

"That's probably the good doctor, now," Agnes nodded toward the kitchen. "…calling to apologize. Better go and answer it."

Katherine giggled. "Should I tell him about Vincent's visit?"

"How will he feel about another man proposing to his fiancé? Is he the jealous type?"

Katherine shrugged. "I've never given him reason to be. Guess we'll find out."

Agnes rubbed the goosebumps on her arm as Katherine ran to answer the phone. *And you might not like the answer.*

Chapter Ten

"Hurry, Grandma. We'll be late!" Maddie said, hopping up and down like a pogo stick.

"Settle down, Maddie. I'm almost ready." Agnes straightened the hem of her suit jacket, and peered at her reflection in the mirror. She shoved the silver chopsticks into her bun; a gift from her husband in 1918. "I'll be ready in a minute. All we have to do is load the two pumpkins into the car. Do you have the quarter Katherine gave you to spend at the carnival?"

"*Uh-huh.*" Maddie held out her handkerchief with the quarter tied tightly into the corner.

"Put it back in your pocket and don't take it out again until you're ready to buy something at the fair. I don't want you to come crying to me, saying you lost your money. Do you hear?"

"Yes, Grandma." Maddie stuffed the handkerchief back into her jacket pocket.

"I'll load the pumpkins in your car on my way out, Grandma." Katherine stood in the bedroom doorway, her hand resting on the jamb. "Do you need to take anything else for your pumpkin carving booth?"

"*Huh-uh.* Mildred is handling things. She and Jackson went down early to set up the tables and the decorations. I'm just supposed to bring the two big pumpkins from my garden to add to the ones her brother sent from the Higgenbottom farm."

"How about your cash box? Who has that?"

"The church secretary made up a cash box with $15.00 in change. It's easier to handle the money after the fair if it all comes from the church. She'll bring it around to each booth before we open the fair. Mildred probably has it by now."

"All right. I think we're ready. Come on, Maddie. You can come with me. We'll take Grandma's chocolate cupcakes in my car." She took Maddie's hand. "See you down there, Grams."

Agnes squelched the uneasy feeling that swished through her chest. What could possibly go wrong? It was just a county fair. "Keep an eye on Maddie. Don't let her wander off, Katherine."

"I will…or won't. You know." Katherine giggled, as she carried the cupcakes out the front door.

Agnes put on her coat and checked the lock on the back door one final time. *Don't want another rat attack while we're out.* She grinned at the cat curled on the sofa. "Take care of things, Ling-Ling. Mama will be back later."

Agnes hurried to her 1930 Model A coupe parked in the driveway, swung into the driver's seat and pressed the starter.

Rrrrrrr… Rrrrrr…

"Come on Nelly. Don't do me this way." She fiddled with the choke and tried the starter several more times but to no avail. "Oh, *pshaw*! Wouldn't you know it? Now, what am I going to do? Everyone has already left for the fair."

Maybe Godfrey can pick me up. Hadn't Katherine been surprised when she heard he was back in town? She dashed back into the house and dialed the Sleepy Time Motel's phone number. After eight or nine rings, she hung up. "Just my luck. The manager must be out of the office. How will I be able to carry two pumpkins on my bicycle?"

Unfortunately, a trip to the garage revealed two flat tires on her bicycle. When did that happen? *First the car and now my bike?* Was this more shenanigans by the unknown assailant? Was the whole universe against her this morning? *Guess I'm going to have to hoof it!*

She hefted the two pumpkins off the rumble seat and started down the sidewalk. An eight or nine block walk carrying two pumpkins and her purse was inconvenient, to be sure, but not impossible–nothing a hometown patriot couldn't pull off.

At the end of the second block, perspiration dotted her forehead and the two, ten-pound pumpkins felt like they weighed at least twenty pounds each. She stopped at the crosswalk, set the dead weights on the sidewalk and flexed her arms. *I'm getting quite out of shape. I really must start exercising again.*

Aooogaa!

Agnes turned and waved at the black 1934 Buick that pulled up to the curb.

Homer Blenkinsop, owner of the Newbury Daily Gazette, leaned over and rolled down his car window. "Where you goin,' Miz' Odboddy? You look all tuckered out. Do you need a lift?"

"Homer Blenkinsop! Aren't you just a blessing on four wheels? I sure do. Old Nelly wouldn't start and I have to get these pumpkins over to the Harvest Fair."

"Get in. I'll run you over."

Agnes picked up the pumpkins, opened Homer's truck door and placed the pumpkins on the floorboard. She slid across the mohair seat and slammed the door. "Are you on your way to the fair?"

"*Nuh-uh!* I'm heading down to the newspaper. Going to spend a few hours working with young George Wilkey. I hired the boy part-time a couple weeks ago. Not much time for training during the week when it's so busy getting the paper out. George was all gung-ho to join the Navy soon as he turned seventeen, but he got turned down at the Navy Recruiting Station, so I offered him a job."

"Yes, I know about that. I was one of the citizen representatives at the draft board the day George came in. He wanted to join up, but I didn't think it was a good idea. I convinced the committee that since Mrs. Wilkey had already lost one son to the war, she shouldn't have to risk losing George. I'm glad you're giving him a chance to learn the newspaper business. That's a great opportunity." She reached over and patted Homer's arm. "You're a good man, Homer."

"*Harrumph. Uh*...sure. How's Miss Katherine? Hear there's a wedding in the forecast. We've been expecting her to drop off particulars at the newspaper." Homer stopped at the corner, rolled down his window and stuck out his arm to signal a left run, then turned the Buick into the cross street. Just ahead, traffic slowed as cars pulled into the parking lot at The First Church of the Evening Star and Everlasting Light. Homer stopped the car in front of the church steps. "This okay?"

"Oh, my! Folks are almost finished setting up the booths. I must hurry. Thanks ever so much for the ride, Homer. Stop by later if you get a chance and bring the missus. I'll be right next to the booth selling war savings bonds." She opened the door, grabbed her purse and her two pumpkins and hurried away before Homer had a chance to reply.

Up ahead, friends and neighbors scurried across the parking lot, setting up tables, stretching canvas awnings over two-by-fours, and carting boxes and bags of decorations to various locations.

Agnes waved to Edith Braithwaite, standing amidst boxes of war bonds and government posters. "Good morning, Edith. Getting everything set up already? Aren't you the busy one?"

Jackson Jackson stood on a box at the pumpkin carving booth, stretching a length of red, white, and blue bunting across the wooden framing over the table.

Love those patriotic colors!

Agnes's best friend, Mildred Higgenbottom, handed him the hammer and a nail. "Well, it's about time, Agnes. I thought you were coming down early to help. It's a good thing Jackson was here to help me with the booth." Mildred squinched her eyebrows as she scolded. "I couldn't very well hang this bunting by myself."

Agnes set the pumpkins on the ground. "It's been one of those days. Katherine left early with Maddie and I had car trouble. I'd still be hoofing it if Homer Blenkinsop hadn't come along to give me a ride. What can I do to help?"

"We're going to need a tub of water to wipe down the tables

and clean up the kids after they carve their pumpkins." Mildred said, gesturing toward the wash tub on the low table. "You and Jackson might take that tub over to the church. We don't need it too full."

"Got it. Come on Jackson. I'll carry one side and you the other." Agnes grabbed the tub as Jackson stepped down from the box.

"You sure you can finish up here alone, Missus Higgenbottom? You still has that other bunting to hang. Maybe Miz Odboddy could find another feller ta' help her with the water."

"That's a good point. I do need help with the other bunting. Oh, dear. Agnes? Can you manage without Jackson?"

"Don't worry. I'll snag someone along the way to the church. You two finish up here. I won't be but a few minutes." Agnes hefted the tub and started down the aisle between the booths toward the church. She nodded to Mrs. Warbuckle in the balloon and dart booth. When she didn't return the greeting, Agnes turned away from the booth. *She's heard the gossip and thinks I robbed the market.* Her breathing quickened as she strode awkwardly along with the tub bumping her knees. How many others would think the same?

As Agnes approached Katherine's booth, she waved. "Good morning, dear. How are things?" Katherine's dessert table looked enticing, laden with pies, cakes and platters of cupcakes. She had layered boxes at varying heights and covered them with bright, colored tablecloths, nicely displaying the goodies at different levels.

Agnes paused, eyeing the cupcakes she and Maddie worked so hard to decorate. Each cupcake boasted a big red strawberry swimming in soft peaks of snowy Three Minute Icing, like a red igloo in a snowbank. *Our cupcakes look better than the others.* "I think I'll just buy the cupcakes we made, Katherine. At least we know they're good. Who knows about some of these others? Your booth looks lovely, by the way." She fished out a five-dollar bill, previously nestled somewhere in the depths between her bosoms. "Thought this might come in handy." She chuckled and handed the bill to Katherine.

"I'll put them on the back table until we go home. I've got them priced at $1.75." She counted out her change and handed it to Agnes.

"Keep the quarter. Just give me the bills," Agnes said, stuffing the bills back into the neck of her dress. "I'm on my way to the church to get a tub of water. Good luck today."

"How will you manage that? You won't be able to carry it back by yourself. You're going to need some help." She looked left and right for a likely helper.

"Don't worry. I'll just grab a man on my way to the church." Agnes started away.

"Don is around here somewhere," Katherine called. "If I see him, I'll send him to the church."

"Good idea. Thanks." Agnes trudged on with her cumbersome load. Every man she spied along the way had been commandeered either by his wife or another church lady to assist in setting up their respective booths. "Wouldn't you know, with men as scarce as hen's teeth, where's a man when you need one," Agnes muttered as she climbed the church steps. "Guess it's just a sign of the times."

Agnes yanked open the church door and started down the side aisle toward the kitchen, fussing in her mind how she could carry a wash tub half-filled with water without help. *I'll cross that creek when I come to it.*

As she reached for the kitchen door, she heard voices down the hall in one of the adjoining Sunday school class rooms. *Ah-ha! If that's not a man or two, my name isn't Agnes Agatha Odboddy!* Smiling at her good fortune in locating a man not yet shanghaied by another church lady, she set the wash tub on the floor and headed toward the voices. Hopefully, it wasn't Pastor Lickleiter and a parishioner engaged in spiritual counseling. Their raised voices suggested otherwise. Even a dissertation about the realities of eternity in Hell wouldn't be that spirited!

She opened the classroom door a crack and listened, not wanting to intrude if it was truly a *coming to Jesus* moment. *What?*

Dr. Don and Vincent stood nose to nose, their faces flushed and fists clenched, looking as if they intended to start WWIII right in the middle of the Sunday school room.

Chapter Eleven

Agnes clasped her hand over her mouth. *What on earth!* She could hardly believe her eyes.

Standing toe to toe, Don shook his fist in Vincent's face. "I don't think you've quite got the picture, buster. Did you actually propose marriage to my fiancé last night? You're no gentleman. How inappropriate is that?" Don's voice cut through the air like a whip.

"I told you…" Vincent's voice was quiet, but determined. "I had no idea she was engaged. But, now that you mention it, doctor, she didn't exactly turn me down." Vincent smirked and flexed his muscles. The pair turned and sidestepped. Their body language reminded Agnes of a pair of roosters in Mr. Higgenbottom's chicken yard.

Agnes pulled the door shut and covered her mouth to stifle a giggle. Now, wasn't this interesting? Doctor Don was worried that he'd lose Katherine. Served him right. All that fussing and fighting about Maddie. Agnes cracked the door open again.

"My grandma used to say, 'if you can't stand the heat, get out of the kitchen,'" Vincent said. "As long as Katherine allows, I'll keep asking, so deal with it." He turned and moved toward the door.

Agnes scurried across the hall, yanked open the kitchen door and plunged inside. *Phew! That was close.* It wouldn't do to have the young bucks know she overheard them. Wait. The wash tub was still sitting in the hall, and she needed help to carry the water.

She opened the door to see Vincent knotting and unknotting his fists, stomping down the hall toward the outer door.

"Oh, hello there, Vincent," Agnes called so sweetly. "Fancy, meeting you here." Oleomargarine wouldn't melt in her mouth. "Could you help me for a minute, please?"

Vincent stopped and turned back, his face still flushed.

Agnes smiled as innocently as a mound of the Three Minute Icing on her cupcakes. "You see, dear, I need to fill this wash tub with water and carry it back to our pumpkin carving booth. You're such a strong, strapping young man. I just know you can help me with that," she said. *That's not likely to have the same effect as when I was an undercover FBI agent in Paris, wheedling information from unsuspecting German officers, but....* "Um... We'll pass right by Katherine's booth on the way back." The mention of Katherine's name was likely to have a more positive effect than when she served drinks in the European nightclubs back in 1918.

With obvious effort, Vincent controlled his temper, unrolled his fists, and strode back down the hallway. He lifted the wash tub. "Sure thing, Mrs. O. Glad to help. Where's the kitchen?"

"Right over here. Thank you, Vincent. I'll make sure Katherine knows how much you helped. We can use all the credit we can get, right?"

They filled the tub and each taking a handle, hauled it back toward the pumpkin booth, without spilling a drop.

Vincent went all gooey-eyed when they passed Katherine's baked goods booth. "Morning, Miss Katherine."

"I see Grandma hornswoggled you into helping," Katherine called as they moved down the aisle toward the pumpkin carving booth. "Come on back when you're done. I'll sell you a cookie."

Vincent's face lit up like the jack-o-lanterns the children planned to carve. "I'll be back before you can say Yankee Doodle Dandy."

"Here's the water." Agnes said, placing the wash tub on the ground beside the pumpkin carving table. "My! Doesn't everything look nice?" Sheaves of cornstalks bound with twine stood in the four corners of the booth. Several dozen pumpkins were piled on the ground.

Vincent flexed his muscles and stretched the kinks from his back. "If there's nothing else, Mrs. Odboddy, I'll just run down and say hello to Katherine before she gets too busy."

Agnes shooed him away "Run along, then. Thanks for the help."

Vincent sidled toward the edge of the pumpkin booth and plunged down the aisle.

Agnes turned to Mildred, counting the money in the cashbox. "Everything looks great. You and Jackson did a good job with the decorations."

Off to the side of the booth, a table covered with newspapers and various knives, waited for the merry-makers to try their hand at carving a jack-o-lantern. Agnes pointed to a sign hanging over the table:

Pumpkin Carving Contest – Entrance Fee – 50 cents – Age Limit – 16 years

First Place – Smoked Ham – Donated by Wilkey's Market

"We're giving a prize for the best jack-o-lantern? I didn't know that." A large ham wrapped in netting hung from the corner. "Donated by Mrs. Wilkey?"

"Yep." Mildred smirked, giving the ham a pat. "She brought the ham before you got here this morning."

"That's a surprise. She probably doesn't remember this is my booth. Mrs. Wilkey is dead-set on seeing me tossed into the clink and throwing away the key."

"Agnes. If you were in her shoes, you'd be upset too. Don't think about it today. Let's just have fun with the kids."

"You're right. I'll try." Agnes sighed and glanced around the colorful booth. "I'll bet we'll have the most popular booth at the fair. With the ham for a prize, every mother in Newbury County will enter her kid in the pumpkin carving contest, whether they want to or not." She chuckled as she counted the pumpkins on the floor. "We only have thirty pumpkins. We'll have to limit the entries to the first kids that sign up."

Mildred gestured toward the back of the booth. "Jackson set up another table behind the canvas where the older children can work."

"I think we'll have to make appointments for the kids throughout the day. I had no idea Mrs. Wilkey was donating a ham. Oh, my! This could get out of hand. Won't we need more knives? And what about some chaperones? Can't have the kiddies chopping off their fingers."

"I'll commandeer some of the parents to stay and monitor the kids throughout the day. Don't worry. We'll make it work."

Agnes folded her arms across her bosom, pleased to have more pleasant things to occupy her mind than the rat on her front porch and Chief Waddlemucker's threats of her potential arrest. Or for that matter, Vincent's suggestion that a Nazi agent was pillaging across the country, headed straight for Newbury!

Perhaps even the confrontation she witnessed between Don and Vincent was of some concern. Katherine had best put a stop to that, or who knows where that might lead?

Katherine moved a plate of cupcakes from one side of the table to the other. Her gaze swept over the booth, from the cash box delivered by the church secretary to the large, brightly colored propaganda posters on the back wall featuring clever slogans and smiling people. *You Can Make A Difference. Plant A Victory Garden. Buy War Bonds.* Slogans and pictures designed by the government, intended to boost the citizens' morale, encourage patriotism, and promote conservation of food and supplies.

She walked closer to the signs and ran her fingers over the colored paper.

War! The country had barely recovered from the Great Depression, finally getting men back to work and lives back on track. Hadn't she and Stephen, her first fiancé, just declared their intention to marry when he lost his life at Pearl Harbor? Why was life so cruel to play such tricks? Just when they least expected it—just when they thought things couldn't get any better—and then there was a tiger...

Pearl Harbor. That unexpected, unprovoked attack on an unprepared nation took Stephen's life and thousands of others, throwing the country into chaos and war. Katherine blinked back tears. *And like that sleeping tiger, America awoke and struck back with a vengeance.*

She glanced again at the slogans on the wall. *Women Power in the Workplace.* Women had a huge role, building planes and battleships, but even more was needed. The government had created a fair rationing program, printed and coordinated the delivery of ration books. They had to deal with trade issues in foreign countries. Most importantly, citizens were encouraged to buy savings bonds to support the war effort. It would take more than the men on the battlefield to win the war. Victory would come only with the additional efforts of the women in the factories and the determination and dedication of the home front warriors to fight the tiger of war. Women like grandma.

If everyone at home fought as hard as Grandma, the enemy would run for cover.

"Hey, Katherine. A penny for your thoughts. You look like you're a thousand miles away." Vincent leaned on the table, eyeing Grandma's chocolate frosted cupcakes on the back table. "Why so serious?"

"What? Oh! Vincent. I guess I was daydreaming." Katherine's face warmed. She glanced quickly around. *Where's Don?* She leaned closer, almost hoping he was lingering somewhere near. Would he be jealous if he saw her talking to Vincent? *Serves him right!* "Thanks for helping Grandma with the wash tub. Do you want to buy a cupcake?" She lowered her head and looked up through her dark lashes. *What am I doing? I'm actually flirting with him?*

Vincent nodded. "Agnes snagged me over in the church. Is there anything I can do for you? I'm happy to stay and help any way—"

"I should have known I'd find you here." Dr. Don strode up to the booth, scowling, fists on his hips. "I thought you were leaving." He moved toward Vincent.

Katherine stepped between them. *Be careful what you wish for.* "Don. That's no way to talk. Vincent just offered to help out. That's why we're here today, right? We need all the help we can get. To help the kids?" Katherine waved toward the church.

Dr. Don's face reddened. He lowered his hands. "Sure. You're right. We do need help. I expect your grandmother needs someone to help the kids carve pumpkins at her booth.

"Hey! There's a thought, Vincent," Don said with a grin. He jerked his thumb down the aisle. "Why don't you go down and help Agnes today? I can help Katherine sell cookies."

"*Uh*…okay. Maybe I'll see you later, Katherine." Vincent turned and walked toward Grandmother's booth.

Katherine glared at Dr. Don. "What the heck was that all about? You looked ready to knock his block off. What's the matter with you?"

"You know what's wrong. That jerk's got no right to come into town and make trouble between us. Imagine, proposing like some Romeo in a three-penny theater act."

"You know very well, his being here has nothing to do with our problems. We were having trouble long before he stepped a foot inside my door. Really, Don, this is not the time, nor the place, but we need to get a few things straight." Katherine's arms crossed her chest. The back of her neck warmed.

"Oh, I don't know," Don said, tossing his blond hair. "This seems as good a time as any. What's wrong with right now? It's not just Vincent, is it? The biggest problem we have was you bringing that kid home without a word to me, and expecting me to be happy about it."

So there it was–the problem in a nutshell. "That *kid's* name is Maddie. Yes, I've already agreed that it was a mistake not to talk to you first, and I've apologized. But it's done now, and if you can't go along with me, then I guess… The child is my responsibility. It's too late to change anything. I can't exactly throw her out like the dishwater." Tears pricked Katherine's eyes. *Oh, why did he have to start up with me here? People are staring.*

Don reached for Katherine's arm. "Things were good between us until Maddie came into the picture. I wish I'd never laid eyes on that brat." He turned on his heel and stomped away.

"What a terrible thing to say." Hearing a sound beside her booth, she looked up.

Maddie stood, not five feet away, her face pale, her eyes wide. She turned and raced away. Within seconds, she ducked behind one of the tents and was out of sight.

How long had she been there? Long enough to hear everything they said? "Maddie! Come back!" Katherine hurried into the aisle. "Maddie! Let me explain."

Katherine glanced at her watch. *A quarter past ten.* Fair-goers had already gathered in front of the various booths. She scanned the crowd. Should she find someone to man the booth and go after Maddie, or should she let Grandmother deal with it? *Darn that Don Dew-Wright. What that poor kid must think, hearing his nasty remarks…and mine.*

"Are you all right?" Pastor Lickleiter's wife hurried toward Katherine. "You look upset. Is there anything I can do?" She squeezed Katherine's arm.

"Oh, I'm so glad to see you. Can you watch the dessert booth for me for a bit? Everything is priced and the cash box is right there. Something has come up. I must go."

"Of course, dear. I'll stay as long as you need me."

Katherine hurried down the aisle toward the pumpkin carving booth. Had Maddie run to Grandmother? *That's what I would do, if I was upset.*

Music from the merry-go-round drowned out the voices and shouts from the various displays. Agnes stood beside the table with the wash tub and watched the crowd walking up and down the aisle, stopping here and there to shop or play the games at each booth. Several ladies with children in hand glanced her way, but hurried past the pumpkin carving booth.

Her good spirits tumbled. Apparently, not even the possibility of winning a ham had tempted mothers to bring their child to carve a jack-o-lantern with an accused thief behind the counter. "Do you think gossip about the burglary has already spread around town?" Agnes grumbled to Mildred. "People are avoiding our booth like the European plague. If it's because of me, I should leave."

"Don't be ridiculous," Mildred said. "We just opened. There's hardly anyone here yet. Give them time." She smiled and waved as a church lady hurried past the booth.

Several customers had gathered at the war bond booth next door where Edith Braithwaite busily filled out paperwork. It didn't look as if the limited number of early visitors had affected her business any.

Agnes started at the distant sound of a roaring animal. Heads turned toward the back of the parking lot where the performing tiger was housed. She planned to take Maddie to the tiger show around noon. Not that it was good to make an animal jump through hoops and other such nonsense, but the performance should bring in the crowds, and the church would benefit from the added attraction. Surely, some of the visitors would find their way to the baked goods and other church-sponsored booths. Maybe even to the pumpkin carving booth.

"Grandma." Katherine rushed up to the booth, breathing hard, her hair flying. "Have you seen Maddie?"

"Not since we got here. I thought she was with you." *What has that child done now?*

"Don stopped by the booth and started up with me again. We didn't realize that Maddie was nearby, listening. He said some dreadful things about her. Now she's run off, God knows where. I thought I'd start here in case she came to you."

Agnes glanced at Mildred and then to Katherine. "You go on

back to your stand. I'll look for Maddie. My presence here is putting a damper on things, anyway." Agnes stepped around the counter holding the wash tub. "I'll be back as soon as I can, Mildred."

"Take your time. Don't worry about anything here. I'll get Jackson to help if we get busy."

Katherine took Agnes's arm and hurried her back to her booth. "Last time I saw her, she was headed toward the church. Where did Vincent go? I thought he might come back when Don left. Maybe he could help look for Maddie."

"I haven't seen him since he helped me carry the wash tub." They stopped in front of the dessert table. "Good morning, Mrs. Lickleiter. Sorry to rush off, but I must go."

"Let me know if you find her, Grandma," Katherine called. "I'm so angry at Don right now, I could kill him!"

"Really, Katherine." Mrs. Lickleiter clicked her tongue. "That's no way for a Christian lady to talk."

"Don't worry, dear, I'll find her." Agnes called as she hurried toward the church.

At the end of the aisle, Agnes darted between parked cars in the parking lot. Why would Maddie run away because of something she heard Don say? If she was upset, it was more logical to think she would run *to* Katherine, not *away* from her.

Agnes stopped, turned and gazed back toward the carnival booths. Wasn't it more likely Maddie was upset by something she heard Katherine say, rather than Don? Maybe Katherine hadn't shared the whole story. Maybe she was having second thoughts about raising Maddie, now that it threatened her relationship with Don. If she had to choose between Maddie and Don, what would she do? Hopefully, it wouldn't come to that.

Agnes reached the church steps.

Beep... Beep...

Godfrey Baumgarten pulled his car into a parking space, opened his car door, and stepped out. "Wait up, love-bunny. I've come to serve you, any way I can," he said with a grin.

As conflicted as she felt about Godfrey, she was delighted to see him now. "Thank goodness. I desperately need you." *Oops!* That was awkward. No telling how he would interpret that remark.

"At your command." Godfrey reached for her hand. "What do you need, lambkins?"

"None of that, now," she said, slapping his hand away. "This is serious. We've had a minor incident and Maddie has run off. You need to help find her. Can you head around that side of the church? She may still be nearby hiding in the bushes. I doubt she'd leave the area. I'll look inside the church."

"Of course, snook-ums. Don't worry, we'll find her. I'll meet you back here in about ten minutes." He started down the sidewalk and then stopped, turned and put his hand over his eyes to shade them from the sun. "Agnes? *Uh…* This Maddie…What breed of dog is she?"

Agnes stomped her foot. "Don't be ridiculous. Maddie's not a dog. She's a nine-year-old child. She's wearing a red and white dress."

Godfrey's face flushed. "A child? And, whose child is this Maddie, again?"

"Maddie is our ward. She's only been with us for a short while. Oh, never mind. I don't have time to explain. Get on your way." Agnes jiggled her hand. "I'll go into the church. Little girl. Red and white dress. Go." She scurried up the steps.

"Right! Got it! Red and white dress. Back in a flash." He trudged toward the corner of the church. "Maddie! Where are you? Come out, come out! *Ollie Ollie Oxen Free*!"

Agnes slowly shook her head. "That man. What will he think of next? Maddie…a dog? Good grief."

The large double church doors squeaked as she pulled them open and stepped into the cool vestibule. Morning sun streamed through the stained glass windows causing dust motes to dance through the colored streaks of light that splayed across the wooden pews. She shivered, sensing the *presence of God*. She always felt closer to God in the church, but it was somehow different with the pews filled with friends and neighbors. Today, in the cool, empty auditorium, it was just Him and her. She dropped into the last pew and bowed her head. "Lord, it's me, again. Agnes Agatha Odboddy. I've got another problem. I know. It seems like the only time I talk to You is when I'm in trouble. You know all about the market robbery and Chief Waddlemucker, so I won't go into all the details again. This time, it's Maddie. She's missing. Wherever she is, Lord, I know You'll keep her safe, but could You please help me find her, so I can bring her home? I'll get back to You about what I'm willing to sacrifice, but if You don't mind, I don't have time to think about it right now. Thanks ever so much. Amen."

Sacrifice? That probably wasn't the best word to use. It wasn't that she was *bargaining* with God, because that would be wrong. It was just her way to thank Him for helping her when she was in need. Satisfied with her humble request and with more confidence in her success now than when she came through the door, Agnes rose from the pew. She strode down the center aisle toward the pulpit flanked on each side with flower stands filled with lilies and gardenias.

Chill bumps rose on her arms as she approached the front of the church. The cloying fragrance of the gardenias filled the air. Her stomach seized. *Uh-oh! Something is wrong.* Whenever she had encountered the scent of gardenias and lilies, it had been the forerunner of a catastrophe. Douglas and John's funerals… Katherine's hospitalization several years before... Just the slightest hint of the scent of lilies and gardenias turned her stomach. *Please, God, not Maddie!*

Agnes stroked the chill bumps on her arms and glanced around the empty church. Her gaze traveled beyond the pulpit onto the church stage. A bronze cross hung over three rows of choir chairs. A banner reading *Jesus Saves* hung over the piano. Off to the left stood the baptistery, one of its curtains pulled across in front, the other torn off its track, drooping half outside the partition enclosure, a darker streak in its center as the water wicked up the cloth from the water in the baptistery. *What happened? What if...*

The hair rose on the back of Agnes's neck. She tiptoed up the steps onto the stage, past the pulpit, past the choir chairs toward the baptistery. *I don't want to look. I can't look.* She had to look. She took a deep breath and stepped closer to the edge. *Don't be ridiculous. What do you expect to find? Maddie? Floating face down in a pool of blood-stained water?*

Chapter Twelve

Katherine wrung her hands. Grandmother was quite capable of finding Maddie. Still, it was hard to wait. *I should have gone to look for her myself.* Katherine stepped out of her booth and gazed up and down the walkway. She so desperately wanted to see Agnes and Maddie. Dare she hope that Maddie would come back on her own?

Where were the men in her life when she needed them? Which one did she most want to see right this minute? Vincent–or Don? Of course, it had to be Don, even if she would like to slap him silly for the way he had carried on in front of Maddie. They were going to be married next month...weren't they?

Vincent's face blocked her thoughts of Don. Then, why was she thinking about another man?

Would it be best to postpone the wedding until Don came to his senses about Maddie? And, what about her confusing feelings for Vincent…whatever they were? She couldn't marry Don if she had the slightest question of her complete love for him.

It was time she and Don had a serious talk about their future. Katherine closed her eyes. Maybe she already knew what was right. Constant quarreling over a major issue was no way to start a marriage. She shook her head, trying to clear away the cobwebs of her conflicted thoughts.

"Daydreaming again?"

Katherine's heart quivered as her eyes flew open. "Vincent! You startled me. I guess I *was* daydreaming again. I've got a lot on my mind. You didn't happen to see Grandmother, did you?"

"Not since we brought back the water. I've been down at the shooting range. Why? Is she looking for me?"

"Maddie's run away and Grandmother is looking for her."

"Oh! Poor kid. I'll look for her. Which way did she go?"

"Toward the church. Thanks. I'm really worried."

Vincent hurried toward the church. He turned and waved. "I'll catch up with you later. You still owe me those cookies you promised."

Katherine's face warmed as guilty pleasure coursed through her chest. "This is most confusing." She looked around. Was someone listening? *Oops! Chief Waddlemucker.*

The chief stepped up to the counter, eyeing the cakes and pies. "Morning, Katherine. I see you're not too busy. This looks like a good time to talk. Unfortunately—"

"Why not?" Katherine's eyebrow rose. "You can't make my day any worse than it already is."

The chief pulled out his handkerchief and mopped his brow. "Sorry if this adds to your troubles. I guess you know, there's gossip that we questioned Agnes about the Wilkey Market break-in." His plump face flushed. He glanced down the aisle. "Is Agnes here today?"

Katherine put a hand over her eyes and nodded. "She's around here somewhere."

The chief tucked his handkerchief back into his pocket. "I knew this would upset you. What else is going wrong?"

She sighed. "Maddie's run away and Grandma's out looking for her. She should be back soon, one way or another." She looked up. "As long as you're here, do you want to buy something? Our ladies have been saving their sugar ration coupons for this event. Mrs. Williams's apple pie looks wonderful. Maybe Mrs. Waddlemucker would rather have a cake?" She pointed at a layer cake with cookie crumbles sprinkled on top. "This one looks delicious."

"That does look good. Can you save it for me? I'll have to come back and pick it up when I get off duty." He removed his wallet from a back pocket and pulled out a bill. "Can you change a ten or is it too early?"

"Yes, I think I can." Katherine took the cash box from under the table. "The cake is $2.00. I know that's a lot, but it's for the kids."

"It's worth it…for the kids. Always glad to help the kids."

Katherine counted out the bills. "Three, four and a five makes ten," she said. "Thanks." She moved the cookie-covered delicacy to the back table and set it beside Grandmother's cupcakes. "I'll put your name on it." She laid a cloth tea towel over the top of both desserts.

Chief Waddlemucker stared at the bills in his hand, pinched the corner of the five-dollar bill and pulled it clear of the ones. He held it up to the light and squinted. "Any idea where this fiver came from?"

Tingles crept up Katherine's neck. "I guess it was in the cashbox. No. Wait. It could have been the one Grandmother gave me. She bought cupcakes a while ago and paid with a five. Why? What's wrong with it?"

Katherine surmised from the deep frown etched into Chief Waddlemucker's forehead that as bad as things were before he arrived, they were about to get a whole lot worse.

The chief waggled the bill in the air. "I hate to say this, but this bill is counterfeit!"

Back at the church, Agnes crept closer toward the stage that held the pulpit and choir chairs. Surely, this was another example of her over-active imagination. She gazed around. *Dark, empty church. Chill in the air. Silence.* Even her prayers for Maddie had put her into a melancholy mood, more susceptible to the powers of her wild ruminations. Hadn't her fancifulness gotten her into more trouble over the past several years than one old woman should experience in a month of Sundays?

That's odd. She approached the marble baptistery tank on the left side of the pulpit. Usually completely concealed behind velvet curtains, one drape was torn away, covering half of the four by six foot rectangular tank. She held her breath and moved toward the tank, fully expecting to see…what? *Stop imagining, Agnes. Don't even think about…about…*

She peered over the edge into the tank. *No blood-stained water! Just the velvet curtain bunched up in a heap in the corner.* So much for her wild delusions. Wait! That lump was too large for just curtains. Something lay concealed under…

Just the smallest fragment of red cloth stuck out from beneath the folds. Panic flooded her heart. *Maddie's red dress?*

"Oh, God, no. No! Maddie?" Agnes slung her leg over the edge of the tank and yanked back the curtain. The breath whooshing from her chest almost made her light-headed.

A man lay crumpled in a fetal position in the corner, his head turned away. One of his shoes had come off revealing a red sock. Blood oozed from a gash in the back of his head.

Head pounding, Agnes turned his face toward her. *Dr. Don?* She laid her fingers on his throat. *Yes, there's a pulse.*

"Hello? Is anyone in here?" Vincent's voice echoed from the back of the church, near the vestibule.

Relief rushed through Agnes. She rose to her knees and peeked over the edge. "Here. I need help!" Thank goodness. She peered through the darkened church as Vincent hurried down the center aisle. "Over here. Dr. Don's been hurt. Run find a phone and call an ambulance." She pointed to the right of the pulpit. "That way. Behind the choir chairs. There should be a phone in the pastor's office."

"Right." Vincent disappeared through the door she had indicated.

Agnes wound the corner of the baptistery curtain around Don's head. Though the heavy cloth was cumbersome and resembled a giant Turkish turban, it served as a compress and might staunch the bleeding.

If help arrived in time, maybe it wasn't too late to save Don's life. She buttoned Don's sweater tighter across his chest, shoved his shoe back onto his foot, and then pulled his turbaned head into her lap.

Agnes closed her eyes. Who would do such a thing? Wasn't Dr. Don beloved by his hospital staff? He was always the children's favorite doctor. With war-time medical services in high demand and doctors in short supply, wouldn't an assailant think twice before attacking one of the few remaining physicians in town? Or was that giving an assailant too much credit? Maybe the attacker had a personal grudge? Was Dr. Don hiding a secret life from everyone? Something that would make him a target for murder?

Poor Katherine. How could she bear to lose another fiancé? Hadn't she had enough sorrow in her short life?

Several minutes passed. *Where is Vincent?* She listened to the faint sound of the merry-go-round. Her lips moved in a prayer for the man crumpled in her lap. The music stopped, plunging the church back into silence. She imagined children climbing off the colorful horses and others climbing back on. Why hadn't help arrived? Why didn't Vincent come back? Was he having trouble getting through to the hospital? She laid her hand across Don's damp forehead. He could die while she waited for help.

Agnes's quick breathing sounded loud in the stillness of the church. She put her hand on Don's chest as it gently rose and fell. His shallow breath barely made a sound. The merry-go-round started up again.

Bang! The front door crashed open.

Finally. A man's voice called out. "Lady? Where are you?"

Agnes raised her head and peered over the edge of the baptismal tank. From the looks of the man's clothing, he might be one of the carnival workers. Vincent must have rounded up some help after he called the hospital.

"I'm here–inside the baptistery!"

Just then, Vincent rushed down the center aisle. "The ambulance is on its way." He leaned over the half-wall. "How's he doing?"

"He's still breathing if that's–"

"What happened?" The carnival worker interrupted. "What do you want me to do?"

"Quit asking silly questions and get in here. Can't you see? Someone has conked Dr. Don in the head, and he's bleeding all over my blue serge suit."

"It's counterfeit? How can you tell?" Katherine leaned closer to inspect the five-dollar bill clutched in Chief Waddlemucker's hand. Passers-by stared and then hurried on their way, likely seeing the expression on the chief's face. "Are you sure?"

"*Humph.* Don't you think I know my own business, missy? I'm an expert in these things. Look at the color. The green dye is fading into President Washington's face. Even a half-wit could see this is a fake. I don't expect you to be as versed in this stuff as I am, but really, Katherine…couldn't you see—"

"No, Chief, I couldn't. This half-wit has never seen a counterfeit bill in her life. I didn't even consider the possibility that a Newbury citizen would pass a fake bill for a dozen cookies at a church carnival."

Chief Waddlemucker's face flushed. "My apologies. Of course, you're right. I didn't mean…" He tucked the bill into his shirt pocket. "*Humm…*You said this might have come from Agnes? Where is she? I need to talk to her." He turned to leave. "I'll be back later to pick up my cake."

"Wait. I didn't say it came from Grandma. It might have been one of the bills already in the cash box." Katherine picked nervously at a loose button on the front of her blouse.

"Right. Always that possibility." The chief gave her a mock salute and hurried off.

Mrs. Kindlebaker sidled up to the booth, eyeing the pastries.

"Hello, Katherine. I'd like a dozen of these cookies, please. My boys love chocolate chip cookies."

Katherine shook her head to dispel the thought of Grandma passing the bill. She slid the cookies into a brown paper bag, took Mrs. Kindlebaker's dollar, and opened the cashbox. A whole eighty-five cents for a dozen cookies! Katherine counted out the change. "So, how is the family, Mrs. Kindlebaker? I hear your son's doing well at West Point." She took a deep breath to settle her racing heart.

"Oh, my, yes. Going to be an officer, he is. We're mighty proud of him, we are." She took the coins from Katherine and dropped them in her purse. "Nice to see you, Katherine." She grabbed her cookies and hurried off toward the merry-go-round.

"Give your son my best." Katherine called after Mrs. Kindlebaker, as she shoved the cash box back under the table.

"Katherine?" A tiny voice quavered toward the back of the booth.

Katherine spun around and pulled back the canvas. "Maddie? Oh, my goodness. Come here. Where have you been? I've been so worried." She dragged the child into the booth and hugged her, kissing the top of her soft blonde head. "Why did you run away? Was it because of what you heard Don say?" She lifted Maddie's chin and looked into her eyes.

Maddie's blonde braids swung as she nodded, her eyes sparkling. "Dr. Don doesn't like me and it's my fault that you're mad at him." Tears rolled down her cheeks.

"No, honey. That's not true. Sometimes grown-ups argue for silly reasons. It doesn't have anything to do with you." That was a lie, but what was she supposed to say to a nine-year-old? *Yeah, it's your fault. Don doesn't want you and I do.* "I love you very much, Maddie. Dr. Don and I will work out our differences. Don't worry about it.

"Now, did Grandma find you? She's looking for you."

"She's in the church. I hid in the back so she couldn't see me. I got scared and ran away. Are you mad at me, Katherine?"

Katherine's brow furrowed. "Maybe a little, because you made us worry, but not now. I'm just glad you came back by yourself."

"Will Grandma be mad with me? I'm sorry." Maddie ducked her head and snuffled.

Katherine sighed. "She won't be mad when she knows you're safe. You'll see."

An ambulance whined, the sound growing louder as it came into the church parking lot. "What do you suppose has happened?" Katherine stepped away from her table and looked both ways. "Someone must have taken ill." Nothing looked amiss. She wished she could run over to the church to see why the ambulance was there. "I hope Grandma hasn't had an accident at the church."

Maddie's face paled. She hesitated. "Is the bad man still there?"

Katherine's stomach jittered. "What bad man would that be, sweetheart?" Her chest tightened. "What are you talking about?" *Something is terribly wrong, I just feel it.*

Maddie burst into tears and threw herself into Katherine's arms.

"Never mind. There's no bad man here now." Katherine hugged Maddie and patted her back. "Let's not think about it, okay? Grandma will be here any minute now, you'll see."

"Here. Let me give you a hand, Mrs. Odboddy." Vincent grabbed Agnes's hand and helped her climb over the marble baptistery wall. "There you go."

The ambulance attendants removed the blood-stained curtain and placed a compression bandage on the back of Don's head. They lifted him onto a stretcher, maneuvered it out of the baptistery, and set it on the floor in front of the pulpit. They checked his vital signs and examined him for further injuries.

Agnes stared at the blood stains on her hands and her left hip where she had cradled Don's head. "Oh! There's blood on my skirt."

The ambulance attendant reached into his bag. "Here. Maybe this will help." He handed her a towel, then stooped again and felt the pulse in Don's neck and wrist. "He's stable. Let go." The attendants lifted the stretcher and moved down the aisle toward the exit.

Agnes dried her hands and then swiped the towel across the bloodstains on her skirt. She handed the soiled cloth to Vincent. "Didn't help much. Do you need this?"

Vincent shook his head. "I'm good. Come over here and sit down." He took her arm and led her to the front pew. "Now, tell me what happened."

"I was looking for Maddie. I thought she might have come in here to talk to Pastor Lickleiter. I saw the curtain pulled down in the baptistery and—"

"What tomfoolery are you up to now, Mrs. Odboddy?" Chief Waddlemucker's ponderous belly loomed near Agnes's face. "Without a doubt, every time there's trouble, I can count on finding you right *squack* in the middle of it."

"Haven't you heard?" Agnes glared at the chief. "I spend my days finding rats on my front porch and looking for people conked in the head. Instead of harassing innocent citizens, why don't you figure out who is causing all the trouble around here?"

Chief Waddlemucker's eyes blinked rapidly. "Well…I…I… No need to… *Ahem!* Well. So what brought you in here? How did you happen to find the good doctor—?"

"Agnes! Pumpkin-bunny. Are you all right?" Godfrey rushed up the center aisle, breathing hard, and his face beet-red. His knees cracked as he knelt on the rug beside Agnes, grabbed her hand and brought it to his lips.

Agnes jerked her hand away. "Don't be so silly. You can see that I'm fine." She glanced at Chief Waddlemucker's startled expression. *What he must be thinking! That Godfrey!*

A muscle twitched beside Godfrey's eye. His hand shook. "I saw the ambulance pull up outside. I knew you were in here, but they wouldn't let me in." His gaze drifted between Chief Waddlemucker and Vincent. "Chief?"

The ambulance whined. Godfrey glanced toward the back of the church and then back to Agnes. "I looked all around outside the church. I couldn't find the child." He sucked in his breath.

Agnes gave Godfrey a wan smile. "I thought Maddie might be in here. Then I found Dr. Don in the baptistery. Vincent showed up about then, so he went to call the ambulance."

"Vincent?" Godfrey turned a lop-sided smile toward the young man. He extended his hand. "Godfrey Baumgarten. I'm Agnes's… *umm*…friend. You've known Agnes long?"

"He's an acquaintance I met… Never mind where. I'll explain it all later."

Chief Waddlemucker raised an eyebrow. "Wait. You said this guy showed up right after you found Dr. Don?" Chief Waddlemucker pulled out a tablet and pencil and addressed Vincent. "What was your business here in the church? Why were you here?"

Vincent opened his mouth to answer, but Agnes cut him off.

"He and Don had an argument, earlier. I'm assuming he came back to…apologize. Isn't that why…?" Agnes's gaze flew to Vincent's face; her hand to her mouth. Why *was* Vincent in the church? He came up the aisle almost the same moment she found Dr. Don. *Was he already here before I came in?*

"An argument, you say?" The chief stared at Vincent.

"Not really an argument," Vincent said. "More like a discussion. Surely, you don't think…" He reached for his wallet. "Here. Let me show you my identification."

"Just exactly what were you…discussing?" Chief Waddlemucker licked the end of his pencil.

Vincent slid his wallet back into his pocket. "I…I asked Katherine to go out with me…*umm*... The doctor objected." Vincent pursed his lips. "But, that's not why I was in the church. Katherine sent me to look for Maddie. I thought she might be in here."

Agnes lowered her head. By admitting he argued with Don,

Vincent just made himself a suspect. *And I had to open my big mouth. When will I ever learn?*

"Sounds like your *discussion* with the good doctor maybe got out of hand and you knocked him in the head?"

Vincent shook his head. "You've got it all wrong. I'd never—"

The chief took his arm. "I think you better come down to the station. We'll finish our discussion there."

"Oh, surely, Chief," Agnes interrupted. "Vincent is above suspicion. He's FBI!" She gripped Godfrey's arm. *I shouldn't have said anything. Will Katherine blame herself for Don's attack? Or blame me for opening my big mouth.* Either way, she might be right.

The chief lowered his voice. "No one is above suspicion, as I'm sure you know, Agnes, being a person of interest in your own legal entanglement." He glanced at Godfrey, still kneeling by Agnes's knee.

"As if I didn't have enough to deal with already, with robberies, counterfeit money showing up and now what looks like an attempted murder. I don't need all this job security!" He snorted. "If you'll be good enough to drop by the station later today, Mrs. Odboddy, we'll take your statement. Good day!" The chief propelled Vincent toward the door. "Come on, buster."

"Mrs. Odboddy," Vincent called over his shoulder. "Believe me, I didn't do it."

Godfrey took Agnes's hand again. "My little love-apple. I don't understand any of this. Sounds like I'm not the only one with some explaining to do."

Agnes rolled her eyes and pulled her hand away. "I'll explain everything later. Right now, I have to let Katherine know what's happened, and we still need to find Maddie."

Godfrey stood and offered Agnes his hand. "Then, isn't it good that I've got all the time in the world. I'm not going anywhere. Let's get out of here and find that kid."

Agnes stood. "What do you suppose the chief was talking about—counterfeit money? My stars! What's next?" She took Godfrey's arm.

"I hope Katherine has an extra apron I can borrow to cover my soiled skirt."

In the distance, the tiger roared. Was it the harbinger of more trouble, or just getting close to feeding time?

Chapter Thirteen

Sales were brisk back at Katherine's dessert booth where she sold cakes, cookies and cupcakes. Coins and a stack of dollar bills grew in the till as the goodies flew from the booth. At the rate of sales, they'd have $20-$30 before lunch. Katherine sifted through the bills, holding each up to the sunlight, checking to see if it looked like the suspicious five-dollar bill Chief Waddlemucker found earlier.

What could be keeping Grandma? She glanced down the walkway past the apple dunking booth, hoping to see Grandma or Vincent returning. How could she let Grandma know that Maddie was safe back at the dessert booth?

The whine of an ambulance caused Katherine's stomach to churn again. Visions of Grandma being loaded inside popped into her head. Surely, someone would have come to tell her if Grandma had taken ill.

What was it folks said? *No news is good news?* That wasn't always true. Following the attack on Pearl Harbor and the report that the U.S.S. Arizona had sunk with thousands of reported casualties, she had waited on pins and needles for six days for some news of her fiancé, Stephen. Hadn't she raced to the phone every time it rang, hoping against hope that he would call and say he was on shore leave when the attack occurred? Or, that he was one of the few survivors? Hadn't she ambushed the mailman every day, praying for a letter from Stephen?

When Stephen's name finally appeared in a list of the deceased in the newspaper, she had collapsed. For two weeks, she drifted between days drenched with tears and nights full of nightmares, visualizing his body floating in the sunken ship.

She shuddered, forcing the memories from her mind. The shadow of a customer fell across the chocolate cake on her table. She looked up. "Good morning, Mrs. Castleberry."

The customer was a lady from church, clutching a toddler by the hand and another babe in her arms. "Can I interest you in this lovely chocolate cake or a dozen brown sugar cookies? It's all for the children's Bible School this fall."

Mrs. Castleberry paused. "Not today, Katherine. Little Arnie has embarrassed himself," she shook the toddler's hand, "and me without any spare clothes. I was just on my way back to my car. Sorry."

"Wait." Katherine eyed the tears dripping off little Arnie's chin. His light blue shorts were stained and damp. "I'm sure it was an accident. Come here, Arnie. I have an extra cookie here. Do you know any little boy who might want to eat it?" She held out a cookie.

Arnie grinned, pulled away from his mother's hand and grabbed the cookie.

"Thanks, Katherine." Mrs. Castleberry struggled to balance the baby and open her purse. "What do we owe you?"

"Not a thing. It's my treat. Have a good day!" Arnie's smile was more than enough payment for the cookie. She waved as the little family hurried toward the parking lot. *Maybe someday I'll have a little one like that.*

"Katherine!" A familiar voice called from two booths away. "Oh, good. You've found Maddie." Agnes waved to the child seated on the floor coloring in her book.

Godfrey Baumgarten trailed behind Grandma, his face aglow as he gazed at Grandma.

"There you are, Grandma. I heard an ambulance. I was worried. What happened?"

Grandma's face reminded Katherine of a day at the ocean when, without warning, drenching rain drives picnickers off the beach.

"I'm afraid I have some disturbing news. I was in the church looking for Maddie and I found Don unconscious in the baptistery. Apparently he was struck in the back of his head."

Katherine's hand flew to her mouth "Is he all right?"

Grandma shrugged. "He's on his way to the hospital. There's more." Grandma cast her eyes down. "I sort of told Chief Waddlemucker about Don and Vincent's argument this morning. Unfortunately, he hauled Vincent off to the station. You had better—"

"Vincent arrested?" Katherine's face tingled. *They were arguing here, too.* Her head swarmed with dizziness. Was she going to faint?

Grandma reached for Katherine's arm. "Come sit over here. Now, dear, I'm sure everything will be all right. Do you want me to drive you to the hospital?" Customers scurried past the dessert stand, stopping at the dart and balloon booth across the aisle. "Perhaps we can get someone to watch… Oh, there's Mrs. Lickleiter. Yoo-hoo, Mrs. Lickleiter, can I have a word, please?"

The pastor's wife hurried up. "Katherine? What's wrong this time? My goodness, you are having a bad day, aren't you? You look positively peaked. Perhaps you should go home and try a good old fashioned steam treatment. Putting a towel over your head over a bowl of boiling water and a quarter cup of apple cider vinegar relieves a headache in no time. I can stay and take care of things here."

Katherine lowered her head. "I wish I had time for that. My head *is* splitting. Apparently, Don's been hurt. If you could stay for the rest of the day, I'd appreciate it." She turned to Grandma. "No need for you to come, Grandma. I'll take my car and then call Chief Waddlemucker. There's probably nothing we can do for a while, anyway."

Grandma nodded. "Sounds like a good plan. I have to go down to the station later and give my statement. I'll keep Maddie with me. Now, don't stress, Katherine. I'm sure Dr. Don will be fine. As for Vincent, the chief said they just wanted to sort out a few things."

"You run on, Katherine," Godfrey chimed in. "I'll hang around and help Agnes."

Katherine grabbed her purse and sweater and touched Maddie's cheek. "Maddie, we haven't had a chance to talk yet, have we? I have to run now, but we'll have a long talk tonight when I get home, okay? Don't worry." She pulled Maddie into a hug.

Tears welled in Maddie's eyes. "Will Dr. Don be okay? Why did that man hurt him?"

Katherine stooped down level with Maddie's face. "Did you see who hurt Dr. Don?" Her hands felt like chunks of ice. Come to think of it, Maddie had said something before about *the bad man* in the church, but it had slipped her mind. Was Maddie in the church when Don was attacked? Cold shivers crept up the back of her neck. "Grandma? Did you know anything about Maddie witnessing the attack?"

Agnes shrugged. "News to me. Maddie? Did you see who hurt Dr. Don?"

Maddie shrieked. She shook her head and threw her arms around Katherine's leg. "I'm sorry. I didn't mean to look. I won't tell anyone!" Great wrenching sobs shook her body.

Katherine hugged her until she quieted. "It's okay. We aren't angry." She wiped the tears from Maddie's face. "There, there, now. It's all right. You're not in trouble. You stay with Grandma, okay? I'll be back later and we'll talk more about it."

"Okay." Maddie hiccupped a few times and scrubbed her face with the back of her hand.

"Grandma. Don't question her now. Let her settle down. We'll discuss this later, okay?"

Agnes took Maddie's hand. "I have an idea. Why don't you and I go and see the tiger. When we come back, you can carve a jack-o-lantern at Grandma's booth." She squeezed Maddie's hand. "How does that sound?"

"Godfrey, while we're gone," Agnes said, "will you go down to the pumpkin carving booth and lend Mildred a hand? I should be back within an hour."

Godfrey's lower lip turned down. "You mean I can't come with you to see the tiger? I haven't seen a tiger all morning. I had really hoped to see one before lunch."

Maddie put her hand over her mouth and giggled. "You're funny."

Godfrey tousled her hair, waved and ambled down the aisle toward the pumpkin carving booth.

"Come along, Maddie."

"Does the tiger bite, Grandma?"

"I doubt it, dear; maybe just a little, if he's very, very hungry."

Katherine waved and hurried toward the parking lot. *If seeing a tiger can't get her mind off all this trouble, nothing will.*

Taking Maddie to see the tiger would do Grandma a lot of good, too. At the very least, watching the show would give her a chance to forget about rats on the porch, or her imminent arrest and Don's attempted murder. Not to mention, the return of an old boyfriend, bent on re-igniting a less than smoldering romance. Any one of those issues was a ticking time bomb.

Chapter Fourteen

Within the hour, Katherine pulled her car to a stop in front of the Newbury Hospital. She sat for a moment, her heart pumping against her chest. *Stay calm. Everything will be okay.* First priority was to see that Don was going to be all right. She grabbed her purse and hurried inside. Her mouth felt so dry, she had to swallow twice before she could speak to the receptionist at the information desk. "I'm Dr. Dew-Right's fiancé, Katherine Odboddy. Can you tell me where I can find him?" She took a deep breath and blew it out. *Steady. Keep calm.*

The receptionist ran her finger down a page on her desk. "He's still in the emergency room," she said. "Straight down the hall and to the left."

"I know where that is. Spent some time there last year." Katherine strode down the hall wondering if she should stop at the gift shop. No. If he was still in the ER, they wouldn't let her bring in flowers. She'd have to wait until he was roomed or released. Her stomach did a flip-flop as she reached the entrance to the ER. Would he make a full recovery? How would it affect their wedding? If there was a wedding… She shook her head to dispel the questions.

Katherine followed a volunteer through the emergency room to Don's bedside. "How is he?" She clutched her hands to keep them from trembling.

The girl shrugged. "You'll have to talk to the doctor. Here he is."

She pulled back the curtain surrounding Don's bed.

Don's pale face blended into the pillowcase. Asleep or unconscious?

Tears pricked her eyes. Would she lose another fiancé, like Stephen, before she had a chance to marry? A lump caught in her throat. *What am I, the Evil Fiancé, cursed to spinsterhood all my life?* With a gentle touch on Don's arm, she whispered, "It's me, Katherine."

Don turned his head toward her. His eyes fluttered open. "Katherine?" He reached for her hand and drew it to his cheek. "What kept you? I missed you."

"I just heard about the…*umm*. I came as soon as I could. Are you all right?"

Don's lips twitched in a smile. "It's a good thing he hit me in the head. Anywhere else, I might have been hurt." He chuckled, and then grimaced. "*Oww!* It only hurts when I laugh."

Katherine sighed, leaned down and kissed his cheek. If he could still make jokes, he should make a complete recovery.

"Do you have any idea who did this? Was it…? *Umm*…did you see who hit you?" She held her breath, waiting for his answer.

Don shook his head. "*Oww*…Shouldn't have done that, either," he whispered. His hand moved to the nurse's call bell.

A nurse appeared at the door. "Yes, Dr. Don. Is there something you need?"

"Can you help me sit up a little higher?"

"Sure thing." She turned the crank at the end of the bed and Don's head rose a few inches. "How's that?" She plumped a pillow behind his back and straightened the sheet up to his chest.

"Much better. Thanks." Don's cheeks pinked up. He reached for the glass on his nightstand.

"Here. I'll help you with that." Katherine carried the tumbler into the bathroom, filled it, and handed it to him. "Can you remember what happened at the church?" She pressed him with the question again and caught her breath, almost afraid to hear his answer. *Please, Lord, don't let him say it was Vincent.*

"I was walking around the carnival, trying to cool off after our little spat." His gaze dropped to the blanket covering his chest. "Katherine. I'm sorry about that. I was way out of line. Forgive me?"

"We both said things we shouldn't. Go on. What happened next?" She smoothed a wrinkle from the sheets, avoiding his eyes.

"I was walking past the merry-go-round and a kid came up to me. He handed me a note and said some guy gave him a dime to give it to me."

"A note?" She sat up straighter in her chair. "That's odd. What did it say?"

"It said, 'Meet me in the church. This involves your fiancé. Come alone.' I couldn't understand what it meant."

"Oh, Don." The shiver at the back of her neck spread through her chest. She rubbed the chill bumps on her arms. "What's going on? Why is this happening?"

Don shook his head.

"So, go on. You went to the church. Who was there?" Katherine's hands felt like chunks of ice.

"I went to the church and waited, determined to get to the bottom of it. I have to admit, I thought it had something to do with you and Vincent. When no one showed up, I started to feel guilty. I'm sorry. I should never have thought..." Don leaned back and his head sagged into his pillow. He shut his eyes.

"Are you in pain, Don?"

A nurse yanked back the curtain. "Dr. Dew-Right? I need to take a blood sample and change your bandages." She frowned at Katherine. "You need to wait outside for about twenty minutes. You can come back when I've completed his medical treatment."

"Why don't you go the cafeteria and get a cup of coffee, Katherine?" A wan smile touched Don's lips.

"Okay. I won't be long." Katherine kissed his cheek, patted his hand and pulled the curtain back around his bed. She left his room and stepped into the hall. Where was the telephone? Surely there was a phone in the ER, or nearby. Should she call Chief Waddlemucker, check on Vincent and give him an update on Don? If only she could talk to Grandma. Wouldn't it be nice if someone invented those little wrist radios like Dick Tracy wore in the funny papers? Then she could talk to Grandma any time she wanted.

There. Just down the hall–a telephone booth. She hurried in, pulled the door closed and ran her finger down the list of names and phone numbers printed on a paper beside the phone.

The First Church of the Evening Star and Everlasting Light

Northern Farmer's Bank of Newbury

Newbury Police Department... *Ah. Here it is.* Better call the station first and tell Chief Waddlemucker about the note that led Don to the church. She dropped a nickel into the phone, put her finger in the hole of the 6, and circled the telephone dial… Each time she removed her finger from the dial, it circled back, clicking as it passed each number, back to its starting point. With the last click, the phone *beeped* several times and then rang at the police department.

Katherine shivered when someone answered the phone. "Newbury Police Department. How shall I direct your call?"

"Chief Waddlemucker, please. It's urgent. This is Katherine Odboddy."

"Can I take a message? He's in an interview room."

"No. Please tell him that I have information about the attack on Dr. Dew-Right this morning. He'll want to talk to me, right now."

"Yes ma'am. Please wait. I'll see if I can get a message to him."

Katherine watched through the pay phone window as patients came and went through the ER. She dug through her purse to see if she had more coins. If the chief didn't come soon, the operator would ask for more money.

When an ambulance arrived with a woman in the late stages of labor, there was a stir of excitement among the waiting patients. The voices in the emergency room stilled in sympathy as the attendants brought the moaning woman through the outer doors.

As Katherine whispered a prayer for her safe delivery, Chief Waddlemucker came on the line. "Hello. Chief Waddlemucker. Miss Odboddy? Now tell me what's so important, you have to drag me out of my…*um*… interview with your Grandma's friend?"

"You were interviewing Vincent? Have you arrested him?"

"I'm not in the habit of sharing investigations with you, young lady. What's on your mind?"

"I'm at the hospital. I just talked to Don briefly. He says he received a note asking him to meet someone in the church. My name was mentioned in the note. That's what convinced him to go."

"*Humm…* That is interesting. But, I don't see… Why ask Don to meet at the church?"

"Maybe he thought no one would see them talking there."

"Who was it? Did he identify Vincent?"

"I'm not sure. The nurse tossed me out of the room before he got that far in his story. I thought you'd want to know that he was lured to the church. Why would Vincent set up such a scenario with a note and all? There was nothing to gain. They'd already met and quarreled."

"*Humm…*It doesn't clear Vincent, but I see your point. We just released him. I sent Sergeant Hickenlooper and Sergeant Crenshaw back to the carnival to warn the church ladies to be on the look-out for more counterfeit money."

"That's a good idea."

For the first time this week, Katherine felt almost encouraged. Someone was creating havoc in their lives. And it hadn't taken the townsfolk long to believe that Grandma was a burglar. If they learned the counterfeit money was found in her booth, would they believe she was behind the counterfeiting, too? Releasing Vincent was the first good news she'd heard for a while.

Katherine's attention turned back to the patients in the waiting room. The woman in labor was gone. Probably moved to the delivery room.

A mother rocked a whining infant while another toddler played on the floor near her feet.

A man with a bandaged hand held a magazine at arm's length. *Must have left his reading glasses at home.*

"Katherine? You still there? Is there anything else?" Chief Waddlemucker's voice yanked her back to the present.

"What? I'm here. I'll get back to you if I hear anything else."

"Tell Dr. Don I'll be over to take his statement as soon as I can get free."

"I will. Thanks, Chief Waddlemucker."

"Bye, Katherine."

She hung up the phone. Voices in the emergency room grew louder as she slid open the phone booth door. She glanced at her watch. This might be a good time to spend a few minutes in prayer before she returned to Don's bedside. Always feeling closer to God outdoors, often more so than when in church, Katherine stepped through the door into the courtyard next to the ER, and sat on the shaded bench beneath the willow tree.

She bowed her head and whispered. "Father God, thank you for bringing Don safely through this ordeal. We pray for his continued healing. But, particularly, I need help understanding my own mind regarding Don. I do love him, but…" Again, her mind wandered…

If she loved Don so much, why did she have such confusing feelings for Vincent, a man she barely knew? Was it right to go through with the wedding when she and Don were already in trouble deciding Maddie's future? She *was* wrong, expecting Don to accept a child from such a conflicted background. She had no right to make that important decision without consulting him.

Was this what the divorce courts called *irreconcilable differences* before she even walked down the aisle?

Katherine shook her head. How could she ask for guidance with her head and heart in such turmoil? On the other hand, perhaps that was exactly when she *should* seek guidance. She bowed her head and closed her eyes again. "Lord, please help me know Your will. Which one of them should I—"

Vincent's voice broke through her prayers. "Katherine? Are you all right?"

Butterflies danced in her stomach. Vincent? Here? Now? *If this is your idea of a joke, Lord, it's not very funny.*

Chapter Fifteen

Agnes took Maddie's hand and marched her down the aisle towards the back parking lot to the tiger exhibition. The further from Katherine's dessert booth they walked, the fainter the sounds of The Blue Danube Waltz from the merry-go-round. Numbers of fair-goers increased as they approached the area near the stage where the tiger would perform. Agnes nodded to her neighbor. "Morning, Mrs. Williams. Fine day! So, you've come to see the tiger, too?"

Mrs. Williams shivered. "I'll admit, the idea makes me a bit nervous. They say it's not even in a cage. You don't suppose it's a wild one, do you?"

"Can't imagine they'd let it perform out in the open if it was." Agnes grinned down at Maddie. "I suspect it hasn't eaten any little girls for a while."

"Grandma!" Maddie sidled closer to Agnes's leg. "That's not funny." Her eyes were as bright as sparklers on the Fourth of July. Her lips trembled, and she shivered, much like a child might, entering a Halloween haunted house.

Agnes's heart warmed, seeing Maddie's pleasure. How good to see her smile. Considering her former life, it wasn't likely she had ever experienced anything as exciting as meeting a tiger face to face. For that matter, Agnes had to admit, meeting a tiger was a first for her too.

The spectators gathered in front of a boxcar-like caravan with a painted canvas draped over the front bars, depicting a ferocious tiger leaping through a fiery hoop. Brightly colored yellow spoked-wheels jutted from beneath the wagon, and beside the canvas drape, on each end of the wagon, clown faces were carved in the wood. Apparently, this was where the tiger lived, as well as his method of transportation from town to town.

The crowd stopped shuffling about at the sound of grunts and grumbles behind the canvas. Their gaze riveted on the wagon, eagerly awaiting the first sign of the emerging tiger.

A slight breeze rippled the ladies' skirts and blew strands of Maddie's hair into her face.

Agnes squeezed Maddie's hand and felt her shiver. Was it from the cool breeze, or excited anticipation?

Roar!

The crowd froze. Anxious titters and whispers broke out. A baby wailed.

The door of the tiger's cage creaked. A young man emerged, dressed in a blue and yellow shirt and red trousers. "My name is Wendell." He tipped his hat, revealing long blond hair tied back in a ponytail. He stepped down the metal step carrying a short red and white striped stick resembling a magician's wand. Was that his only protection against a wild tiger? Agnes pulled a hankie from the bosom of her dress and dabbed her forehead.

The trainer bowed to the audience, then glanced back toward the open door. He drew a whistle from his pocket and blew a shrill note. "And this is Shere Khan."

The crowd waited. Seconds passed. Ten… Twenty… Someone coughed. Stars and Stripes Forever began to play on the distant merry-go-round. Where was the tiger?

The young man stepped back toward the door. "Don't be shy, Shere Khan. Come on out and say hello to the nice people."

Shere Khan! Like the tiger in Rudyard Kipling's *The Jungle Book!* Agnes grinned. *I must read that book to Maddie.*

Scratching sounds came from behind the canvas, like the sound one might imagine a tiger would make as it rises from a metal floor.

Again, the crowd waited. A few tittered. Feet shuffled.

An orange nose appeared through the open door and the beast leaped onto the ground. Yellow eyes roamed the crowd.

The spectators murmured and took a collective step backwards. Coming to see a tiger was one thing–actually *seeing* one three feet away, unchained and unrestrained, was quite another.

Maddie cringed against Agnes's leg.

"Shere Khan." The trainer waved his stick in a circular motion. "Wave hello to the nice people."

"Is he dangerous?" Someone called from the audience.

"Only when he's hungry." The trainer chuckled. "Up! Shere Khan!"

Shere Khan sat back on his haunches, lifted his front feet and waggled one foot.

A wave of *oohs, aahs,* and nervous titters broke out in the audience.

The trainer pulled a treat from a bag at his waist and slipped it to the big cat.

The crowd inched forward, clapped and laughed. They weren't afraid. Not really. They knew he was tame. Heads nodded and smiled.

"Shere Khan! Up." The trainer's short stick tapped a large rubber ball.

The tiger leaped onto the ball and rotated his feet backwards. The ball rolled across the ground with the cat balanced on top. Some twenty feet distance, he hopped off the ball.

The crowd exploded with hoots, claps and whistles, and moved closer.

For the next ten minutes, the trainer put the tiger through his paces. After each trick, he gave the cat a treat from the bag at his waist. At one point, the tiger lay on the platform, gazing at the crowd, looking like an enormous, striped housecat.

Agnes dabbed her hankie across her forehead again as her thoughts turned to Shere Khan's distant furry relatives. Too many had fallen prey to the hunter's guns and the clothing industry, now that Hollywood starlets fancied fur coats. Shere Khan's native cousins should be thankful that fox fur coats had recently become more fashionable this season than tiger. Even so, the threat imposed by poachers was still real. She envisioned wealthy and unscrupulous hunters stalking an unsuspecting prey, seeking tiger skin rugs and tiger heads mounted over their bars. She shivered. A foreboding?

It was hard to imagine this gentle giant pursuing an antelope, leaping on its back, killing it with one snap of his jaws. Hard to imagine his jowls covered in the life's blood of the still warm antelope, snarling to fend off predators determined to steal his bounty. Hard to imagine the beast dragging his kill through the underbrush, perhaps to a nearby den where two or three cubs awaited their first taste of meat. Such was a wild tiger's life in the jungle.

This tiger was as tame as Ling-Ling, probably hand-raised as a cub, likely declawed for safety and now totally dependent on a human to provide his meat on the end of a stick. It was doubtful he'd ever seen an antelope, and even if starving, wouldn't know what to do if he saw one.

The trainer's voice snapped her back to the present. "Does anyone want to pet Shere Khan? He's very friendly." The trainer pointed to Maddie. "You?"

Maddie glanced up at Agnes. Was she asking for permission or seeking an excuse to forgo the invitation?

"What do you think?" Agnes touched Maddie's cheek. "Do you want to pet him?"

"I…I…think so. Yes!" She pulled away from Agnes's hand and stepped closer.

"Good!" Agnes nodded and smiled. "That's my brave girl." Not at all like the shy, frightened, child they brought home from Washington D.C. several months before.

Maddie slowly reached out her hand and touched Shere Khan's head, then ran one finger over his ear. She looked up and grinned at the crowd. "He's so soft." She stroked down the tiger's neck and scratched behind his ear.

Shere Khan turned his head toward the caress, opened his mouth and yawned, showing long sharp teeth. His eyes sought Maddie's face and their eyes locked in a gaze that seemed to connect their soul. At last, he blinked and lowered his head onto a giant paw.

Seeing Maddie's delight, several other children rushed forward.

The trainer motioned them back. "Just one at a time." He touched Maddie's shoulder. "Will you let the other children have a turn, honey?"

Maddie nodded and returned to Agnes. "He only likes me. See how he's turning away from the other children?"

Indeed, Shere Khan stood and was ambling back toward the open door of his caravan, apparently having had his fill of public adulation and applause. He appeared ready for a well-deserved nap and within seconds, he was up the steps and out of sight.

"Well, guess the show is over, folks. Our star needs his beauty sleep." The trainer chuckled and turned away. "Come back later. We'll have another performance at four o'clock."

"*Ohhh!*" The crowd mumbled and drifted back toward the game booths and rides.

Agnes reached for Maddie's hand. "Are you ready to go back now?"

Not responding, Maddie stared at the caravan door.

"Maddie?" Agnes gave her hand a shake. "Shall we go back and carve a pumpkin?" She pushed a lock of hair off Maddie's face.

Maddie had not moved. Her gaze was still fixed on the spot where Shere Khan had disappeared. She rubbed her fingers together, seeming unable to relinquish the sensation of the tiger's ear, reluctant to forget the rumble in his throat as she stroked his face.

"Maddie?" Agnes searched Maddie's face. The child seemed lost in the memory of a special shared moment with a creature from the wild, reluctant to move past the experience and return to her life where troubling events were a daily occurrence. "Shall we go, sweetheart?"

Maddie blinked. "I remember when we played together, with baby lambs and goats in a meadow in Heaven, before I was born. See how he looked at me? Did he remember, too?"

"What strange ideas you have, child. Where do you come up with such things?" Agnes grasped Maddie's hand and hurried her away from the stage.

Played together in Heaven? What could have put such a thought into her head? Agnes glanced at Maddie's face. Her eyes were aglow, her smile as innocent as an angel. Her face looked as though she was truly remembering, catching a glimpse directly into Heaven where she had played in a meadow with a tiger.

Goosebumps crept up Agnes's arms. Maybe Maddie *was* remembering. Hadn't Pastor Lickleiter just preached on this text and encouraged the congregation to memorize the Bible verse? *The wolf also shall dwell with the lamb, and the leopard shall lie down with the kid, and the calf and the young lion and the fattened calf together; and a little child shall lead them. (Isaiah 11:6 KJV)*

Wolves? Leopards? Lions? Who's to say there wasn't a tiger among them?

Chapter Sixteen

Katherine put her hand to her heart. "Vincent! You startled me." She glanced anxiously around the patio outside the emergency room. What was there about this man that made her heart jump every time she saw him? She smoothed her hair off her forehead with a trembling hand.

Vincent blushed as he backed away. "I'm sorry. You were praying for him, weren't you? I shouldn't have interrupted. I'll leave you to your prayers."

"No. Please. Come back. I…I *was* praying for Don and for you, too. I'm glad Chief Waddlemucker released you. Is everything settled at the police station?"

"Actually, he had no evidence, so he couldn't hold me. He said, 'Don't leave town, buster.'" Vincent chuckled. "Sounded just like the cops in the gangsta' movies. I wasn't planning on going anywhere."

Katherine lowered her gaze. Her heart beat so fast, surely he would hear it pounding. What was wrong with her? She shouldn't feel this way. She was engaged to be married. Wasn't she? Tears pricked her eyes. "Oh, Vincent, why don't you leave me alone? You have no idea…"

Vincent started. "What? What have I done? I swear I didn't attack the doctor, if that's what you think. You must believe me. Won't you let me sit and talk to you?"

Katherine shrugged and patted the bench alongside her. "I suppose."

Vincent sat.

Katherine's hip tingled where her thigh touched his leg. She scooted away. *This just won't do at all. I should leave before I make a fool of myself.* She stood and backed away. "I've changed my mind. I have to go. Don is waiting for me."

"Before you go, please say you believe I'm innocent."

Katherine stopped at the door. "I believe you. It's just that I…I… have to go." She pulled the door open and escaped into the emergency room. Why was she so confused? If she loved Don, why would she get so flustered when she saw Vincent? "Am I having feelings for him?" Never before had she allowed herself to even think the words, much less whisper them out loud. If it was true, she had to come clean with Don.

Katherine swallowed the lump in her throat. It was time to make a decision. Either break it off with Don, or insist that Vincent stop coming around, getting her all stirred up. It wasn't fair to either of them.

She stood in the receptionist's line until it was her turn at the counter. "May I see Don Dew-Right, now? The nurse asked me to leave while she changed his bandage."

"Give me a minute. I'll check." The receptionist stepped away from the counter.

Katherine gazed around the emergency room, empathizing with a young mother with a wailing infant.

The young woman slid back onto her stool. "Go on back. You can see the patient, Miss."

"Thank you." Katherine walked to the area where the blue-grey curtains circled the patients' beds. *Third bed on the right.* She pulled back the curtain.

Don lay half reclined against a stack of pillows, his head now swathed in a new bandage, his eyes closed against sunlight streaming through the window.

"Don? Are you awake?" Katherine whispered.

He opened his eyes and reached out his hand. "Katherine."

"I'm here. Did I wake you? You don't look well. Maybe I should call the nurse."

"I wasn't asleep. Just thinking about what happened at the church."

Her pulse quickened as she pulled the chair up closer to the bed. "Did you see who hit you?" She held her breath. Would he name Vincent?

"I remember going into the church. I was feeling bad for snapping at you. I don't know what got into me. I saw the way Vincent looked at you. When he said you agreed to go out with him, I was jealous."

Katherine nodded, remembering how she felt when the waitress flirted with Don at the diner the other night.

"When Vincent told me that you didn't exactly turn down his proposal, I had to question our relationship. Do you have feelings for him, Katherine? I thought we had an understanding…" Hadn't he gone straight to the heart of the question she was struggling with?

Katherine leaned forward, her mouth trembled. "I…I…can't answer that, Don. I don't know how I feel. I thought I was in love with you. But, then the issue of Maddie came between us. Quarreling about her future made me question whether we could make a go of marriage.

"Then, Vincent showed up. It came as a complete surprise when he proposed, but I have to admit… I guess I do have feelings for him. I just don't know exactly what they are." She put her hand over her eyes, unable to look him in the face.

Don turned his head away. "It sounds like we should put our wedding plans on hold until we sort out some things. About Maddie and Vincent?"

Tears puddled in Katherine's eyes. She lowered her head. "Maybe you're right–at least for the time being," she whispered.

She stood, moved to the window and stared out at the parking lot. A nurse wheeled a woman to a waiting car and helped her out of the chair. A dog ran past the car and stopped at the foot of a tree to sniff. What was Don thinking? Why didn't he say something? The ticking clock on the wall was the only sound. She turned. "You never finished telling about what happened in the church. Did you see who attacked you?"

Don's hand covered his eyes. "I was sitting in the front pew, praying. Asking forgiveness for saying such terrible things to you. I know Maddie heard me. I was praying for peace about adopting a child from a horrible family background. Praying for strength to face the trouble I knew would surely follow, because it's what you wanted." He sighed and pushed the button on the call bell.

"I never saw the attacker. He must have come up behind me and conked me on the head. That's all I remember. So, if you're afraid that it might have been Vincent... Sorry. Can't help you, one way or the other." Don's face clouded and he turned away from Katherine. "Next thing I remember, I was in the ambulance and—"

The nurse flung back the curtain. "You rang, Dr. Dew-Right?"

"Yes. I have pain in the back of my neck. Could I have another pain pill, please?"

"I'll check your record and see what we can do." The nurse turned to Katherine. "I believe you should leave. Dr. Don is over-tired and needs his rest."

"Don...I don't know what to say. I..." Katherine touched his arm.

"I think we've both said enough. You should go now, Katherine."

"Perhaps I should." Katherine stepped away from the bed, out the door, and then dashed into the emergency room. A man with a bandaged arm held the door open. She mumbled her thanks and stumbled down the hall, tears pricking her eyes. *Now, what have I done? Ruined my chances with Don? What about Vincent? I could lose both of them before this is over.*

Chapter Seventeen

O h, my Lord, a-mercy." Agnes gripped Maddie's hand tighter as they approached the pumpkin carving booth. It was barely an hour since she and Maddie left the area neat and tidy, to visit the tiger. During that short time, the booth had turned into a scene from a Saturday matinee horror movie.

Strings of pumpkin viscera clung to Mildred's arms, her hair, and her dress. Pumpkin shards and seeds littered the ground. Three school-aged children attacked a pumpkin with the ferocity of Jack the Ripper. Twenty-one leering, sneering jack-o-lanterns sat on the table against the back wall. Little name cards beside the savaged victims identified their juvenile assailants.

Orange sludge drifted across the top of the water Mildred used to clean up the kids before they left the pumpkin slaughter house.

Mildred shuddered as she pulled a tuber strand off her forehead. "Thank God, you're back. Once word got around about the smoked ham, the local moms swarmed the place. You'd think we were giving away a brand-new Hudson, instead of a ham. No doubt they realized it was enough meat to feed their family for a week."

"Where are Godfrey and Jackson? I thought they were supposed to help you?" Agnes tied an apron around Maddie's middle and shoved her toward a recently vacated place at the table. As a sticky child passed by, Agnes grabbed his arm. "Hold it, young man. Let's clean you up a mite before you leave. What would your mother say if I turned you loose like this?" She steered the child toward the tub and thrust his arms into the soupy water, and then swiped a fairly clean towel over his face and hands. She thrust the kid into the aisle. "There you go. Off with you. We'll let you know if your jack-o-lantern wins." Agnes turned to face Mildred. "Now, tell me! What's going on here?"

Mildred jerked her head toward the back of the booth. "Godfrey and Jackson are out back with the older kids. The goal is to keep them from killing each other with the carving knives. We've already had one minor incident that drew blood. Probably would qualify more as attempted voluntary manslaughter, than attempted murder. It's doubtful their mothers advised them to deliberately kill off the competition."

"Good grief!"

Two more mothers approached the booth, dragging reluctant children. The women eyed the smoked ham dangling from the top of the booth. Their children stared longingly toward the merry-go-round.

Judging from the ragged jack-o-lantern faces on the back table, previous contestants had finished their mandatory obligations in a hurried and haphazard manner, anxious to run off to more enticing entertainment. From such poor entries, it was going to be hard to choose a winner.

"Maddie, Mildred saved this pumpkin just for you," Agnes said. "I'll help you get the top off. Try not to make a bigger mess than we already have. See if you can hit the garbage can with at least half the seeds."

"But, Grandma. I don't want to carve a pumpkin. I want to walk around and spend my quarter."

"Nonsense! You have all day to spend your quarter. Now, carve." Agnes shoved the knife into Maddie's hand, grabbed the towel and made an effort to wipe the slime off the table around her pumpkin.

What was this generation coming to? Kids these days didn't behave anything like children when she grew up. She would have stood in line for an hour for a chance to carve a pumpkin, even if there *was* a merry-go-round a hundred feet away.

Really.
Almost certainly.
Probably...
Well...maybe.

Maddie's jack-o-lantern was remarkable, even with its crooked smile and slanted pyramid-shaped eyes. Compared to the hasty offerings by the other distracted children, it was definitely a contender for the prize. Not that Maddie could win, since Agnes was manning the booth. Not the least bit prejudiced, of course, it was obvious that Maddie was much more talented than any other Newbury child. Her jack-o-lantern was just an example.

"War bonds. Get your war bonds here. Support a soldier and win the war." Agnes turned toward Edith Braithwaite's voice.

Edith stepped out from her booth and waved. "Pretty exciting, *huh*? How's your punkin' carving goin'? Looks like you're pretty busy over there, too," she called.

Since it appeared that Mildred and Godfrey could handle the few children currently carving pumpkins, and Maddie had finished carving her pumpkin, she and Agnes strolled next door to speak to Edith.

"How are sales?" Agnes picked up a pamphlet from the table, opened it and read a few lines. *War Bond - $18.75. The government will use this money to pay for tanks, planes, ships, uniforms, weapons, medicine, food and everything the military needs to fight and win. This is an investment in your country. Ten years from now, redeem your war bond for $25.00!*

Agnes flapped the paper. "So, that's how the government finances the war. Heavens to Betsy! We put up our hard-earned money now, and it takes ten years to get it back?"

Edith straightened the pile of pamphlets. "You can't think of it that way, Agnes. It's another way you can do yer' part to win the war. You, of all people, must realize financing a war isn't cheap. And you'll get interest on your investment."

Maddie tugged on Agnes's arm. "Grandma? I want to help win the war." She pulled the quarter from her pocket and handed it to Edith. "May I please buy a war bond, Mrs. Braithwaite?"

Edith smiled and shook her head. "That's very sweet of ya', Maddie, but I'm afraid yer' quarter isn't enough to buy a bond. Wouldn't you rather ride the merry-go-round?"

Maddie crossed her arms and shook her head. She pulled her mouth into a pout.

"Wait. Wait! I wasn't through explaining." Edith picked up another small booklet and held it up. "See what I have here? *War Savings Certificate Thrift stamps.*

"If you want to help win the war, you can buy a twenty-five cent Thrift stamp with yer' quarter." Edith opened the booklet lined with squares and pictures of the Minuteman statue. "See? We paste each stamp right here. When you have another quarter, you can buy another stamp to put in this savings stamp book. When yer' booklet is filled with 75 stamps, you can trade it in for a real war bond. And, in ten years when you're ready to go to college, it will be worth $25.00." She picked up another booklet. "We also have savings booklets for ten-cent stamps, fifty-cent stamps, one-dollar, and five-dollar stamps. What do you think of that?"

Maddie handed the quarter to Edith. "Yes, please. I want to start my very own book. There's a boy in my class who collects tin cans and glass bottles after school. He buys savings stamps with the money he earns, because his big brother is in the Army."

Agnes squeezed her shoulder. *What a precious child.* "That's very thoughtful of you, giving up your quarter. Maybe we can buy several every week and fill up the book real soon."

"Well, isn't that nice? That's a fine start." Edith retrieved a stamp from her box and handed it to Maddie. "Just lick the back and stick it right there on page one." She tapped the booklet.

Maddie attached the stamp. "Won't Katherine be proud of me? I'm winning the war!"

Agnes hastily blew her nose and stuffed her handkerchief back into the neck of her dress. Oh, if it could only be true, that an innocent child could end the war by buying a stamp. She shook her head. She would not cry. "Come, Maddie, let's show Mildred your Thrift stamp book."

Who were they kidding? She could buy Thrift stamps, collect cans, knit socks and grow turnips in her victory garden until the cows came home, and it wasn't going to make one whit of difference or save one soldier's life. The war would play out in all its ugliness until the last cathedral was toppled, the last European town blown to smithereens, and the last enemy soldier was beaten into submission. Only then would the boys come home, those who could come home. Only then could they try to put the shreds of their lives back together. Only then…

Chapter Eighteen

gnes and Maddie bid Edith farewell and returned to the pumpkin carving booth.

As they entered the booth, Agnes stopped short. Why was Mildred giggling, holding Godfrey's hand, and making eyes at him?

Mildred hadn't giggled like that since April Fool's Day in 1932, when her late husband sat on the raw egg she put under the seat cushion in his truck. He broke another one when he stepped on the gas pedal, and a third slid from behind the visor and tumbled into his lap!

Why all the giggles now? Godfrey was charming, to be sure, but wasn't he supposed to reserve his charm for her? Jealousy zig-zagged through Agnes's chest. *Stop that. Mildred is my dearest friend. And Godfrey loves me.* But, truth be told, she hadn't been very clear about her feelings for him. Hadn't she continually spurned his romantic overtures and put him off again, just this morning? How many times could she rebuff him before he turned to another pair of welcoming arms? Like Mildred's. Wasn't Mildred an attractive widow who deserved to find happiness?

The pumpkin booth was currently empty of children. Every mother with a child between the ages of eight and sixteen had apparently dragged them to the booth to try their hand at the tempting, ham dangling from the rafter. Thirty jack-o-lanterns leered at Agnes from the back of the booth, displaying a multitude of expressions and carving skills.

Agnes stepped closer to the booth. With heart pounding, she

watched Mildred pick a shred of pumpkin off Godfrey's collar. *That's right, Mildred, flirt away!* Oh, the pain, watching, and not a thing she could do about it.

Godfrey's hand came up and for a moment, he grasped Mildred's hand and then released it. He smiled down at her–that smile that always made Agnes weak in the knees. From the expression on Mildred's face, she was equally affected. It seemed that Godfrey had that effect on every female between the age of eight and eighty.

Agnes stopped outside the booth. Her heart sank. Too late. Too late. She had kept her feelings from Godfrey too long. Like two ships passing in the night, she had her chance, but her resistance had sent Godfrey straight into Mildred's arms. Then again, why shouldn't he love Mildred? She was a wonderful woman. They both deserved to find love, even in their old age.

Maddie paused beside the wash tub as Agnes stepped behind the counter. "And, just what is going on here, may I ask? Am I interrupting something? I haven't been gone thirty minutes and…" *Now, why did I say that?* It sounded downright snotty. "I mean… It looks like I interrupted you cleaning the booth. Can I help?" She grabbed a rag and hastily swiped around the jack-o-lanterns on the table. Her stomach churned. She hoped Godfrey wouldn't see her red face.

"Oh, did you have fun?" Godfrey smiled. "What have you got there, kiddo?" Godfrey pulled Maddie inside the booth and took the booklet she held out to him. "Why, it's a Thrift savings stamp booklet. I heard they were selling stamps as well as the bonds." He glanced up at Agnes. "I've bought a number of savings bonds, myself. I'll be rich in ten years, if I live that long." He delved into his pocket, pulled out a handful of change, and handed Maddie another three quarters. "Go on back and get some more stamps for your book, sweetheart."

Maddie grinned, grabbed the quarters and scampered back to Edith's booth. "Thank you," she called over her shoulder.

"Mildred and I have been through World War III with these kids," Godfrey said. "I think we're finally done for the day." He gestured toward the back table. "No more pumpkins. No more kiddies. Time to turn out the lights!"

"Now, we have to choose the winner." Mildred gestured toward the pumpkins. "We've narrowed it down to these three." She ran her hand over the three jack-o-lanterns in the middle of the table. "What do you think, Agnes?"

A name tag sat in front of each pumpkin. Agnes pointed to the one on the left. "That's Maddie's. She can't win. She was carving for the fun of it. So, I guess it has to be one of these two."

The pumpkin in the middle had round eyes and a snaggletooth grin. The other jack-o-lantern had pie-shaped eyes and a frown with what appeared to be two missing teeth. Both of their faces were such that with a candle inside, their intense expressions would amuse the most discerning trick-or-treater.

"I think this one," Agnes said, pointing to the pumpkin with the missing teeth. This child must have spent a bit of time getting the teeth to look like that. Whose is this?" She turned over the name card. "Wouldn't you know it? It's Chief Waddlemucker's boy, Humphrey. I think he's in Maddie's class at school. He's small for his age, only about knee high to a grasshopper, that one." She grinned. "Won't Mrs. Waddlemucker be pleased with the ham?"

Mildred nodded. "Good choice. That's the one I liked, too."

Of course you like what I like. Especially my Godfrey! Agnes's face warmed. That wasn't nice. Pure-de-jealousy. That's what it was. Straight from high school where girls are best friends one day and hate each other the next, if the friend dares to smile at a boy she favored. Guilt filled her heart. Hadn't she and Mildred been friends for more than thirty years? Wouldn't she give up her life for her? But, was she willing to give up her Godfrey?

An ache swelled in Agnes's chest. "I'm sorry. I have to go." She could not stand there for one more minute and watch Mildred make goo-goo eyes at Godfrey.

"Where are you going?" Godfrey touched Agnes's shoulder.

"Won't Maddie wonder where you've gone? I'm sure she wants you to take her around to the carnival games."

Her upper arm tingled where Godfrey's hand touched her. How on earth could she continuously be around this man, feeling as she did? What if he married Mildred? God forbid. She'd have to move away, that's what she'd have to do. Perhaps she could sell her house and move to Boyles Springs. She'd have to start shopping there anyway, since Mrs. Wilkey wouldn't let her shop at the local market any more.

Agnes opened her mouth to answer, but no words came out. *What did he say about Maddie? Something about the carnival?*

"Grandma! Grandma! Look! Now, I have four stamps in my book." Maddie dashed into the booth waving the Thrift stamp book.

"Yes, I see. We should go and see the displays and games or..." The thought occurred to her that Mildred and Godfrey had worked like dogs, dealing with the crushing onslaught of thirty jack-o-lantern carvers. What with all the water fetching and hunting for Maddie and visiting the tiger, she hadn't done bupkis.

Agnes turned to Mildred. "I'm sure you and Godfrey want to be alone. I'll stay and hold down the fort so you guys can take in the sights." Her face warmed. Why stand in the way of true love? Manhandling thirty sticky children all morning wasn't exactly conducive to a budding romance.

"Don't be ridiculous," Mildred said. "You and Godfrey should take Maddie on the merry-go-round."

"You don't want to go out and about together?" Agnes gulped. Was Mildred being magnanimous, willing to sacrifice her true love for her friend? That should make points with the Big Guy. Why was it so hard to breathe?

Mildred grinned. "Whatever for? He's your boyfriend, not mine."

Sparkles of light danced in front of Agnes's eyes as tears pricked. *Must have something in my eye.* Had she heard Mildred correctly? Mildred wasn't making cow-eyes at Godfrey? How could she have believed even for a minute that her best friend would try to steal him away?

Agnes let out her breath in a big sigh. Once again, her vivid imagination had run amuck. She had fabricated an entire scenario with almost as much detail as Orson Welles when he broadcast his 1938 Halloween night radio show, and the country went bonkers, thinking Martians had invaded the United States. Well, maybe it wasn't quite as dramatic, but pretty close. "So, you and Godfrey aren't—"

"Romantically inclined? Me and Godfrey?" Mildred giggled. "What kind of an idiot do you think I am?"

"Hey! Wait a minute. What am I, Swiss cheese? I'm standing right here." Godfrey chuckled. "I'm not such a bad catch…am I?"

"No, dear. You're perfect." Agnes threw her arms around his neck and hugged the stuffing out of his ample figure. "You're the whole nine yards and back again, and I love every inch of you."

"Agnes! Come quickly. I need you."

Agnes turned toward Edith's voice. Whatever was the matter?

Chief Waddlemucker stood beside Edith, his head lowered, shuffling his hat.

Agnes hastened over to the war bond booth in time to hear the chief say, "…to bring such bad news, Edith, but I knew you'd want to go to the colonel as soon as possible."

"What's the matter with the colonel? Have we been invaded?" Agnes rushed to Edith's side. "I knew I shouldn't have given up serving a shift on the coast watch—"

"Don't be so melodramatic, Agnes," Chief Waddlemucker said. "We haven't been invaded. I just heard on the radio that Edith's husband, Colonel Farthingworth, was in an automobile accident. They've taken him to Newbury County Hospital."

Edith wrung her handkerchief. "Oh, my poor darling. I really must go ta' him. What shall I do about the war bond booth?" She turned her pale face toward Agnes. "Can you help me, Agnes? Someone has to monitor the booth for the rest of the day. It's so terribly important to the war effort. I was planning to take the money home for the weekend and bank it early Monday morning. Could you do that for me, too? I'd be ever so grateful." She grabbed her sweater and purse. "Everything's right there. The cashbox. The booklets. The bonds. You'll see. It's all self-explanatory. Just take the money and fill out the forms. Thanks!" Edith flew out of the booth before Agnes could ask any questions.

How hard would it be to sell a war bond? The selling part wasn't a problem. People either wanted one or they didn't, but there was paperwork that needed to be completed correctly. It would be *on the job training* when the next customer came to buy a bond or a Thrift stamp.

"Don't worry, Grandma." Maddie patted Agnes's hand. "I know just what to do. I watched Edith two times when I bought my stamps. I'll help you."

Agnes squeezed Maddie's head. "Of course you will." *And, a little child shall lead them!* "We'll do it together. It can't be that hard." She opened the cashbox. A chill raced up her neck. The box was over half full of fives, tens and twenty-dollar bills. There had to be over a hundred dollars in there! Not to mention all the quarters, half-dollars, dimes and nickels. Who would have thought that war bonds and saving stamps would be such a hot seller at a church carnival?

Agnes thumbed through the completed paperwork, each one filled out by a customer who had forked over eighteen dollars and seventy-five cents for a war bond. The half-full money box held the unsold bond booklets, as good as cash, once a name was filled in, stamped with the official rubber stamp, and clamped with the metal thing-a-ma-jig lying beside the cash box.

Agnes glanced nervously around the booth. What if Don's attacker was still lurking around? He could have come and smacked Edith in the head, stolen the savings stamps and books, filled out the paperwork with his own name and added the stamp and seal. Was she the only one who thought like a criminal? Edith should never have worked alone in the booth with so much money at stake.

Chief Waddlemucker had left the booth and was half-way down the aisle.

Agnes called after him. "Chief! Come back! A word, please?"

The chief turned and shuffled back, a growl affixed to his lips. "What's wrong now?"

"I don't want any gossip about me being alone with all this money. I'm willing to take it home and bank it Monday, but I'd like an officer with me the rest of the day."

"Right. I should have thought of that myself. I'll have Sergeant Dimwiddie escort you home, if you like."

Agnes shook her head. "Godfrey Baumgarten is here. He can drive me home. I would feel better, though, if an officer stayed this afternoon." She hesitated and then added, "*Uh*…I don't suppose there's any news about the Wilkey Market burglary?" Agnes held her breath. Wouldn't it be wonderful if the chief reported an arrest, and she was cleared of any wrongdoing?

The chief shrugged. "We've questioned several drifters in town, but so far, no leads. 'Fraid you're not off the hook yet, Agnes. But, we'll keep looking. Don't worry. A jury would never convict you on such circumstantial evidence, anyway. Like you said, you could have dropped that handkerchief in the store any time."

"But, I didn't, and you know it. Now, you've arrested Vincent for attacking Don and he was the only one who was trying to help me clear my name."

"I didn't arrest Vincent. We just questioned him. I was just doing my job."

"You're going to *do your job* me right into the jailhouse!"

"Besides, we already released Vincent. I couldn't hold him. Suspicion is one thing; evidence is quite another. My hands are tied until we speak to Dr. Dew-Right. I was on my way to the hospital to question the doc when I heard about the colonel's accident. I'll be on my way, then." He doffed his hat and stepped into the aisle again. "I'll send Sergeant Dimwiddie right over. Can Godfrey stay with you until the Sergeant gets here?"

"I'm sure he can. Thanks, Chief."

As the chief stepped away, a man and woman walked up the booth. "We'd like to buy two war bonds for our children." The woman smiled and opened her purse.

Well, here goes nothing. Guess I'll figure out the paperwork as I go. Agnes reached for the moneybox, the bond booklets, the rubber stamp and the official seal gadget. She handed the sheet to the lady with a pen. "I think you fill out this top part with your children's names and your address. I'm new here, so be patient with me." She picked up a completed form. "Yes, fill in all the information up to that line and I'll complete the rest."

With the completed forms as examples to follow, she figured it out. "I'll need to see your driver's license to verify your identity and then I'll sign it."

She nodded at Sergeant Dimwiddie, who had arrived and taken a seat behind the counter. "Morning. Thanks for coming."

In no time, the forms were completed, money paid and bonds stamped and sealed. Agnes looked over the forms and signed her name at the bottom. "Here you are, one for Arthur and one for Margaret."

Maddie picked up the Thrift stamp booklets. "Would your children like to start a savings stamp booklet? The stamps are just twenty-five cents each. When their book is full, they can trade it in for a savings bond." She shoved the book into the woman's hand.

She and her husband exchanged a smile. "What a good idea." She handed Agnes two more quarters."

Maddie pushed in front of Agnes. "Let me do it. I know how." She opened the box and removed two twenty-five cent stamps, marked two 'x's' on a separate sheet and handed the stamps to the woman. "There you go. Just lick the back and stick the stamps in the book."

"Thank you, dear. Our kids are around here somewhere. I'll have them attach the stamps when we get home. They'll love the idea of helping the war effort." The woman dropped the booklets into her purse and the couple walked away.

"Good job, Maddie. You are an excellent saleslady," Agnes said. "You're really helping the war effort now."

"I know. I'm good at everything, even spelling."

Agnes chuckled. "And, very modest, too, aren't you?" It was good for children to have self-esteem, but when did it slip over into conceit? She'd have to watch this one carefully.

Throughout the rest of the afternoon, Agnes and Maddie sold a number of bonds and savings booklets. By closing time, Agnes began to worry about the cash box full of money. Suppose someone broke into her house again and stole it? Where could she hide it that a thief would never think to look? *I know just the place. No one will ever guess!*

Thus satisfied with her plan, she and Maddie gathered the savings bond material into a cardboard box, folded chairs, and pulled down the posters. Sergeant Dimwiddie helped the men from the church choir dismantle the booth and carry the tables and chairs back to the church.

Agnes carried the money box back to the pumpkin booth. Godfrey and Mildred had cleaned up the booth and Jackson carried the children's jack-o-lanterns to the church kitchen. On Monday, the church ladies planned to turn the pumpkins into pies for the Veteran's Hall.

On the way home, Agnes and Godfrey delivered the smoked ham and the three jack-o-lantern finalists to Wilkey's Market. The top three pumpkins were to be displayed in the store's front window. Mrs. Waddlemucker could pick up her ham at the store.

"Why don't you wait in the car?" Godfrey opened the trunk to retrieve the prize winning pumpkins. "Maddie and I can take the ham and the jack-o-lanterns into the store," he called from the rear of the car. "No sense you going inside and getting Mrs. Wilkey all frazzled up again."

Godfrey stopped at the single stoplight in the middle of town on their way home. Last year, in their infinite wisdom, the city council had voted to install its first stoplight at the one major cross street in the middle of town.

Agnes glanced from left to right. Not another car in sight. "Putting in this stoplight was the biggest tom-foolery that Horatio Puselbuster, ever pushed the town council into voting for. *Humph!* We're the only car in the whole intersection. Why should we have to stop?"

"Stoplights mean progress, babe, like in the big cities. As the head city councilman, Puselbuster is just trying to keep Newbury up with the times."

"I don't give a rat's patootie about Pustlebuster's progress if it's a waste of time. I should never have given up my seat on the town council. They wouldn't have gotten that vote past me."

"You're getting all *het up* for nothing. Can we change the subject, Puddin'-face?"

"Speaking of changing, can you check my bicycle tires when we get home? Both were flat this morning. Just one more thing to worry about."

"Maybe it's not as bad as you think." Godfrey smiled.

While Godfrey checked the tires and Maddie supervised, Agnes hid the savings bond money in her secret hiding place. Completing her covert task, she hurried out to join the pair.

She found Godfrey squatting by the bicycle, examining the front tire. "Well, do I have to buy new tires?" Agnes wrung her hands.

"Don't take on so, Love-kins. They can be fixed," Godfrey said. "Someone just let the air out. That didn't happen by accident."

"Really! Just the next phase of *get Agnes*, huh? At least I don't have to buy new tires."

"If you'll drop me at the corner service station, I'll pump up the inner tubes. I'll have your bicycle good as new in three shakes of a lamb's tail."

Agnes sighed. "Thank goodness. How did I deserve such a handy man in my life?"

"You're just lucky, my dear," he said with a grin that melted Agnes's heart.

Chapter Nineteen

Agnes left Godfrey with the family while she drove down to the station to give Chief Waddlemucker her report about Don's attack in the church. Once inside the police department, she scowled at the officer behind the reception desk. "Agnes Odboddy, here to see Chief Waddlemucker. Tell him I'm in a hurry to get home and make waffles."

The officer raised an eyebrow. "Waffles? What has that got to do with Chief—"

Agnes stamped her foot. "Don't be impertinent, young man. Tell the chief I'm here and be quick about it."

He picked up the phone. "He may be busy. You'll have to wait."

"I don't intend to wait. I'm in a hurry. He'll see me."

The officer dialed. "Chief? You have a visitor. It's that Mrs. Odboddy again. She says she's in a hurry. Shall I— Yes, sir." He looked up. "Go right on in. He's expecting you."

Agnes glared at the officer. "*Told ya'!*" She turned on her heel and stomped into the chief's office. Flumping into the chair in front of his desk, she tossed her purse on the floor. "Well, what more do you expect me to say? I already told you everything I know down at the church." She glanced at her watch.

Chief Waddlemucker laid down his pen, looked up and smiled. "So, here we are again, Agnes. Just like old times. Can I get you a glass of water or some coffee?" He laced his fingers behind his head and tilted his chair back.

"I think not. That muck you drink down here could strip the rust off a radiator."

"As you wish." He pulled a tablet from the top drawer, wrote across the top and looked her straight in the eye. "If you'll just tell me again how you found Dr. Dew-Right in the church and what happened next. I'll take some notes and have them typed up. You can look it over and sign it if you're satisfied with the report."

Agnes repeated the story she told the chief at the church, adding once again that she was convinced, beyond a shadow of a doubt, that Vincent had nothing to do with the attack.

"By the way… Maddie may have witnessed the attack in the church, but she was so upset, we haven't had a chance to question her, since you insisted I come down as soon as I was through at the carnival. So, if there's nothing else, I'm going home and make waffles for my family." She stood and moved toward the door.

"By all means, talk to the child. Call the station if she has anything important to add. The officer on duty can get in touch with me any time, day or night."

Agnes reached for the doorknob. "Chief? Just one more thing. You might be interested to know that someone let the air out of the tires on my bicycle this morning. So, after putting a rat on my porch, framing me for the Wilkey Market break-in, and spreading gossip all over town that I'm the thief, it doesn't look like they're through with me yet."

The chief heaved his ponderous body up from his chair, and moved toward the door. "What exactly do you mean by that?" His forehead wrinkled.

Agnes sighed. "Mrs. Wilkey has informed me that I am no long welcome to shop in her store. She received an anonymous phone call from someone who told her all about the handkerchief, and my being at the store that night. Due to the specific details she received, she's convinced that I'm the guilty party."

"So that's how the gossip got started? Why didn't you mention this before?"

Agnes shrugged. "What difference would it make? Everyone except Vincent thinks I'm guilty. He's trying to help me sort out this mess. He says the FBI suspects a foreign agent may be behind my troubles and he's—"

"Foreign agents? I don't understand."

Uh-oh! Now she'd gone and done it. Chief Waddlemucker wasn't aware of the events on their train trip across the country, or the affairs in Washington D.C. she and Katherine had experienced earlier this summer. "*Umm. Heh. Heh.* Never mind all that about foreign agents. You know me. I see foreign agents behind every cabbage bush. Well, I must be going. Those waffles, you know. *Ta ta!*"

Agnes yanked open the door and scurried out. Poor Vincent. It was her blabbing about his quarrel with Don in the church that got him in trouble in the first place. One of these days, her big mouth was going to get her into a peck of trouble.

She pushed the button on the elevator and glanced over her shoulder. Hopefully, the chief wouldn't follow her into the hall and ask more questions.

The elevator door slid open. Jackson Jackson, the attendant, grinned, his dark eyes glowing and his smile a perfect study in white. "Mizzus Odboddy! Have you been to see Chief Waddlemucker?" He glanced down the hall.

She stepped into the elevator. "How are you, Jackson? How's the family? Well, I hope."

He chuckled. "They's fine. Thanks for askin'. Little Mary is in the fifth grade now, with that child you brung back from Washington."

The elevator jerked to a stop. Jackson pressed the button to open the door. "Now, don't forget, Mizzus Odboddy. With all the able-bodied men off to war, I's here to help the widda' ladies here abouts if you needs anything, anything at all."

"Yes. I know. You've been a big help. I'll be sure and let you know if something comes up." She stepped out of the elevator.

"How is them chickens?" Jackson called as she hurried down the hall. "I heard you sent them to live on the Higgenbottom farm. They was too much for ya', huh?"

Agnes gave him a dismissive wave. Hadn't the chickens sent her on a merry chase last year when they first came to live with her? A visit to the Higgenbottom farm was in order soon. It would be nice to see how the chickens were getting along.

Thinking about a visit to the Higgenbottom farm put her to mind about her immediate plans. *Do I have enough milk and eggs to make waffles for everyone? If not, they're out of luck, since I won't be shopping at Wilkey's Market any time soon.*

Chapter Twenty

Warning! Stay in your homes. Keep small children and animals inside. Radio announcer

Katherine waved her grandmother toward the sofa where Godfrey waited, and hurried into the kitchen. "Go sit down, Grandma. I'll make the waffles."

Grandmother hung her coat on the hall tree and called to Katherine. "That would be lovely. Thanks, dear."

Katherine pulled the waffle iron from the cupboard, placed it on the kitchen counter and plugged it into the wall socket. "You set the table, Maddie, and get the honey and jam from the icebox while I mix up the batter. Then you can fetch Grandma and Godfrey for supper. I should have several waffles ready by then."

She beat an egg, milk and flour into Grandma's green Pyrex mixing bowl. She flipped the switch on the radio next to the sink and tuned it to a local station. A little music might put her in a better mood, after her upsetting talk with Dr. Don at the hospital.

The big band sounds of Tommy Dorsey with soloist Frank Sinatra filled the kitchen with uplifting jazz music. Katherine hummed along as Frank sang *In the Blue of Evening.*

Maddie had placed the last spoon on the table, and Katherine poured batter into the waffle iron when an announcer's voice interrupted the music.

Attention, Newbury residents. This is a public service announcement. While tearing down the carnival rides at The First Church of the Evening Star and Everlasting Light parking lot this afternoon, the trainer found the cage door open and the tiger missing. He reported seeing the tiger safely in his cage the previous hour. Searchers failed to find the animal despite a diligent search of the church grounds. The tiger is presumed to be wandering freely around the Newbury city limits.

Warning! Stay in your homes. I repeat. Keep small children and animals inside. Chief Waddlemucker's search party is combing the neighborhoods in and around the church. Stay tuned to this station for updates on this life-threatening event!

Katherine glanced at Maddie. *Life-threatening? Grandma said he was a tame as a kitten.*

The child's face was as white as a sheet. She turned pleading eyes toward Katherine. "He's probably trying to find me. He loves me. Will they shoot him when they find him?"

Katherine shook her head. "I'm sure they'll find him real soon. He'll be fine."

In truth, the risk to the poor tiger was grave. Not many people in town knew how tame and gentle the big cat was, even allowing the children to pet his head. Wasn't it more likely that some trigger-happy homeowner, seeing a Bengal tiger in his back yard, perhaps with his eye on the family cat, might shoot the animal? Why did the announcer have to say 'life-threatening event?' Couldn't he have said the tiger was tame and ask the public to notify the police if it was seen?

Maddie threw her arms around Katherine's waist and sobbed. "They'll kill him, won't they? They'll shoot him dead!"

Katherine patted Maddie's head. Her heart wrenched. There really was no good way to reassure Maddie. "There, there, Maddie. I'm sure they'll find Shere Khan sleeping in a big dog house somewhere. Don't worry." Katherine closed her eyes and whispered a prayer for the safety of the big cat. How could they protect Maddie from the inevitable? She was sure to hear the news, however this thing ended. She would be heart-broken if the tiger was destroyed.

Katherine lifted the waffle iron lid and peeled the golden brown waffle away from the top of the iron with a fork, placed it on a plate, and filled the iron with batter for the next waffle.

"Grandma? Godfrey? You'd better come in here and eat," she called. "I've got a waffle ready.

"Maddie. Now, stop crying and run wash your face. Everything will be fine. You'll see."

Maddie fled down the hall, wiping tears from her cheeks.

Grandmother and Godfrey came into the kitchen and sat at the little wooden table covered with a red-checkered tablecloth. Grandmother placed half of the waffle on Godfrey's plate. "We heard the radio announcer. Maddie's taking it hard."

Godfrey buttered his waffle and spread apple butter over the top. "Poor kid. Isn't that the carnival tiger you took her to see, Agnes?"

Agnes nodded. "Maddie took quite a shine to him. Even said she remembered playing with him in Heaven. Lord knows where she came up with that idea. I hope they can get him safely back to the trainer. I'd hate to think…"

Maddie walked back into the kitchen, her eyes puffy from crying. Her lip trembled as she slid into a chair. "Can I have a waffle?"

Katherine took the second waffle from the iron, split it in half and placed it on Maddie's plate. "There you go. Now, do you want honey or jam on top?" How she wished she had never turned the darn radio on.

The buttery scent of cinnamon wafted up as Agnes sliced a bite from her waffle. "Maddie, dear. I have an idea. How about we drive out to the Higgenbottom farm after church tomorrow? Do you remember we told you that we used to have chickens? That's where they're living now. We could drive out and say hello. I hear they have baby chicks."

Maddie looked up, her eyes bright. "Katherine said you named one Mrs. Whistlemeyer. That's a funny name." The corner of her mouth turned up and a bit of color returned to her cheeks.

Oh, the ability of children to be turned from their grief with the smallest cheerful suggestion. Wouldn't it be great if adults could be more like children? But no, when tragedy strikes, adults feel they must hold on to sorrow, wallow in it, savor it, roll it around their tongues, lay awake nights worrying, and deny themselves joy of any kind, lest others think them heartless and unfeeling.

"I remember Mrs. Whistlemeyer." Godfrey chuckled, shoving a bite of waffle into his mouth. "One of my *favowites* …" He swallowed. "…favorites as feathered friends go."

Katherine giggled and ladled more batter into the iron. "And, don't forget Chicken Mildred, and Sophia, and Myrtle! What a bunch they were, waking us up at the crack of dawn every morning. So what about it, Maddie, shall we plan a trip out to the farm? Grandma can call Mr. Higgenbottom and see if they'll be home tomorrow."

"I can do that." Agnes stood, picked up her plate and set it in the sink. "It sounds like fun. Should we invite Vincent?" She tipped her head, gave Katherine a sideways grin, and wiggled her eyebrows.

"Grandma? There you go. I'm an engaged woman…well, possibly an engaged woman. I don't even know what I am, anymore. I should probably go to the hospital tomorrow afternoon and sort things out with Don. I can't run off with Vincent, even if you and Godfrey are there." She ran her hand over her face which had warmed considerably since Grandma mentioned Vincent. "If you don't mind cleaning up, I'm going to my room. I really need to think." Katherine hastened down the hallway.

"Poor Katherine. Who would think after losing Stephen at Pearl Harbor, she'd find herself in a love triangle with two men who hate each other," Grandma whispered.

Several hours later, Maddie and Katherine were in their bedroom, reading a chapter from Little Women.

Agnes and Godfrey sat together in the living room, listening to an episode of The Green Hornet on the radio.

"Keep low, Kato, the villainous embezzler is parked just up the street."

"Right, Green Hornet. We want to take him alive. Evil though he may be, he deserves his day in court, his constitutional right, as an American citizen!"

The local station broadcaster broke into the broadcast, intermittently, to update the public with running tiger reports, each more sensational than the last, as radio stations are wont to do, hoping to attract more listeners. Agnes heard her friend's name and gasped.

Mildred Higgenbottom, on Broad Street, reported strange noises coming from her side yard. Upon reaching Mrs. Higgenbottom's house, Chief Waddlemucker found her refuse can tipped over and garbage scattered around. Neighbors reported seeing Mrs. Higgenbottom's dog running down the road. We can only speculate that it was chasing the tiger.

Godfrey chuckled. "If Mildred's Chihuahua chased it down the street, it shows just how ferocious the beast is, right?"

"Humph! The poor tiger is obviously terrified. It's been a pampered pet all its life. Probably doesn't know what to do on the loose and wishes it had never left—"

The wild tiger sightings that have terrified local residents all evening, once again brought Chief Waddlemucker's search party to Doubleday Drive where Mr. Crockhold reported the beast in his back yard, stalking one of his hens. Mr. Crockhold fired his shotgun at the tiger as it raced away. He said, 'I hit the critter, all right. He won't be sitting down any time soon with birdshot in his rump.' Now, back to regular programming. Morgan Burkinbower, signing off for KFUG radio."

Bang! Bang! (Scream) "Zounds, Kato! He's getting away. Head him off on the corner!"

"Right!" (Sounds of running feet and garbage cans falling) "Hold up there, you scoundrel..."

"Wild tiger, my aunt Fannie!" Agnes snorted. "That reporter is going to get the poor thing killed. He's making it sound like it's a man-eater. Now that it has birdshot in his rump, it's likely to make it even harder to capture him." Agnes swallowed a lump in her throat. "I can't imagine what Maddie will do if they kill it. She had almost a spiritual connection with the creature."

Godfrey nodded. "I'm sorry, Agnes. Come over here and sit beside me. I have something to tell you. I hope you'll be as thrilled as I am."

Agnes's throat went dry. Was he going to propose? What would she say if he did? "What is it?" Agnes moved slowly across the room to the sofa chair and sat.

Godfrey took her hand.

This is it! The moment she'd been waiting for. Or was it? She pulled her hand away and glanced toward Katherine and Maddie's bedroom. How would things change if she married Godfrey? Perspiration daubed her forehead. She swallowed.

Godfrey recaptured her hand. "Last month, before I came to Newbury, I heard that the Newbury Crest Theater was for sale. I contacted the company and bought the place with my FBI severance package. There's even a small apartment upstairs and—"

Agnes caught her breath. "So you're definitely settling down in Newbury?" Dare she hope he would stay this time, or would he leave again when the first fly-by-night scheme came his way, like he had before?

Godfrey nodded. "The sale is final next week. So, I'm gainfully employed and I'll have my own place. What do you think of that?"

Agnes's heart pummeled. No proposal, but, a definite plan for the future. That was good enough for now. "So, you *are* staying in Newbury. Why didn't you tell me sooner?"

"I didn't want to say anything until I was sure the sale was going through. Now I'm sure. Are you pleased?"

Was she pleased? Why shouldn't she be pleased? Wasn't it her heart's desire that he retire in Newbury? Hadn't she hoped he would settle down this time? Purchasing a business suggested that he might finally be serious about their relationship.

"Of course I'm pleased." She threw her arms around his neck and kissed him. "What old widow woman wouldn't be pleased to have another eligible bachelor move back to town? And to think you're rather fond of me—"

"Rather fond, indeed. In fact, that's what I wanted to talk to you about. I—"

This is a public service announcement. Citizens fled in panic when the ferocious tiger escaped into the dense Fryholder-Steinbeck woods. The search is suspended until seven o'clock tomorrow morning when searchers will reconvene at the corner of Fryholder and Steinbeck roads. Again, keep children and small animals indoors. Report any tiger sighting to the Newbury Police Department. This animal is considered extremely dangerous.

Agnes's face squinched into a grimace. "Well, at least Shere Khan can get a good night's rest tonight without risk of being shot by another traumatized Newbury citizen."

Chapter Twenty-One

Katherine, Agnes, and Maddie returned home following a rousing Sunday *go-to-meetin' revival* at The First Church of the Evening Star and Everlasting Light, changed their Sunday clothes, packed a picnic basket and were ready to visit the Higgenbottom farm.

Katherine called the hospital nursing staff who reported that Don was doing 'as well as could be expected'. Wasn't that statement loaded with innuendo and wiggle room? Katherine decided to join the family, and visit Don at the hospital later that evening.

Katherine quickly quashed Grandmother's suggestion to invite Vincent along on their outing. Though they had talked of visiting the farm with Maddie on the night he first arrived, Katherine thought such an invitation would further complicate her sticky situation with Dr. Don.

"Will we see baby chicks?" Maddie struggled to pull her gingham dress over her head, while Katherine laid a pair of coveralls and a blouse on the bed.

"Grandma spoke to Mrs. Higgenbottom last night. She says fifteen baby chicks hatched three days ago. She says it's the perfect time to visit." She giggled. "The roosters that used to live with Grandma are walking around, about to bust their buttons with pride."

Maddie stepped into her coveralls. "Is Godfrey coming with us?"

"He should be here any minute."

Maddie frowned.

What an odd reaction. Katherine picked up the brush and ran it through Maddie's hair. "Don't you like Godfrey?"

"*Uhh.* He's all right, I guess. Is he going to marry Grandma?" Maddie ducked her head and turned away.

Was she afraid that if Grandma married Godfrey, he might reject her too, just as Dr. Don had? Perhaps she thought she'd be on the street before they cut the wedding cake. Or was it simpler than that? Typical childish jealousy. Not wanting to share Katherine and Grandma's attention with anyone?

"Now, Maddie. Don't worry. Godfrey and Grandma have never even talked about getting married. Even if they did, it wouldn't change anything. You'll either live with me and Don, *if we get married,* or you'll stay with Grandma. Godfrey has nothing to do with those decisions." Katherine pulled Maddie into her arms. "Does that sound okay?"

Maddie struggled to smile. "I wish that Dr. Don liked me."

"Dr. Don likes you fine. Our problems have nothing to do with you. In fact, we may not get married for a long time. Here, let me finish your braids and we'll go and see those baby chicks." *Liar, liar, pants on fire.* She gave Maddie a hug.

"Katherine? Did they find Shere Khan last night? I said a prayer for him this morning in church."

"I did too. I haven't heard anything on the radio today. I'm sure they'll find him and he'll be home soon." Katherine separated Maddie's hair, braided it, and then tied a red ribbon on the end of each braid. Now that a little time had passed and she had calmed down, maybe this was a good time to question her about what she saw in the church yesterday. Katherine couldn't afford another sleepless night worrying.

"Maddie, about yesterday… When you were in the church, did you see who hurt Dr. Don?" Katherine's heart raced. Vincent's future could be in the hands of a nine-year-old girl. She held her breath. "What did you see, honey?"

Maddie shrugged. "I saw a man with red hair. He was real tall."

"Red hair?" Katherine caught her breath. "Are you sure?"

"*Uh-huh*. He sneaked up behind Dr. Don and hit him. Dr. Don fell down. I was scared, so I hid behind the church bench. When Grandma came in, I ran outside."

Red hair! "Have you seen the man before? Would you recognize him if you saw him again?"

Maddie shrugged and put the end of her braid in her mouth. "I just saw him for a little."

Katherine hugged Maddie. "Never mind." She pulled Maddie's hair from her mouth. "You were very brave to tell me. I'll call the chief and tell him what you said so he can find the man that hurt Dr. Don."

While Agnes finished packing the picnic basket and added boiled eggs, carrot sticks, fruit jars full of milk and peanut butter cookies, Katherine spoke to the chief. She hung up the kitchen phone as Godfrey's car pulled up the curb.

Agnes hurried to answer the door. "Godfrey's here now," she called over her shoulder. She opened the door before he knocked. "Morning, Godfrey."

"Good morning, love."

Agnes gestured him into the house. "Katherine just talked to Chief Waddlemucker." She picked up her purse and a sweater, and turned to Katherine. "What did the chief say when you told him what Maddie saw at the church?"

"I guess her information clears Vincent, if the chief believes it."

Godfrey held the door as Katherine pulled on her jacket. "Looks like you're ready to go."

Agnes took Maddie's hand and shooed her out the door. "Can you grab that picnic basket, Godfrey? If we don't hurry, those baby chicks will be all grown up before we even get there!"

Agnes pointed through the car window at the colorful chickens strutting across the Higgenbottom barnyard. "Look! It's Chicken Myrtle and Chicken Mildred! Look how they've filled out. Must be the country air and clean living."

Godfrey pulled his Hudson to a stop in front of the big red barn. He hurried around to open the passenger door for Agnes. "Here you go, my princess." His hand swept out like a court courtier.

Agnes's cheek grew rosy and warmed as she stepped out of the car. She ducked as a swallow dove past her head. "*Whoa!* The attack of the barn swallows. Just like last summer." Another swallow dive-bombed past her, veered to the left and swooped back up to the nests below the eaves where dozens of mud condominiums and swallow townhouses adorned the edge of the roofline. "Aren't they something? Look, Maddie. See how they make little mud houses? Next spring, that's where they'll raise their babies."

Maddie stared. "Oh!"

Chicken Myrtle and Mildred scuttled closer to the car.

Agnes clapped her hands. "Hello there, Mildred. Myrtle." Would they remember her? She knelt and put out her hand. How many mornings had she fed the little darlings at the crack of dawn to keep them from waking the neighbors? But, unlike elephants, it was doubtful that two such scallywags would remember her, even though it had only been several months since they came to live at the farm. How she had missed their kitchen chats.

Chicken Mildred moved closer and pecked at Agnes's fingers, probably expecting they held some treat.

Agnes stroked a finger across the top of Mildred's feathered head. "You do remember me, don't you?" It made her feel better to think so, even if it wasn't true.

Mr. Higgenbottom's pickup truck rumbled down the driveway toward the barn and jerked to a stop in a cloud of dust. He leaped out, leaving the cab door open, pulled off his hat and slapped it against his leg. "Hello! Hello! Nice to *shee* you again, Mizzus Odboddy. Just got back from the feed store. So, you brought the family to *shee* the baby *chicksh?*" He chuckled.

Agnes grinned. Same old Mr. Higgenbottom, lisp and all.

"Come on in. The *hensh* are inside. The mamas are all aflutter with their new babies." He took Agnes's arm and led her toward the barn.

Katherine and Maddie trailed behind Mr. Higgenbottom, while Godfrey brought up the rear.

Inside the barn, they paused beside a small fenced-in area where a black-faced sheep was housed. "*Thish* is Heidi. *Shesh* got a lame back leg." Mr. Higgenbottom moved on to the cow in the next pen. "Hilda's having trouble with digestion. She's on a special diet. And, here are the baby *chicksh*." Three hens clucked and picked at corn scattered amongst the straw in the next pen. Clustered behind each hen, five or six chicks about the size of a baseball, wearing varying shades of brown and red fluffy feathers, trailed behind. Imitating the hens, they picked at the straw.

Agnes studied the scene for a minute, noticing how the chicks followed first one hen and then another. "How does she know which ones are her babies?"

Mr. Higgenbottom chuckled. "I don't *shaposh* it makes much difference," he whistled. "They just follow the closest hen." He stepped inside the enclosure and grabbed one of the chicks. He held it out to Maddie. "Do you want to hold it?"

"Yes, please." She cuddled the chick in both hands. "It's so soft." Her face lit up. "I thought all baby chicks were yellow."

"Bantam *chicksh* are brown and black, like their mamas."

Agnes touched the chick. "This must be Mrs. Whistlemeyer's baby. I can see the same devil-may-care look in its eyes." Probably not exact science, but her opinion, none the less.

"Really, Agnes," Godfrey chuckled. "I doubt there is a recognizable familial trait in a chicken's eye." He glanced around the barn at the vintage farm tools hanging from the ceiling. "Quite a collection you've got here, Mr. Higgenbottom. Been collecting vintage tools long?"

"*Thesh* are my pop and grandpappy's *toolsh*. The Higgenbottom's have farmed this land for almost a hundred years."

"Fascinating. You must have some stories to tell." Godfrey ran his hand over an old leather yoke hanging on the wall, once used by oxen to till the fields. "Bet you're glad those days are gone. Walking behind a pair of oxen and a plow all day must have been exhausting."

"Grandpappy was the last to use oxen to till the soil. Pop used a team of horses. Ahead of his time, he bought a tractor back in the 30's and that's what we use now." Mr. Higgenbottom gestured to the large green tractor parked on the opposite side of the barn where one of Agnes's former boys sat perched on the steering wheel. "*Shophia* uses it most days," Mr. Higgenbottom chuckled, spittle spraying from his mouth.

Agnes pointed. "Looks like Sophia's ready to till up your north forty this afternoon."

At the sound of a shriek from the direction of the house, Mr. Higgenbottom raced to the barn door. Where previously the air had hummed with the chittering of the swallows in the eaves and Mrs. Whistlemeyer and Chicken Mildred's gurgles, all usual barnyard noises had ceased, leaving a chilling silence. A breeze whispered through the nearby willow tree. A loose screen rattled against the farmhouse window.

Agnes and Godfrey followed Mr. Higgenbottom to the barn door with Katherine and Maddie several paces back.

Agnes stepped outside and blinked in the bright sunlight, not quite believing her eyes. A shiver crept up the back of her neck. Perspiration blossomed on her chest. "What…!" Instinctively, she reached back to stop Maddie and Katherine. "Stay back."

Mrs. Higgenbottom stood beside the kitchen door, a dead chicken dangling from her hand, her other hand raised to her mouth.

Mrs. Whistlemeyer danced at her feet, scratching and picking at bugs in the barnyard gravel seemingly unaware of any danger. The rooster looked up and froze as Shere Khan crept toward Mrs.

Higgenbottom, his tail switching, his orange and black striped head lowered. A trickle of blood oozed down his hip.

Driven by pain and hunger, instinct had kicked in. Locked and loaded, saliva dripping, the pampered tiger inched toward the dead chicken Mrs. Higgenbottom held close to her breast.

"Mother. Stand still," Mr. Higgenbottom shouted, all trace of his lisp disappearing. "Don't make any sudden move." He turned and disappeared into the barn.

Before Agnes could move, Maddie had yanked her hand free from Katherine, and raced across the barnyard toward Shere Khan.

"Maddie!" Agnes made a grab for her and missed. She started to rush forward, only to have Godfrey grab her arm and pull her back into the barn. "No! Don't go."

Maddie stopped several feet from the stalking tiger. "Shere Khan. You remember me. It's Maddie. Come back, Shere Khan. Lie down!" She reached her hand toward the tiger.

At the sound of Maddie's soothing command, the tiger turned toward her. For a moment, he held her gaze, then shook his body from shoulder to tail, and dropped to his belly.

Oh, my goodness! Is he purring? Agnes held her breath, her heart pounding, her lips moving in a prayer. She grabbed Katherine's hand and squeezed.

Without a sign of fear for her own safety, Maddie knelt beside the tiger and scratched behind his ear. "There, there," she crooned. "It's all right. Grandma's here. She'll make everything all right. She'll help you get home safe."

Shere Khan yawned. He fluttered his tail, sending up little puffs of barnyard dust. The muscles in his shoulder rippled as he flicked a fly off his back.

Maddie smiled and looked back toward the barn. Her smile melted when she saw Mr. Higgenbottom lift a rifle to his shoulder. Clearly, he meant to put an end to the tiger-mania that gripped the town and appeared to threaten the life of his wife and a child.

Maddie threw her body across the tiger and spread her arms. "No! You can't. I won't let you."

And there goes the last trace of a timid, traumatized child. Nothing will stop her now! Agnes grabbed Mr. Higgenbottom's arm. "That's not necessary. See? The tiger is tame. He's lying down." She raised her hand to her eyes and called to Mrs. Higgenbottom. "Step back inside, Mrs. Higgenbottom. Call the police department. Tell them to bring the trainer to collect his cat. No need to bring a posse. He's just a big kitty-cat out for a stroll." She cautiously advanced toward Maddie and Shere Khan. Everything was fine now, right?

As she stepped closer, Shere Khan rose and tossed Maddie to the ground.

ROAR!

The tiger moved toward Agnes, his stance tense, his wild eyes suddenly locked on Agnes's face. He lowered his head and growled. Was he protecting Maddie? Her presence was one thing…anyone else? Something else again.

Terror filled Agnes's chest. *Maybe he's not as tame as I thought.*

"Maddie?" Agnes called. Her voice trembled. "Can you get up and back away now, very slowly, dear? Shere Khan is upset. He might hurt you." Agnes's chest felt so tight, she could hardly breathe. It was doubtful the tiger would purposely hurt Maddie, but he was confused and hungry, and probably in pain with the birdshot in his rump. Who knows what a hungry, frightened, injured tiger might do? At the moment, the usually tame tiger was an unpredictable, wild animal. *Oh, dear God, protect Maddie. If You'll just keep her from harm, I promise, I'll…*

Here we go again! What offer could she make this time? She'd used every bargaining chip she could think of, trying to barter away the burglary charges. She was already into the Big Guy with a commitment to attend church every Sunday for three months, come rain or shine. What was left? The only major sacrifice she had left was to agree to give up her henna rinse every other Tuesday. Is that what it would take to save Maddie? Must she allow her hair to go as grey as a Brillo pad?

Her gaze moved from the tiger's snarling mouth to the child crouched beside him. *Okay, Lord, I give up. If You'll protect Maddie, I promise that I'll stop... That I won't...*

A sudden movement caught her eye. Clutching the chicken, Mrs. Higgenbottom raced past the tiger toward their 1928 Ford pickup. She stopped about eight feet from the truck and heaved the dead chicken through the open cab door, and then dropped to the ground, her apron pulled over her head.

Shere Khan's head snapped up, following the trajectory of the feathered delicacy as it appeared to fly from Mrs. Higgenbottom's hand into the truck cab. A momentary primal killer instinct must have surged through his breast. He leaped up, bounded toward the truck in two leaps, soared over Mrs. Higgenbottom's crouched body and landed in the cab of the truck.

Mrs. Higgenbottom jumped up and slammed the truck door, trapping the big cat inside.

All that was visible through the truck window was the wisp of Shere Khan's tail as the hungry cat crouched on the seat, devouring an unexpected *capon a la tartare.*

Mrs. Higgenbottom dusted feathers and dirt off the front of her apron. "That should hold the critter until the authorities arrive."

Mr. Higgenbottom raced over to his wife, "*Schweetheart!* Whatever made you think to *tosh* the chicken in the truck?"

"I was just on my way to take the dead chicken down to the hogs when I saw the tiger stalking Mrs. Whistlemeyer. Then, here came little Maddie. It just popped into my head on the spur of the moment. Looks like it worked, huh? The tiger should be okay in the truck. Once he's had his lunch, he'll probably curl up and take a cat nap until the trainer and Chief Waddlemucker get here."

"This *callsh* for a celebration. Why don't we all go in the *housh* and have some lemonade." Mr. Higgenbottom squeezed his wife's shoulder. "My little hero *shaved* the day!"

"Mrs. Higgenbottom *shaved the day* more ways than she knows, and I didn't have to promise…to…to…" Agnes closed her eyes and ran her hand over her hennaed hair. She fingered the silver chopsticks in her bun. *Thank you, Lord. Just…thanks…*

Chapter Twenty-Two

Mrs. Higgenbottom nodded toward the porch. "Won't you ladies have a seat? I'll bring some lemonade while we wait for Shere Khan's trainer. The menfolk have disappeared back into the barn to gab." She hurried into the house and returned with a pitcher of lemonade and six glasses.

Agnes accepted a glass of lemonade. "This is lovely. Maddie's gone with the guys to play with the baby chicks."

Within the hour, the trainer arrived and freed Shere Khan from the pickup truck. Once again on the ground and with his trainer near at hand, the tiger lay down and rolled like a kitten. After a good head scratch, the young man snapped the chain to his collar.

A flatbed truck rumbled down the driveway carrying a traveling cage. It backed up close to the pickup truck. The driver jumped out, hurried around and unlatched the cage.

"How did he get out of his cage in the first place?" Katherine asked.

"Good question," the trainer said. "It looks like the cage was opened on purpose while we were tearing down the carnival. Probably some teenagers, playing a prank."

"*Humph!* Some prank." Agnes frowned. Hadn't they had their fill of pranks this week? Still unnerved by the tiger's previous erratic behavior, she pulled Maddie further away. "Who would let a tiger out of its cage? Couldn't they have guessed the panic it would cause?"

The trainer shrugged. "Maybe that was the whole idea. Time to go, big boy." He tapped his stick on the side of the cage door. "Up, Shere Khan!"

The tiger crouched and leaped into the cage with ease. "He's safe and sound, at last. We'll have him back to his caravan in no time." He unhooked the chain from the tiger's neck, slipped him a treat and latched the cage. "Anyone who would let a tiger loose is either sadistic or a fool. I mean, he's tame, but the poor thing was scared and hungry. That guy who took a shot at him probably thought he was apt to eat the cat, what with the fool radio announcer calling him ferocious and wild. Lucky he only used birdshot. I'll make sure we install a padlock with a key on the cage door tomorrow." He slapped the truck. "Okay. That does it. Let's go."

Maddie moved closer to the back of the truck. "Good-bye, Shere Khan. I hope you come and visit us again." She looked up at the trainer. "Are you coming back next year?"

The man smiled. "I hope so, sweetheart. I'm sure Shere Khan wants to see you again. Thanks, folks, for helping us get him back unharmed." He waved, jumped into his car and started down the driveway.

As the truck followed the trainer's car onto the highway, Agnes knelt and wiped a tear off Maddie's cheek. "Don't cry. Shere Khan is going over to Boyles Springs to meet some other children."

Maddie's lip trembled. "Are you sure he'll be okay, Grandma?"

"As sure as God made little green apples. He'll be fine. You saw how much he trusted his handler. He loves him. You'll see him again. Just wait and see. Now, I think we've had enough excitement for one day. Here's Godfrey now. Say good-bye to the chicks and we'll get on home. I want to bake a rhubarb pie this afternoon and I could use some help." She took Godfrey's arm. "Are you up to it?"

"I'll help you eat it," Godfrey said. "Rhubarb pie is one of my favorites."

Agnes gave his shoulder a tap. "From what I've seen, anything you can get a fork under is one of your favorites."

"Can't argue with that." Godfrey grinned and opened the door into the back seat for Katherine and Maddie. As Agnes slipped into the front seat, the episode with Shere Khan kept running through her mind. Who would purposely let the tiger out of his cage?

Maddie sat at the cluttered kitchen table with her crayons and papers while Katherine swept the floor. "Maddie. Move your chair so I can reach under you. Better yet, why don't you take your crayons out onto the front porch? Grandma and Godfrey will be back in a minute from the garden with the rhubarb for a pie."

Maddie hopped up and scooted her chair to the side. "See my picture of Shere Khan, Katherine? I want to have a tiger when I grow up."

"*Uh-huh...*" Katherine leaned on the broom, while thoughts of Vincent and Don swirled through her head. Would Don come to his senses about Maddie or would their relationship be doomed from the start? And, if they should break up...

Maddie pulled on Katherine's skirt. "Katherine? Did you hear me? I said I'm going to have a tiger someday. He'll wear a diamond collar and I'll call him Shere Khan."

"Oh, yes. A tiger. Very nice." Katherine smiled. "But, don't you think you would rather have a puppy or a kitty like Ling-Ling?" Katherine peered through the window and waved to Grandmother in the victory garden, cutting stalks of red and green rhubarb. She handed her basket to Godfrey and started down the next row.

Godfrey followed Grandmother around the garden, looking much like the puppy Katherine thought would better suit Maddie.

Katherine smiled at the besotted expression on Godfrey's face. *Now that Grandma has her puppy, which puppy do I want?* Vincent or Don. A decision would have to be made, and soon. She turned to face

Maddie. "I guess you know, if you had a tiger, he'd have to live in a cage. Did you think about that?" Fantasies were fun, but it was time to interject a bit of reality into Maddie's make-believe world.

Maddie shook her braids. "No. My tiger will sleep on my bed—"

Ring... Ring...

"Just a minute, Maddie. I need to get the phone." *Maybe it's Don!* Katherine's heart quickened. "Hello?"

"Hi. It's Vincent. Are you busy? Do you have time to talk?"

Vincent! Her hand holding the receiver quivered. "I have a few minutes. We just got back from the Higgenbottom farm. I suppose you heard–"

"I…I wanted to make sure you were all right. I just came back from the coffee shop. I overheard Homer Blenkinsop gossiping with the guys. They said you and your grandmother captured the tiger. Was Maddie there? I'll bet she was scared."

Katherine chuckled. "Then, you'd be wrong. She walked right up to Shere Khan and started petting him. Scared *us* to death! Then Mrs. Higgenbottom threw a dead chicken into the pickup and—"

"A what? A chicken?"

Katherine giggled, and burst out laughing. "*Uh-huh.* You should have seen it. Shere Khan leaped into the truck and Mrs. Higgenbottom slammed the cab door and trapped him inside. Funniest thing I've ever seen." She held her stomach. "She couldn't have timed it better if she'd choreographed it."

"So, the tiger's back where he belongs. That's good." Vincent didn't speak for a few seconds. "Katherine. I didn't call about the tiger. Well, of course, I wanted to make sure you were okay, but there's more.

"About what?"

"Your name came up and I—"

"You mean our capturing Shere Khan?"

"No. About the counterfeit bills showing up around town. That Blenkinsop guy said a bill turned up in the offering plate this morning at The First Church of the Evening Something or Other. He said Chief

Waddlemucker found the first one in your booth at the fair and–"

"And, the townsfolk naturally assume Grandma must be involved." A cold chill clutched Katherine's chest. When was this gossip going to stop?

Vincent sighed. "From what I could gather, they figure since Agnes is the thief behind the Wilkey Market, then it's an easy leap to assume she's a counterfeiter, too. I told them I wouldn't stand for such gossip, but having me defend your grandma didn't go very far. I thought you should know. I'm sorry."

A vessel throbbed in Katherine's forehead. She pulled out a chair. "So, I guess no one was convinced–"

"You know how people are. Who knows what they believe? I guess I stopped the gossip in the diner, at least for the moment."

Maddie pulled on Katherine's sleeve. "Katherine. Someone's coming up the front walk. Shall I go to the door?"

"Just a minute, Vincent." Maybe it was those church people who go door-to-door. She nodded to Maddie. "Go see who it is."

Maddie skipped across the kitchen and into the living room.

Katherine wiped her hand across her forehead where a pain stabbed her brow. "So, what do you suggest? Should I call Chief Waddlemucker? I don't suppose he can stop people from gossiping if they're of a mind to."

Maddie pulled on Katherine's sleeve again. "The people at the door are collecting old clothes for the war refugees. What should I tell them?"

Katherine waved toward the back porch. "Give them Grandpa's old raincoat hanging on the peg out there. Grandma said she wants to get rid of it." She turned back to the phone.

"Okay." Maddie retrieved the coat and carried it over her arm back into the living room.

"Sorry, Vincent. Someone is at the door. Maddie's taking care of it."

"You're busy. Maybe I should call later," Vincent said.

"No. It's okay." She rubbed her forehead again. "It's just so hard. I don't think I can stand much more of this." Tears pricked her eyes. "I wish I could get away… Maybe Maddie and I should leave town for a while." She dabbed her eyes with a tea towel from the rod by the kitchen window where Chicken Mildred used to perch. She remembered the day the only thing she had to worry about was a chicken roosting on the towel rack. Was there a lesson there somewhere?

"I'm doing all I can to find out who's behind this," Vincent said.

"I know you are, but you don't even know who to look for or why this is happening. Maybe Grandma just stepped on the wrong toes again."

"I'll keep asking questions. Something might turn up."

Grandma stomped onto the back porch, and stopped to pull off her garden shoes.

Godfrey followed with the basket of rhubarb.

"I have to go. Grandmother's here now and I need to tell her about your call. I'll talk to you soon. Good-bye." She hung up the phone. Wasn't this a fine kettle of fish? Explaining the latest news to Grandma was the last thing in the world she wanted to do.

"Have a seat, Grandma. We need to talk."

Chapter Twenty-Three

Agnes paced the floor, still fuming over that rascal, Homer Blenkinsop and his wagging tongue. "I don't understand. I just talked to him yesterday. We've been friends for years. Why wouldn't he give me the benefit of the doubt?"

Katherine held up a cup of tea. "You must sit down, Grandma. Here's your—"

"How could he spread such lies? Haven't I given my time and energy for every worthy cause inside Newbury's city limits? Now, the whole town has turned against me. They're treating me like vipers on a hot rock. They think I'm a thief *and* a counterfeiter?"

Godfrey reached for Agnes's arm as she passed. She made another loop around the kitchen, pummeling her fist into her hand, tears sparkling in her eyes. "What shall I do? What shall I do? I can't stay in Newbury with so much hatred directed at me. Should I sell the house and move? What should we do, Katherine?"

Godfrey stood and grabbed Agnes's hands. "There, there, now lambie-pie. You must calm down. You're going to have a coronary. Sit down here beside Katherine and drink your tea. I don't think you need to sell the house this afternoon." He raised her clasped hand to his lips. "What can I do to make you feel better?"

Agnes pulled away, sank into a chair and put her head in her hands. Up went her chin. "You're right. I'm not going to let a bunch of flibbertigibbets tear me down. I'm innocent. It's just a matter of time until the real thief is brought to justice."

Agnes's gaze fell on the kitchen counter where the stalks of rhubarb lay. She shoved back her chair and hurried to the sink. "No more wallowing in self-pity. I said we were going to bake a pie and that's exactly what we're going to do."

She tied her apron around her ample midriff, shoved the chopsticks more firmly into her bun, and tossed the rhubarb into the sink. "Godfrey? Run out and pick me a couple of apples. Now, where did I put that…?" She turned to Katherine. "Don't just sit there. Help me find Mrs. Yeager's recipe for Rhubarb-Apple Pie." Her hand fluttered in the general direction of a cupboard over the stove. "I think it's in my recipe file box."

Katherine pulled down the old red plastic card file and thumbed through the tattered cards. "Here it is. Rhubarb Pie Supreme. Wasn't she your neighbor across the street years ago before Mrs. Williams moved in?"

Agnes nodded. She took the card from Katherine and scrutinized it. "Yes. This is the one I remembered. She always made the best rhubarb pie for the church socials." Agnes assembled her large yellow Pyrex bowl and her measuring cups and spoons from various cupboards and drawers.

The screen door screeched and Godfrey returned, holding out his offering. "Here, queen of my heart. Three pretty apples like the roses in your cheeks, fresh from yonder tree."

Agnes squinched her nose at Godfrey. "Katherine, why don't you make the pie crust while I prepare the fruit?" Agnes turned on the faucet to wash the apples and stalks of rhubarb.

Katherine shook her head. "Your pie crust is always better than mine. You'd better do it. Maddie and I will work on her reading and spelling." She went into the living room and called Maddie in from the front porch.

"When there's baking to be done, that girl disappears faster than Houdini," Agnes said.

Godfrey grinned. "Then, I guess it's just you and me, light of my desire."

"Oh, you and your endless balderdash. Okay. You can help me. Let's start with the fruit. *Cream two tablespoons butter with one-half cup brown sugar and one-half cup white sugar.*" She brought the sugar canisters to the table, measured both kinds of sugar and dumped them into the bowl.

Godfrey picked up the card. "Here, I'll read and you measure. *Work in two level tablespoons flour with a pinch of salt.*" He glanced up at Agnes. "How much is a pinch of salt?"

"Oh, you know. Just a pinch…" Agnes brought her flour canister to the table and popped off the lid. "Oh, my stars!" She slammed the cover on the canister and jumped back. Her hand flew to her mouth.

"What's wrong, punkin-raider? Are there ants in the canister?"

"Oh…*um*…really, it's nothing. It's just… Oh, dear." She lifted the lid again and tipped the canister toward Godfrey.

Godfrey's eyes flew open as Agnes's WWI service pistol clanked against the side of the canister.

"I forgot I'd put this here for safe-keeping. I'll just get the flour sack from the cupboard."

"Why…Why on earth did you…? Never mind." Godfrey waved his hand. "Nothing you do surprises me anymore. I'm sure you'll have an explanation that makes no sense whatsoever."

Agnes pulled the flour sack from the cupboard and set it on the table. "Of course there's a good explanation. I brought the gun into the kitchen for protection. You know what's been going on around here. I wanted it handy in case I needed it in a hurry. Since it's loaded, I didn't dare leave it anywhere Maddie might get hold of it." Agnes measured two tablespoons of flour from the flour sack and added it to her bowl. "I didn't think there was much chance she'd look in the flour canister and find the gun. But, I have to admit, it sort of slipped my mind that I put it there. Perhaps it would be better if I returned it to the top of my closet." She chuckled. "Shall we get on with the pie? What's next?"

"It says; *mix with one pound of rhubarb washed and cut into pieces, and three apples cut into very small pieces.*"

"Right." Agnes lit the oven with a match, washed and peeled the apples, and cut them up into a bowl. "So," she called over her shoulder as she chopped the rhubarb. "I've been thinking about the counterfeit bill that turned up at Katherine's booth yesterday. I'll bet it *was* the five-dollar bill I gave her. I was trying to remember just exactly where I got it."

Godfrey crossed his arms and leaned on the table. "Shouldn't be too hard to figure out. Where were you when you last bought something?"

"My best recollection is Wilkey's Market, when I bought the cocoa for the cupcakes. Mrs. Snodgrass was at the counter, but I can't remember if she paid with a five or not.

"I gave Mrs. Wilkey a ten for my purchases and she gave me change, including a five. If the counterfeit bill came from me, I'm sure that's where I got it. So! Either Mrs. Snodgrass passed it to Mrs. Wilkey, or it was already in her register. One of them must be the counterfeiter." She wiped her hands on the tea towel beside the sink and turned to Godfrey. "That's got to be it."

"Now, Agnes. Old Mrs. Snodgrass? Or the widow Wilkey? You're jumping to conclusions again. If it came from the cash register, who knows how long it might have been in there?"

"It was very early in the morning. I expect we were her first customers."

"The bill could have been there from the day before. Someone might have passed it late in the afternoon. There's really no way to know for sure *where* the counterfeit bill came from."

"Mrs. Wilkey did say she leaves money in the register overnight. So, why are folks so convinced that I'm the counterfeiter?"

"Because…because… Really, Agnes. How should I know? When people get scared, it makes them feel better to blame someone else. You were the last one to handle the bill before Chief Waddlemucker spotted it, so obviously, *you* must be the guilty party. See how it works?

People are like sheep. They follow the loudest *bleat* and at the moment, it's coming from Homer Blenkinsop's big mouth."

"So, maybe I should find Mr. Homer Blenkinsop and tell him to shut his fat trap."

"What good would come of that? You'd likely end up having a quarrel and make an enemy. I suggest you call Chief Waddlemucker and tell him what you just told me. Now, what about the pie crust?" He glanced at his watch. "It's getting late and I'm looking forward to a piece of warm rhubarb pie."

Agnes brought down her mother's large amber-colored glass mixing bowl from the cupboard. She opened her *Better Homes and Gardens* cookbook, turned to the Pastry and Pies section, and ran her finger down the page to plain crust. "Here it is. I'm going to make a double crust, so I need this one.

"Two cups flour." She shoved the cookbook across the table and tapped the recipe. "Here, you read it." She measured the flour and dumped it in the bowl.

"Okay." Godfrey straightened his glasses and read, *Add one teaspoon salt. Cut in two-thirds cup shortening until the mixture resembles small peas. Add five to seven tablespoons of cold water, one tablespoon at a time.* How can shortening and salt resemble peas? I don't get it."

"It means you take a fork or a pastry cutter and squish the flour and salt into the shortening until the chunks are the *size* of peas. Watch." She ran the fork through the ingredients repeatedly, squishing and tossing the mixture until the chunks squished into little chunks, then added a few drops of water until it formed soft dough. "That's about right. See?"

"Okay. *Form dough into two balls for double crust. Flatten one at a time on a lightly floured surface. Use rolling pin to roll out the dough. Roll from center of ball to the edge, making a round disc approximately three-eighths-inch think.*

"I think I've got that part. I've done it a zillion times." Agnes quickly rolled out the dough, flipped it over the top of a pie pan, and trimmed the crust to fit the pan. She dusted the crust with a sprinkling of flour. "Go back to the pie recipe and finish reading."

Rhubarb-Apple Pie. Mix sugar and flour mixture with the rhubarb and apples. Put in an unbaked crust and add a top crust. Bake in hot oven, 425° for fifteen minutes and then reduce heat to 325° and bake for thirty minutes longer. "Shucks! Must we wait that long?"

"Goof-ball." Agnes filled the pie shell with the fruit mixture and attached the second rolled crust to the top. She wet the edge of the bottom pie shell and pinched the two crusts together. After trimming the excess crust, she pressed ridges all around the edge of the pie with her thumbs. "Cut slits in the top to let out the steam, sprinkle sugar on top, and pop in the oven."

"It looks delicious already, my heart's flower. We make a pretty good team, don't we?"

Agnes rolled her eyes and squeezed his arm. "Couldn't have done it without you. Now, if you'll excuse me, I'd better put my pistol back into the locked box in my bedroom. Let's hope I won't need it any time soon."

"From your lips, to God's ears."

Chapter Twenty-Four

Katherine! Are you ready for breakfast? Is Maddie dressed? The school bus will be here any minute." Agnes spread apple-butter on her toast. Getting breakfast cooked and Maddie ready for school was always hectic on Monday mornings. Maddie was a dawdler and particularly following the weekend, even with Katherine's help, it was a struggle to get the child dressed, fed, and out the door in time to catch the bus.

"I'm braiding her hair. Almost done," Katherine called from the bathroom.

Agnes poured a little milk into Ling-Ling's bowl and set it next to the stove. She opened a jar of last summer's canned peaches and placed it on the table. "Girls! I'm dishing up the oatmeal. Come and get it while it's hot."

The girls hurried into the kitchen, Maddie with red ribbons on the ends of two neatly plaited braids, and Katherine with her hair fashioned in a victory roll at the nape of her neck. They pulled out the kitchen chairs and sat.

"You both look so nice." Agnes smiled at Maddie and set the bowls of cereal on the table. "Maddie, would you get the milk from the icebox?" In the past, they would have had bacon and eggs for breakfast, but since the attack on Pearl Harbor, eggs were scarce and bacon was nearly impossible to buy as most meat, including bacon, was sent to the troops overseas. Most mornings lately, breakfast consisted of hot oatmeal. At least, with canned fruit on top, the oatmeal was almost palatable. She sighed. How long could the war last? She couldn't wait for the day they'd have bacon on the table again.

While Katherine spooned a golden peach from the jar into her bowl and another into Maddie's, Agnes filled their mugs with coffee. She poured milk over Maddie's cereal and a dollop into her coffee, and took a sip. Since coffee was rationed to one pound per adult every six weeks, their one pot in the morning was particularly enjoyable. Rationing was a sacrifice they willingly endured for the war effort, but, oh, how she missed her coffee throughout the day!

I should have put brown sugar on my cereal like my mother used to do. Agnes's spoon clanked against her bowl. She smiled at Maddie. "Did you get all your homework done, sweetheart?"

"Yes. We have a spelling test today. Katherine helped me study my words yesterday. Do you want to hear me spell bicycle? B-Y-C-I-C-L-E."

Agnes shook her head. "No, sweetheart. B-I-C-Y-C-L-E." The *B-I* part of the word means two. Like two wheels on a bicycle. That's how I remember it. I missed it in a spelling bee, myself, years ago. Can you remember that?"

"I think so." Maddie leaned down to stroke Ling-Ling's back. "B-I means two, like Ling-Ling's name." She giggled.

"Hurry and finish your cereal. The bus will be here in a few minutes." Agnes tipped the last drops of coffee into her mouth, stood, and placed her bowl and cup in the sink.

"So, what's on your agenda today, Grandma?" Katherine asked as she cleared the table and set the milk back in the icebox.

"I have to bank the war bond money this morning and…" Agnes turned toward the back porch. She blinked, unable to believe what she saw…or rather, what she didn't see. The red peg, usually hidden beneath Douglas's grey raincoat, glared nakedly in a patch of sunlight streaming across the back porch. "Where's Douglas's raincoat?" *Jumping Jehoshaphat! How could it disappear overnight?*

She hurried out to the back porch. There lay the stacks of newspapers piled in the corner ready for the next paper drive day… The shelf of canned fruit, handy to reach when she needed something extra for dinner or breakfast… The wringer washing machine in the corner…

She pawed through a pile of clothes on the floor, waiting for her to hook the washing machine hose to the faucet and run a batch of clothes through the washer.

Panic surged through her chest. "Where's Douglas's coat?" It was hanging right there on the peg when they got home from the carnival Saturday evening. "Katherine? Please tell me you moved the coat somewhere." Agnes stood in the doorway, wringing her hands. Her head felt about to burst. *Don't panic, Agnes.* Surely there was a reasonable explanation. Agnes stared at Katherine's stricken face. *Oh, dear God. What has she done?*

"I…I… Grandpa's coat? That old thing that's hung out there for years? We donated it to…to…someone who came to the door yesterday afternoon. You said you wanted to get rid of it." Katherine hurried to Agnes and peered into her face. "What's wrong?"

Agnes flopped into a kitchen chair, her hands over her eyes. "I put the Savings stamps, books, and the seal in a shoe box in my closet, but I hid the war bond money in the lining of the coat."

"You did what?" Katherine's eyebrows rose. "In the coat lining? Whatever for?"

"I wanted to hide the money where nobody would think to look, in case the burglar came back again when we weren't home. I ripped a hole in the lining and stuffed the money inside. I safety-pinned it shut." Her stomach clenched.

Katherine threw up her hands. "Heavens to Betsy! Why…why didn't you just put it under your mattress or in the cookie jar? Wouldn't that have been safe enough?"

"Because that's the first place a burglar would look. There was several hundred dollars in there." She paced back into the kitchen and slumped into a chair. "I have to get the coat back. Which organization took it?" Agnes's heart pounded so loud, it was hard to catch her breath. Dots of perspiration sprinkled her forehead.

Katherine glanced at Maddie, now frozen in her chair, her fist in her mouth. It appeared she understood the seriousness of the situation. "I don't know. I was on the phone. Maddie went to the door. I told her to give them the coat. Maddie? Do you remember? Did the lady say which…?"

Maddie jumped up, knocked over her chair, and raced shrieking, down the hall toward her bedroom.

"She thinks she's in trouble. I'd better go." Katherine hastened from the kitchen.

Agnes knuckled her eyes, feeling as though she had a knot the size of golf ball in her throat. Wasn't it bad enough that the town thought she robbed Wilkey's Market and was passing counterfeit bills? Now, with the war bond money missing, even more reason to call her a thief! She yanked the receiver off the wall phone and dialed Godfrey.

"Hello?" A yawn suggested he was not yet fully awake.

"Godfrey? I desperately need you. I…I…" She sobbed, a lump in her throat.

"Don't say another word, buttercup. I thought I'd never live to see the day I'd hear those words. You have no idea how long I've waited. I'll be right there, my darling snuggle-bunny."

"No. Wait… You misunderstood. I didn't mean—" The phone line buzzed in her ear.

"Great! On top of everything else, now I have to deal with a puddling love-sick puppy."

Agnes sat across the kitchen table from Godfrey, staring into a cold cup of coffee, a headache raging across the top of her head.

Head down, shoulders slumped, Godfrey was the epitome of grief. "What did Maddie say? Can she remember which agency came?"

Agnes shrugged. "She wouldn't stop crying until we assured her she wasn't in trouble. She can't remember anything except a white truck. Katherine drove her to school and went on to work. That's all I know." She lowered her head into her hands.

"Well, cheer up, kitten-puss. All we have to do is figure out which charity took the coat." He stood and opened the nearest cupboard. "Where's your phone book?"

Agnes nodded toward the bottom cupboard near the phone. "There, next to the sack of potatoes."

Godfrey retrieved the book, tossed it on the table and sat. "Okay. So, let's try the Salvation Army first." He licked his thumb and leafed through the book. "*Ah*. Here it is." He stood and pulled the receiver off the wall phone. "Shall I call or do you want to talk to them?"

Agnes took the phone from him. "I'll do it. This is my fault. I shouldn't have put the money in the coat without telling Katherine what I was doing. What's the number?"

"MU2-5549"

She dialed the number. "Hello? Salvation Army? Were you, by chance, collecting old clothes in the Winterfield neighborhood yesterday afternoon? Someone came to our house and–"

"Sorry, ma'am," the volunteer wheezed. "We don't work of a Sunday. The Lord's Day of rest, you know. We're open six days a week, but the staff is all volunteers, you know, and some of them have families. They're entitled to some time off, don't you think? Did you say you have some old clothes you want to donate? That's very kind of you. We have a volunteer that lives out your way, even though his wife is an invalid, and hasn't been out of the house for six months. Bless his heart. She's suffering from heart disease, you know. He gives us as much time as he can. He could stop by and—"

"I didn't say I had anything to donate and, quite honestly, I don't give a hoot about what days… Oh, never mind. Thanks, anyway." She hung up the phone, her mouth turned down in a scowl. "Honestly. That woman."

"Really, passion flower. That was rather rude. You really shouldn't talk like that to—"

"Oh, hush up, Godfrey! You should have heard her. She just kept blathering on and on. I couldn't get a word in edgewise. So, I guess you gathered…they weren't here yesterday. What's the next name in the book?" She wiped her hand over her forehead. "My head is killing me."

"Are you sure you want to do this now? Maybe you should take a headache powder and lie down. I could make a few calls, and—"

"Not on your tin-type! I got myself into this mess. What kind of knucklehead would I be if I just *lie down* and let you bail me out?" Agnes took the phone book from his hand.

"I know you mean well, Godfrey, but I really must do this myself."

Godfrey's face crumpled.

Now she was six shades of a stinker. He was just trying to help. She grabbed his hand. "I'm sorry I snapped. I know you want to help. I'm upset and taking it out on you. Forgive me?"

He shrugged, his head turned, not meeting her gaze.

Still mad. She patted his hand. "You know what? I think there's one piece of rhubarb pie left. I could warm it in the oven, if you like…" She jerked her head toward the icebox. "Pie? Warm pie? What do you say? Forgive me?"

"Well, when you put it that way." He grinned. "I wouldn't want to hurt your feelings."

While Agnes lit the oven, Godfrey located and wrote down the names and phone numbers of three more charitable agencies.

Agnes called the first two without success. By the time Godfrey's pie was warmed, she was on the phone with *Gently Used Clothes and Shoes, Inc.*

"Good morning. By chance, was your truck in the Winterfield neighborhood yesterday?"

"Yes, ma'am." The volunteer took a deep breath. "Our truck was out your way yesterday, collecting clothes for the Polish refugees and underprivileged. Did we miss your house? I can have—"

"Hallelujah! My granddaughter donated a man's raincoat and I need to get it back as soon as—"

"I'm afraid that's not possible, ma'am. We toss all our donations together into large bins once they come back into the warehouse, for sorting and processing, you understand. There's no way to know just which bin the coat might be in this morning."

"Wait. You don't understand. The coat was donated by accident. It was my husband's coat and there's a great deal of money…I mean…" Agnes gulped. "I mean, it holds considerable sentimental value to me because my husband died during WWI, you see, and it's all I have left of him. I really must get it back. Please? Won't you please look for it? You'd recognize it right away if you saw it. It's kind of greyish-tannish-brownish, like, with a belt and big black metal buttons, and—"

"I'm sorry. We couldn't possibly spend time looking for a specific garment. We're much too busy. I'm sorry. I really can't help you." The phone line went dead.

Agnes hung up the phone and shook her head. "They have it, all right, but they won't look for it. This is terrible. What am I going to do?" She ran her fingers over her chin and mouth. "*Humm*…I wonder…" A smile barely curved the corner of her mouth.

"Agnes? What deviltry are you concocting? I can see that look in your eyes. You're up to something. Spill it." Godfrey pinched the last crumb of pie with his fork and popped it in his mouth.

"It's really nothing, my dear. I'm just thinking that I haven't done nearly enough to help those poor unfortunate refugees. Perhaps I'll go down there, and do some shopping."

"Agnes? You know how you are. Don't you go and do something stupid, now."

"How am I, Godfrey?" Agnes put her fists on her hips and glared. Her eyebrows squinched down. "Tell me. How stupid am I?"

"I...I... I didn't mean it to come out quite that way, pigeon-puss, it's just that you're...you're..." Godfrey ducked his head. "You're prone to be impulsive and...sometimes you get yourself into hair-brained predicaments...*um*... Oh, pshaw! You know what I mean." He glanced up with a sheepish grin. "And, in spite of everything, I love you to the moon and back, and that's a fact."

Chapter Twenty-Five

Katherine drove into the parking lot at *Curls to Dye For*, pulled the hand brake and turned off the key. She sat for a moment, staring at the back door, her hands on the steering wheel. Poor Grandmother. *It's my fault.* She shouldn't have let Maddie take the coat without asking Grandma. What was she thinking? There must have been several hundred dollars in the coat, though the exact amount was unclear. Grandma probably didn't even count the money before stuffing it in the lining. As if things weren't bad enough without this.

How much more must they bear? *Lord? If we're being punished for something, I'd sure like to know what it is, so we can stop doing it.* She slammed her fist on the steering wheel.

"Hello? Katherine? Is everything all right?"

Katherine jerked her head toward the man's voice outside her car window. Homer Blenkinsop? "Oh!" She cranked down the window. "Hi, Homer. You startled me. I was just thinking." She nodded toward the salon's back door. "My shift doesn't start for a few minutes."

She opened the car door and stepped out, then reached back and grabbed her purse, sweater and lunch pail. Should she confront him about gossiping? Grandma would.

Grandma would grab Homer by the collar and ask him what the heck gave him the right to spread gossip about her passing counterfeit money? Maybe she should take a lesson in 'brave' from Grandma.

Here goes nothin'. "Say, Homer… A friend of mine overheard you talking about me and Grandma down at the diner. Why do you think Grandma and I are the ones passing counterfeit money around town?" She stared into Homer's eyes. Her face warmed. *Is he going to yell at me?* She put her shaking hand behind her back.

Homer stammered, "I...I... *er*..." He batted his eyes and pulled off his hat. "I don't think I ever said that. I said, *umm*...something like...if the counterfeit bill showed up at your booth, maybe you knew something about it. Or, something like that. *Heh! Heh*." His lips quivered in a guilty smirk.

Katherine held his gaze. "That sounds like you were suggesting I must be printing them. How stupid would I be to pass the fake money in my own booth?"

Homer's cheeks turned rosy. "I...I guess I never thought of it that way. *Er...um*...I gotta' go now." He slammed his hat back on and scuttled across the parking lot, jumped in his pickup truck and drove off.

Well, at least she gave him a piece of her mind. Wouldn't Grandma be proud? Which was fine, but it didn't change the accusations or the problem of Grandpa's missing coat. Grandma was in big trouble if the war bond money wasn't turned into the office today, or tomorrow at the latest.

Katherine squared her shoulders and entered the back door of the beauty salon. She considered whether she should go to the bank and pull some money from her savings account. Grandma could take that to the war bond office. If the coat should be found, which was doubtful, and if the money was still in the lining, which was even more doubtful, Grandma could repay her. If not, what would it matter, compared to getting Grandma out of trouble?

Agnes ran her hand over the top of her henna-colored hair. "My head is killing me, Godfrey. I really must lie down." Agnes handed him his hat and opened the front door. "Why don't you come back later tonight and we'll have dinner together."

"Whatever you say, my gypsy-queen. I'll see you later. I have a surprise for you."

"That's nice." Agnes shoved him out the door. She watched through the front window until Godfrey's car turned the corner. Then she ran her plans past Ling-Ling, as she poured a bit of milk into her bowl. "I'll go down to the *Gently Used Clothing and Shoes* warehouse this morning. I'll bet the coat is already on the sales floor for sale. I'll just buy it back. Easy-Peasy. So, what do you think of that?"

Ling-Ling lapped her milk, showing no particular indication of approval or disapproval of her plan. But, knowing that cats found human events tedious and boring, and seldom have much of an opinion one way or another, Agnes took no offense. She figured the cat's indifference indicated approval of the plan. She put on her jacket, shoved her chopsticks firmly into her bun and headed out the door.

She paused by the car. Maybe she should have left Katherine a note, telling her where she was going. No need. She'd be back long before Maddie got home from school. She hopped into the car and drove straight across town to the address in the phone book.

The *Gently Used Clothing and Shoes* warehouse was housed in a red brick building next to the railroad tracks on the outskirts of town. Mannequins in the front windows wore outfits perhaps more fashionable a decade ago, but still clean and in wearable condition.

A light breeze blew leaves around Agnes's ankles as she paused to read a sign posted by the door. It stated that in addition to being a retail outlet, refugees could come between ten o'clock and two o'clock, allowing each family member in need, six items of clothing and a pair of shoes. That certainly sounded generous.

She glanced at her wristwatch. *Almost ten-thirty*. She pulled the door open.

Inside the retail area were rows of clothing; women's-wear on the left, children's in the center and men's-wear on the right. Rows of shoes lined the far wall by style and size. Toward the back, racks of men's jackets and coats.

Agnes hurried toward the men's coat racks, all hanging in order of color. This should be easy. She scanned the coats. *No, no, no, no!* None were the right color or the right material. As she reached the end of the rack, a voice startled her.

"Can I help you?"

Agnes turned to face the clerk. The lady was elderly and plump, with her hair greying at the temples. She had a nice smile, a red nose and a wart on her chin. "Have you been here long?" The wart wobbled as she spoke.

Agnes gazed at the wart. Why on earth wouldn't she get that thing removed? Hadn't she ever heard of cancer? "What? Oh! Not long. I arrived just a short while ago."

"If you need help with anything at all, I'm at your service. We also have a list of agencies that can provide any assistance you might need. Do you have children? No, I can see, your children must be grown. Did any of them come with you?"

Agnes raised her eyebrows. *Nosy, isn't she?* "No. My granddaughter's at work today."

"Wonderful! So nice to have family around us, and she's working already. How resourceful. So, what can we do for you today? Our ladies clothing is over there." She pointed toward the women's section.

Agnes shook her head. "Actually, I'm looking for a man's raincoat. A tannish-greyish-brownish one with big metal buttons."

"That's a rather specific request. Most folks who come here aren't quite so picky. They're usually thrilled to find anything that fits." She thumbed through the raincoats and pulled out a tan one. "How about this one? It's tan. I'm sure your husband would like it." She held up the raincoat for Agnes's approval.

"No. That's not it. I said tannish-greyish-brownish. That one's much too tan."

"I see." The clerk shrugged. "Well, all the available raincoats are here, so if you can't find one you like…"

"What about the ones that were just donated? Maybe one in your back room would fill the bill. I have money. I can pay." She patted her purse.

"Oh, that's not necessary. We make provisions for your kind but it takes a lot of hands to keep this program working for you people, you know. Many hands help lighten the load, as they say. I must say, have you considered volunteering? Your English is so good, you'd be a wonderful volunteer. We see so many of you folks who can't communicate worth a plug nickel." She grinned and the wart on her chin wobbled from side to side.

Agnes stared at the women's wart. "Just exactly what do you mean by *my kind* and *you people*? Do you mean a woman of a certain age? I may look old, but, I'm quite spry. And, I'm not looking for charity. I can pay whatever it costs."

The clerk's eyes opened wide. "Aren't you a Polish refugee?"

"Do I look like a Polish refugee?" Agnes glanced down at her faded house-dress. *I knew I should have changed my dress.*

"I am so sorry, ma'am. I misjudged you. My mistake. We're a charity organization, you see," her cheeks a rosy red. She pointed up at the sign on the wall. "We provide gently used clothing at good prices to the underprivileged, but it's free for refugees and their children. In exchange, we ask for two hours of volunteer service per family member, here or at another specific charity agency."

"Sounds reasonable. This is a democracy, after all. The United States would never give handouts to able-bodied folks capable of helping themselves, now, would we?" Agnes said.

This wasn't getting her any closer to Douglas's raincoat. The coat must still be somewhere in the back room. She'd have to get back there herself and find it. *Aha!* "So, listen. I wouldn't mind volunteering today. I have a few hours to kill."

"Really? That would be just hunkie-dory!" The clerk grinned. The wart quivered. "What's your name again?"

"I'm…*uh*… I don't believe I mentioned it. I'm Hilda…*um*… Meddler-Burns…from Boyles Springs. I'm sure you've heard of us. The Meddler-Burns stove factory? We're very big on the West Coast." Perspiration beaded Agnes's forehead. As an almost regular church goer, it went against her grain to actually tell a bold-face lie, but since she was on an undercover mission today, it seemed reasonable to give an alias until she checked out the lay of the land.

"Of course. We've had a Meddler…*um*…stove all my life."

That's interesting. Since I just made it up! Agnes grinned. "You can call me Mrs. Burns."

"Nice to meet you, Mrs. Burns. I'm Juanita. Juanita Blenkinsop." She extended her hand.

"When can you start?"

Blenkinsop? What were the odds that she was related to Homer Blenkinsop? Probably not very much, considering that Blenkinsop was such a common name.

"How about I start right now? Show me what to do." Agnes gazed around the showroom, as though looking for a broom and a dustpan to start tidying up the place.

"Come with me. I'll introduce you to the ladies, and give you a tour of the warehouse so you get an idea of how things work."

"Oh, I think I'd just like to…sort of wander around and check out everything myself, if you don't mind." *And, find Douglas's raincoat and get the heck out of here.* "I'll just introduce myself to the ladies as I go. They can show me what they're doing, and—"

"I don't think so. We want to keep an eye on you for a while... *heh...heh...* I mean, I don't want you to get lost or hurt or anything... *heh...heh...* Come along. Step lively, now."

Agnes sighed and followed Juanita through the maze of clothing and into the work room. How could she find the raincoat if someone was watching her every minute?

Along the back wall, three washing machines rumbled. A volunteer pulled a batch of wet clothes from the tub and fed them through the wringer rollers where they tumbled into a wicker basket. The smell of perspiration and wet clothes hung in the air. Through an open door, Agnes saw a clothesline with blouses and dresses whipping in the breeze.

Two more volunteers stood at ironing boards with large baskets of clean clothes at their feet. As one completed ironing a lady's blouse, she placed it on a wooden clothes hanger and hung it on a rack half-filled with blouses. The other volunteer leaned over a little girl's dress with an iron.

Oh, please don't make me iron. I hate to iron! Agnes's gaze moved on to a mound of clothes lying in the middle of the floor. She could see a greyish-tannish-brownish item of clothing poking out from the bottom of the pile. It was all she could do to keep from rushing to the pile and pulling out the item, but she'd have to wait for an opportunity when no one was looking. This was going to take longer than she thought. She could be here all day. *I should have left Katherine a note.*

"Do you wash and iron everything that comes in?" Agnes asked, as if interested in the handling process, which, of course, she was not.

"Only the things that need it," Juanita said. "Unfortunately, some items come in soiled. It means so much to the refugee ladies to get a nice, clean, ironed blouse. The majority of clothing is clean enough to be sold *as is* to the public for a discount price. A penny saved is a penny earned, you know. Everyone loves a bargain."

Who knew so much effort went into a charity run second-hand shop? "But, there are so many." Agnes nodded toward the stack of clothes on the floor where the greenish-tannish-brownish item, just out of reach, tortured her imagination. "How can you possibly process all these clothes?"

"That's why we need so many volunteers. We have to handle every item and make a decision whether it needs washing and ironing or can just be sent out front for sale. Some items are in such bad shape they're discarded and sent to a mill to be processed into paper or cardboard. Let's start you here on this ironing board.

"Milly, here, will answer any of your questions." She nodded to Milly. "This is Mrs. Burns. She's going to help us today."

Milly smiled and pushed a damp strand of hair off her forehead. "Great. I could use a break. I've been here since nine o'clock." She stepped back from the ironing board. "Guess you know what to do with an iron. I'll just run and grab a cup of tea. You can keep working on those." She nodded toward an overflowing basket of wrinkled clothing, and then scurried away.

"Well, *ta-ta* for now," Juanita said. "I'll check back with you later, Mrs. Burns." And, off she went, leaving Agnes staring at the ironing board and the basket of clothes, deeply regretting her hasty decision to volunteer.

Now, what had she gotten herself into? She glanced at the woman at the next ironing board. With her no more than three feet away, there was no opportunity to check out the grayish-tannish-brownish item partly protruding from the pile of clothes not more than eight feet away.

Agnes shrugged, set her purse on the floor and picked up the iron. When she had pressed several ladies' blouses and hung them on the rack, Milly returned from the break room.

"Thanks for taking over. I needed that. Juanita said to tell you that you can take that mop and pail over there and scrub the bathroom floor." She pointed over her shoulder to a closed door.

Agnes's shoulders slumped. *From purgatory to hell's fire...* Could things get much worse?

"I know. It's not a very nice job, but somebody has to do it and it usually falls to the most recent volunteer, so it looks like you're it!"

Well, isn't this peachy-keen? Now, I get to scrub toilets. How could she search for Douglas's raincoat if they kept her busy doing scud work all day?

Never one to approach a commitment half-heartedly, Agnes tackled the bathroom. Within half an hour, she had it clean and shining.

For the rest of the day, Juanita kept her scrubbing, ironing, working the intake table and sewing on buttons. Agnes kept her head down and willingly completed every task.

Along about mid-afternoon, Agnes returned to the sparkling clean bathroom, closed the door, and unlatched the window. Clearly, with no opportunity to search for the raincoat during the work day, she would have to return after the facility closed to retrieve the coat she was sure lay in the pile of clothing near the ironing boards.

As the day wore to a close, Agnes got to know Milly and Juanita, and realized the importance of the program for the immigrants. She considered volunteering again, another day. That is, if she wasn't in the Newbury jail house for breaking and entering Wilkey's Market, or Tehachapi Women's Prison, for passing counterfeit bills. For that matter, it wasn't impossible to think she might end up in the Federal Correctional Institution in Danbury, if she couldn't find Douglas's coat and return the war bond money.

Good grief. I never did look good in black and white stripes!

Chapter Twenty-Six

Curls to Dye For Beauty Salon, Myrtle speaking. Oh, hi, Maddie… Katherine?" Myrtle glanced up. "Yes, she's here. I'll call her." Myrtle put her hand over the receiver. "It's Maddie. She sounds upset," she whispered, and handed the phone to Katherine.

What's wrong now? Katherine laid down a comb and patted her client on the shoulder. "Excuse me, Mrs. Plumbinder. I'll just be a minute. I need to take this."

The elderly lady's curlers bobbed. "No problem, dear. I'm in no hurry." She laid her head back against the chair and closed her eyes.

Katherine's gaze passed around the beauty shop and over the shelf of bottles and boxes containing shampoos and henna rinse, noting that it was time to buy more conditioner. A basket of wet towels lay near the back door. Clean towels were stacked beside the table next to a Hollywood movie magazine touting the latest fashions and hair styles.

"Hello, Maddie? What's wrong?"

"Grandma didn't come get me, so I walked home," Maddie whined. "She's not here and the door is locked, and I can't get in the house."

A stitch caught in Katherine's throat. "Where are you calling from, sweetheart?" *Why didn't Grandma pick her up from school? Where is she?*

"Mavis heard me crying on the front steps." Maddie sniffed. "She said I should come to her house and call you. What should I do, Katherine? If Grandma doesn't want me anymore, where will I go?" A sob burbled through the phone.

"Now, don't take on so, honey. Of course, Grandma wants you. She loves you. I'm sure she'll be home any minute now. Why don't you stay and play with Mavis's puppy, okay? I'll come home as soon as I finish Mrs. Plumbinder's hair, okay?"

"Okay. I love you, Katherine." Maddie sniffed.

Katherine's heart jerked. "I love you too, sweetheart. Bye." She hung up the phone.

Myrtle peered around the corner. "Is everything okay at home?"

"Maddie came home from school and Grandma's not there. You know how Maddie overreacts, and sees the slightest problem through the lens of her insecurities. No one's home so she's convinced that no one loves her. She's having another emotional break-down."

"If you have to leave, I can finish your client."

"I'm almost finished. Maddie's with the neighbor. She'll be okay for a little while."

Yet another example of Maddie's emotional problems, it exemplified Don's reluctance to adopt her. They'd likely be up half the night with Maddie's tantrums.

Why hadn't Grandma picked her up at school? There must be a mighty good, or bad, reason. Oh, wait. She and Godfrey were going to look for Douglas's raincoat today.

Myrtle snickered. "Maybe she and Godfrey went to lunch and lost track of time. You know how young lovers are."

"Grandma never leaves Maddie alone, especially now, with all the recent troubles. Something must be wrong. She left the door locked, so she must have intended to be home by the time Maddie got out of school."

"Why don't you go on home? I'll finish up Mrs. Plumbinder."

"Would you? Thanks. That would be great. Maddie was really upset," Katherine said.

Myrtle shook her head. "The poor kid."

"And, we try so hard…" Katherine untied her apron and retrieved her purse from the corner locker. She approached the older woman, who appeared to have dozed off in her chair. Katherine touched her arm. "Mrs. Plumbinder?"

The woman blinked.

"I'm sorry. I didn't mean to startle you." Katherine chuckled. "I have to run home unexpectedly. I hope you won't mind if Myrtle finishes styling your hair."

"Not at all, dear. Is everything all right at home?" Mrs. Plumbinder sat up straighter in her chair and readjusted the drape around her neck.

"I'm sure it is. I'll see you next week, okay?"

Katherine hurried to her car and started the engine. *Whatever are you up to this time, Grandma?*

She honked the horn as she pulled into her driveway. She was not surprised to find Maddie waiting at Mavis's front window, watching for her return.

Maddie and Mavis pushed open the screen door onto her front porch. "Thanks for watching her, Mavis," Katherine called, stepping out onto the driveway.

Mavis took the puppy from Maddie's arms. "Run on now, Maddie. Come back anytime."

The distraught child raced through the yellow-rose hedge, threw herself into Katherine's arms, and burst into tears.

"Now, that's enough." Katherine crouched and wrapped her arms around her. *Crocodile tears, no doubt, but real enough to her.* "There's no need to cry. You're a big girl. You did just the right thing when Grandma wasn't here. You went to our friend's house and asked for help. There's always someone who cares and will help when you're in trouble. All you have to do is ask. Can you remember that?"

Maddie swiped way her tears. "I…I guess so. But, why didn't Grandma come?"

Katherine hugged her. "I'm sure there's a good reason. I'll bet Old Nelly got a flat tire or ran out of gas and she couldn't get there in time. See? There's no need to be upset, now, is there?"

"I guess not. I just got scared."

"I know. If it happens again, you'll do just what you did today and you won't be scared…will you? Now, come on inside and we'll get some milk and a snack." Katherine stood and steered Maddie toward the front door. She waved to Mavis, and mouthed, "Thanks!"

Agnes laid a dress on the table and smoothed out the wrinkles, checked the buttons, the hem and the underarms. *Will this day ever end? I've seen enough old clothes to stretch from Newbury to Sacramento and back.*

Juanita approached the intake table. "How are things going, Mrs. Burns. Any questions?"

"Not yet. Just helping with this batch of clothes. This one has a smudge on the front, though, so I guess it needs washing." She tossed it into a basket headed for the washing machine.

"You're catching on very quickly." Juanita said, glancing at her wristwatch. "It's three o'clock. I'll bet you're about due for a cup of tea."

Agnes's head jerked up. "Three o'clock, already? I was supposed to pick up… Oh, dear. Is there a phone I could use?"

"There's a pay phone in the break room." Juanita pointed toward the back of the warehouse.

Agnes retrieved her purse and hurried to the break room, inserted a nickel into the wall phone and dialed Katherine's beauty salon.

"Hello? Curls to Dye For Beauty Salon. Myrtle, here. How can I help you?"

"Myrtle? It's Agnes. Can I speak to Katherine?"

"Oh dear. She's not here. Maddie called and… Where are you? Maddie walked home and found the front door locked."

Agnes rolled her eyes. "I know. I got busy and lost track of time.

So, Katherine's gone home already? That's good."

"She just left. She's probably there by now. Is everything all right?"

"No time to explain. Thanks. I'll call her at home. Bye."

Agnes dropped another nickel into the phone and dialed her home phone. She waited, and tapped her foot. *Ring...ring...ring...* No answer. "Why isn't she picking up?"

"Yoo-hoo! Agnes?" Juanita Blenkinsop called from across the warehouse. "Are you coming back? Another truck just arrived. We need you at the intake door."

Agnes waved. Maddie would be fine, once Katherine got home.

Planning to call again later, she hung up the phone, retrieved her nickel from the slot, and hurried to the Intake door where a driver unloaded bags and boxes of donated clothing. *Back to work!*

If Juanita would just leave her alone for five minutes, she could find Douglas's raincoat and be out of there. *The old gal sticks to me like flypaper.* She squared her shoulders and picked up a bag of children's clothes. No choice but to come back after closing time. She bent her head to her task, shook out the children's shirts and jeans, and spread them onto the table.

Katherine had barely steered Maddie through the front door, and sat her at the kitchen table with a glass of milk when the phone rang. *Grandma!* She grabbed the phone, "Hello? Grandma?"

"No, it's me, Don."

"Don?" Why would he call her from the hospital? Had something happened to keep him from coming home tomorrow as previously planned? "Is everything all right?"

"I'm fine. I just called the beauty shop. Myrtle said you left early. Apparently Agnes called the shop a few minutes ago looking for you, too."

"She did? I wonder why she didn't call here. Did she say where she is?"

"Myrtle didn't go into it. Just said she called. *Uh...* Katherine? Can you come by the hospital this evening? We need to talk."

Here it comes. A twinge seared her stomach. "Is it good news or bad news?" She held her breath.

"Don't be so melodramatic. I don't want to go into it on the phone, but we need to discuss a couple of things. Can you come or not?"

He's breaking up with me. Not that she'd blame him, with all that was going on. She glanced at the chicken clock over the stove. Almost four o'clock. "Why don't I come down now? I'll have to bring Maddie." *I hope he won't make me cry.*

"Fine. I'll see you in a few minutes. Good-bye."

"Maddie, finish your milk. We're going down to the hospital to see Dr. Don."

"Can't I stay with Mavis?" Her hand shook as she drained the milk from her glass.

"Not this time."

Chapter Twenty-Seven

hanks for your help today, Mrs. Burns." Juanita raised an eyebrow. "Can you come back tomorrow?"

"I…I don't know. Obligations, you know. I might be able to make it. Perhaps for part of the day. It was very…interesting. I enjoyed it."

"That's fine. I hope you can work it out." Juanita glanced at the clock. "It's after five o'clock. Time to close up the store, so, thanks again." It was clearly a dismissal.

What's she in such an all-fired hurry about? Agnes gathered her purse, went out the front door to the front parking lot where she had parked her car.

Agnes started Old Nelly and pulled out of the parking lot, then circled the block and parked half a block from the warehouse, still able to see the back entrance.

Storm clouds had gathered over Newbury again, darkening the sky. The pavement was damp from intermittent cloudbursts. Agnes watched Milly and three other volunteers exit the back door and drive away. Still no Juanita! Until everyone was gone, she didn't dare proceed with her Black-Ops operation through the bathroom window. *Break in, find the raincoat and leave. Easy Peasy!*

There was every possibility that Juanita had discovered the open bathroom window and locked it. That would be the end of access to the warehouse.

She shook her head. *I won't think about that now.* If the bathroom window was unlocked, she wouldn't exactly be breaking and entering. She'd just be…*entering!*

A few minutes later, Juanita came out of the warehouse and climbed into her car.

Agnes ducked out of sight and held her breath until Juanita's car turned the corner and rumbled down the street. She straightened up and tucked the chopsticks back into her bun. *I'll wait another five minutes to make sure she doesn't come back.*

Her heart pattered, anticipating her next move. A quick in and out and she'd be home free with the raincoat in hand. Once the money was retrieved from the lining, she could bank it in the morning. None would be the wiser that she had lost the war bond money from the harvest festival.

Katherine's car spluttered to a start. The windshield wipers zigged and zagged, wiping away large drops of rain. She turned to smile at Maddie, hunched beside her in the front passenger seat. "Are we ready?" *Ready or not, here goes nothing.*

Maddie sat with her head down, picking at her fingernails.

"Everything okay, sweetheart? Is there anything you want to talk about?" Katherine's gaze returned to the road. She stopped at the corner, cranked down the window, put her arm straight out the window to signal a left turn, and stepped on the gas.

Maddie shook her head. "Do I have to go in Dr. Don's room? Can I wait in the car?"

"I don't think so." She patted Maddie's cheek. "I know what. You can wait in the children's play area." They probably weren't going to have a conversation she should hear, anyway. "But, I'm sure Dr. Don would want to see you."

"*Uh-huh.*" Maddie examined her shoes, turning her foot from side to side.

They drove in silence the rest of the way to the hospital. Katherine eased into the parking lot, found a spot to park near the entrance, and yanked on the hand brake. "Here we are."

Maddie wrinkled her nose at the scent of flowers mixed with the sting of disinfectant just inside the lobby door. "It smells funny in here," she said.

"I guess the nurses get used to the smell after a while." Katherine said, patting Maddie's curls. A staff member wandered past, his eyes glued to a clipboard.

They walked down the hall toward the children's play area. Only one other child was there, playing on a slide. "Now, you'll stay right here in the play yard until I come back, okay? Don't go anywhere else."

A young woman sitting near the swings smiled at Katherine. "I'll be here for several hours. My mother's in surgery. I'll keep an eye on your little girl, if you like."

The young woman looked familiar. *Where have I seen her before?* "Would you? That would be great. I won't be more than an hour, I don't think…maybe even less. Thanks."

Or, five minutes, if Don wants to call it quits. Her heart wouldn't be broken if he did. Was that a sign that she was ready to let go? She was so tired of arguing about Maddie.

Maddie climbed on a swing and begin to pump. How could she love the child more? The bond between them was as strong as if she were her own flesh and blood. *If Don asks me to choose between him and Maddie, I choose Maddie.* There. She had finally admitted the truth. A sense of peace settled over her heart. If Don forced such a choice, it was obvious that she shouldn't marry him.

She waved to Maddie. "I won't be long. I'll bet by the time we get home, Grandma will be there." She left the play area and headed toward the second floor.

Katherine stopped outside Don's hospital room. *Should I have brought flowers? Too late now.* The next ten minutes would change her life, one way or another. She pasted a smile on her face, pushed open the door, and paused just inside his room. *Deep breath! Deep breath!*

Don lay in the bed, a pillow plumped behind his head, chatting with a pretty nurse, her blonde hair styled in a soft waves around her face. She pulled the covers straight, tucked in the edges and stood. "There, that's better."

Don winked. "Thanks, doll. That's great." He looked up. "Katherine! You're here already."

"I said I was coming right down." *He's flirting…again.*

"Yes, but…I guess I thought you might…*um*…wait until your Grandma came home." He glanced at the nurse. "Thanks." A slight flush on his cheeks faded as the nurse nodded and strode toward the door.

Katherine kissed Don's forehead, and then sat in the chair beside the bed. "So, can I get you anything?"

"I'm fine." Don tugged on the sheet and the bedspread. His face flushed as he rolled his neck and winced. "Might as well get right to it. I've been offered a job at the Mercy Hospital in Sacramento. They want me to head up their Surgery Wing. I'd be Chief of Surgery, with all the benefits that go with the title."

Katherine started and sat back in her chair. Where was he going with this? Breaking up or asking her to go with him? "Oh? That is news."

Don glanced at Katherine and then ducked his head. He cleared his throat. "It's quite an honor for a doctor my age. I'm tempted to accept the offer…but…I thought we should talk about it first. What do you think? This is a big decision. It involves both of us." He glanced around the room, not quite meeting Katherine's eyes.

"Chief of Surgery. That is quite an honor." She picked at a hangnail on her thumb. "Last time we talked, I was under the impression you didn't think there was an *us*. What exactly are you suggesting? That we should get married, now? That I should leave my life in Newbury, my job, Grandma…and…and come to Sacramento with you? What about Maddie?"

Indeed. What about Maddie? The big stumbling block that had put a crimp in their relationship in the first place.

Don rolled his eyes. "Maddie could stay with your grandmother. You could always get a job in Sacramento if that's what you want. You wouldn't need to. My salary would be enough."

Katherine shook her head. "I don't think my job is quite the issue. As for Maddie, I don't want to leave her with Grandma. I love her. I want her with me."

Don turned his head away. "So, I guess that's that. Maddie shouldn't even be an issue. She's not your child—"

"She is! She's my child now. And I won't give her up." Katherine stood and paced the six steps between the chair and the door. "If you can't understand that, then I guess… I guess there's nothing more to say." She twisted the ring off her finger and laid it on a table by the door. "I…I wish you success in Sacramento, Don. Really, I do. I want only what's best for you." She yanked the door open and reeled from his room, tears blurring her vision.

"Katherine!" Don's muted voice echoed into the hall as the door swung shut.

Katherine stumbled down the hallway, dashing tears from her face, and headed back toward the play area. She dropped into a chair outside the lab. It wouldn't do to let Maddie see her crying. She already suspected she was the cause of their relationship troubles. No need to involve her further in this situation tonight.

Katherine dabbed her eyes with a handkerchief and blew her nose. *It was my choice. No need to cry about it.* She could leave Maddie with Grandma, marry Don and move to the big city where his new job and prestige would guarantee a comfortable life. But no, she had to go all Mother Theresa on him, playing nursemaid to a child from a criminal family. And where that might lead one day was anybody's guess.

She looked back toward Don's room. Maybe she should go

back. Tell him she changed her mind. *He's a good man and I know...I mean...I think he loves me. He just doesn't want Maddie.* Could she blame him? Was it possible that Maddie's family was behind the break in at the house, for Grandma being framed for the burglary. and the counterfeit accusations, because she took Maddie away from them? Would things be any different in Sacramento? If Maddie's family was behind the trouble, they could just as easily follow her to Sacramento and cause more trouble. Was it any wonder Don didn't want to risk adopting Maddie?

On the other hand, if there was such a risk, could she leave Maddie and Grandma to face things alone in Newbury? *I'm the one who insisted Maddie come back to Newbury with us.*

No. Breaking up with Don was the right decision, whether because of her love for Maddie or duty to Grandma.

Katherine dried her eyes. Better get on home. Grandma would surely be there by now, probably cooking dinner and ready to chat a mile a minute about whatever had upset her day.

OK, Agnes. The coast is clear. Let's get on with it. Once Juanita's car was out of sight, Agnes started Old Nelly, drove into the warehouse parking lot and parked near the back door. Since Juanita had clung to her all day like a fly on a cow patty, there had been no opportunity to check out the greenish-tannish-brownish item, lying right in plain sight under the stack of clothes in the middle of the warehouse.

If the elusive clothing item *was* Douglas's raincoat, it wouldn't take her five minutes to retrieve it. This whole ridiculous mess would be something she and Godfrey would laugh about later tonight over a cup of cocoa!

Agnes pulled Douglas's flashlight from the glove box and crept to the bathroom window. It was too high to reach. She spotted several wooden crates and a steel drum stacked along the wall further down the side of the building.

She tipped the drum on edge, rolled it back to the window, and placed a wooden box beside it. By stepping on the box and then onto the top of the drum, she was able to reach the window.

Large drops of rain dampened the pavement as Agnes teetered on the top of the drum, pushed open the unlocked window, and threw one leg over the sill. *Umph! Oww! Arrgh!*

A car rumbled toward the warehouse. She clicked off the flashlight and held her breath. Wouldn't it be mortifying if Chief Waddlemucker found her, straddled half-in and half-out, of a warehouse bathroom window, six feet off the ground?

The car moved on down the street. Agnes whooshed out her breath. *Wait! What was that?* Had the sound come from inside the warehouse? The hair on the back of her neck stood up. That wasn't possible. Everyone was gone. *I'm just being paranoid!*

She listened for a minute, then hearing nothing further, drew her other leg through the window and stepped onto the back of the toilet. The ceramic creaked under her weight as she stepped down onto the toilet lid. *That's all I need! To break through the lid and get my foot stuck in the toilet!* She quickly hopped to the floor and straightened her skirt.

She turned the handle and pushed open the bathroom door. *Squeak!*

Now. All she had to do was grab the raincoat and get out. Piece a' cake.

With few windows in the warehouse, despite the early hour, with the lights out, it was quite dark inside. She snapped on the flashlight, stepped into the main warehouse and flashed her light toward the pile of clothes where Douglas's raincoat lay. Casting the light back and forth, she carefully tiptoed toward the garment, making sure she didn't stumble over anything.

There. The item in question still lay tucked under the pile of men's clothing. She reached down, grabbed one corner and tugged. It didn't budge. The weight of the clothes held it down. She pulled again. *It's coming…out…from…the stack!* She leaned over further, laid the flashlight on the floor and grabbed the hem of the garment with both hands and yanked.

The stack of clothes toppled toward her head, throwing her off balance. She went down on her knees, *Oww!* Clothing tumbled around her, half burying her beneath jackets, jeans and shirts. Darkness loomed as the garments buried the flashlight.

Agnes shoved a pair of jeans off her head, still gripping the raincoat with one hand. *Where did that blasted flashlight go?* She scrabbled beneath the pile with her other hand until she touched the cold metal and drew it out, casting light on the item clutched in her hand.

Her heart fell as she saw, not Douglas's raincoat, but a workman's trench coat, close to the identical color and texture, but not the item she sought. *Rats! I was so sure!*

Wasn't this a fine kettle of fish! She flashed the light around the warehouse. *Okay, Agnes. Move along.* The coat had to be there somewhere. She'd have to keep looking. She laid the flashlight on a nearby chair, where it cast a beam of light toward the rumpled pile of clothes. Then, she tossed pieces left and right as she pawed through the stack. *It must be here!* They piled all the incoming clothing here. Soon the floor was littered with garments of all shapes and colors, but no raincoat. *Oh, beans!* If it took all night, she'd search every basket, pile and stack in the wretched place.

She paused to think. Maybe they thought it needed washing. It might be over by the washers. She picked up the flashlight and made her way closer to where the washers lined the wall. The light flashed over the round, white porcelain washers that resembled cans of baking powder with legs and rollers on top.

What was that? She spun in a circle, and turned her flashlight toward the wall behind the washing machines. It sounded like machinery next door. *Rumble, rumble, clunk! Rumble, rumble, clunk!* What kind of machine made that kind of sound? She tilted her head to listen. *Rumble, rumble, clunk! Rumble, rumble, clunk!* There it was again. The flashlight shook in her hand. It wasn't a sound she'd heard all day, and she'd been over every inch of the warehouse since ten o'clock this morning. Perhaps the noise in the warehouse and the washing machines had masked the noise from next door.

If someone was still working over there, they might see her light under the door or through the window. They might even think it was a burglar and call the cops.

She flipped off the flashlight. The twilight had turned to darkness. She hoped her eyes would adjust to the darkness. She had to think. A hollow feeling plunged through the pit of her stomach as doubts assailed her mind. *Maybe it's useless. It's just too daunting. If I can't find the raincoat, what shall I do?* How long did she dare keep searching? Nobody even knew where she was and it was after five o'clock!

Only a bit of light came through the windows up near the ceiling. As her eyes adjusted, she could now see enough to keep from bumping into things, but not enough to distinguish colors or textures of the clothing on the floor. Everything looked greyish-brownish-tannish. She could never identify Douglas's raincoat without the aid of the flashlight, even if she happened to find it.

Rain spattered at the windows and wind whistled across the roof… most likely across loose tiles. It looked like Newbury was in for another good storm, just like the other night when she went to Wilkey's Market. A chill crept up the back of her neck at the memory.

Was it an omen that she shouldn't be here? Wouldn't it be wiser to come back tomorrow? She could throw herself on Juanita's mercy and ask her and the other volunteers to help her find the coat. Now that she had gotten to know the ladies, wouldn't they sympathize and help? Why hadn't she done that earlier this afternoon? She would have had to admit she had thoughtlessly stuck the money in the lining of Douglas's coat. Pride. That's what it was. *Pure-de-pride* that kept her from admitting she was three shades of a fool.

Another thought occurred to her. Maybe she should call Edith

Braithwaite Farthingworth and confess. She might put in a good word at the war bond office. Maybe they wouldn't send her to Leavenworth. She shivered at the thought. Or maybe…

As Agnes stood lamenting her past and contemplating her dilemma, her gaze moved along the back wall. *Rumble, rumble, clunk! Rumble, rumble, clunk!* Again, that noise next door. Was it another part of *Gently Used Clothing and Shoes, Inc.*? Could there be a night crew over there, still washing clothes? Maybe that's where they'd sent Douglas's overcoat.

She moved toward the door and reached toward the knob.

LEAVE, AGNES! GET OUT OF HERE!

She started and turned, snapped on the flashlight and flashed it around the warehouse. "Who said that?"

She stood alone in the empty warehouse, next to the washing machines.

Goosebumps popped out up and down her arms. The last time she'd heard such a warning, she was at the watchtower on the beach. Heeding the advice without question had saved her life.

She swallowed a lump in her throat. Her first instinct was to obey. She took a step toward the back door, toward safety, and then stopped.

That time, the *Voice* had warned her for a good reason. She'd been in real danger that day. This was different. She wasn't in any danger, all alone, here in an empty warehouse. *Now, I'm imagining voices, of all things.*

She shrugged, dismissing the warning from her mind and grabbed the doorknob to the adjoining room. Oddly, it turned easily in her hand. She edged it slowly open.

Once inside, the *rumble, rumble, clunk* grew louder.

She stepped through the door and gazed around the small room full of machinery. *What on earth?*

"Agnes Odboddy! What in blue blazes are you doing here?"

Her heart leaped to her throat.

A man appeared from behind the nearest machine. A menacing

grimace replaced the smile she was accustomed to seeing on his face.

"And, now that you're here, my dear," he said with a snarl, "what am I going to do with you?"

Icy needles pricked her cheeks. *Rumble, rumble, clunk* assaulted her ears as printing presses churned out large sheets of United States currency. Forcing her hands to stop shaking, she straightened up to her full five feet, two-and-one-quarter inches and faced her challenger. "Homer Blenkinsop! What exactly are *you* doing here? If that's not counterfeit money you're printing, I'll be a horse's rear end."

Chapter Twenty-Eight

Katherine tucked her tear-soaked handkerchief back into her purse and opened the door into the hospital's covered play area. Rain sluiced down, bending branches on the decorative trees outside the playroom.

Maddie chased a little girl around the swing set while her mother laid down her book, looked up and smiled.

Katherine pulled off her jacket and threw it over a chair. "I'm back." She waved to Maddie, now crawling behind the little girl into the doll house. She turned to the mother. "Looks like the girls are having fun. Thanks for keeping an eye on her." *Where have I seen her before?*

"No problem. I'm Sally Hawkins, by the way." She stood and shook Katherine's hand.

"Nice to meet you. I'm Katherine Odboddy." She took a quick breath as tears pricked her eyes again. "I was here visiting my...my…" *Did she say her name was Sally?*

"Is your loved one okay?" Sally lowered her eyes. "I mean…I'm sorry. I didn't mean to pry."

"Oh, it's nothing like that." Katherine paused. "Have we met before? You look so familiar." *Sally from Joe's Diner? The waitress who spilled tea in my lap? Great! Now what do I say?*

"I'll bet you've seen me at Joe's Diner. I'm a waitress there and…" Speaking the location of the diner aloud also appeared to trigger Sally's memory. Her face turned bright pink. "Oh! I remember you now. I spilled tea in your lap. I am so sorry. Really, it was an accident. I guess I *was* flirting with Dr. Don but…really…I am sorry."

"Forget it. It's water under the bridge. Or should I say tea." Katherine chuckled. "As it happens, Dr. Don and I just broke up, so if you're still interested, I won't stand in your way." Her stomach lurched. She glanced toward the girls, crawling on the rug. "Come on Maddie. Let's go. Grandma should be home by now."

"Wait. You misunderstood," Sally said. "I'm not interested in the doctor. I never was. I'm married. Joe and I own the diner. I was just… just flirting. Joe and I quarreled that morning. Nothing important, but I was trying to make him jealous. And, it worked. I've never seen him so mad. He thought Dr. Don was flirting with *me*! My husband has the crazy idea that I'll leave him if I get a better offer, like, from the doctor." Her cheeks turned a darker red. "Oh, I'm talking too much."

Katherine sat down beside Sally. "It's okay. I get it. I shouldn't have acted that way, either. I was a little mad at Don that morning, too. So, let's say it never happened." Katherine gestured again to Maddie. "We should go now. Say good-bye to your friend."

Maddie hopped up from the floor, waved to Sally's little girl, and took Katherine's hand.

"Oh, there's my husband, now," Sally said.

Before Katherine reached the door, a tall man with a day-old beard opened it. "Thank you." She stepped through the door into the hallway.

Maddie glanced at the man, yanked her hand away from Katherine and darted down the hall. She pulled open the phone booth door and sobbed, huddled on the floor, and wrapped her arms around her knees.

"Maddie. What's wrong?" Katherine squatted outside the phone booth. *This child shall be the death of me yet.* Was she having nightmares during the day now?

Maddie lifted her tear-streaked face, choked down a sob, and pointed back down the hall toward the playroom. "That's the man that hit Dr. Don in the church. I'm scared." She ducked and put her hands over her head.

Sally's husband, Joe? From the diner?

"What's going on here? What's the problem?" A man's voice overhead…

At the touch of a hand on her shoulder, the hair on the back of Katherine's neck tingled. Had Joe followed them? Her gaze moved up past khaki pants, a black belt and a blue shirt.

Vincent leaned over them, his eyebrow raised. "Katherine? What's the matter?"

Katherine stood. "Oh, Vincent... Thank goodness, it's you." She swallowed against the tight feeling in her throat, and nodded toward Maddie, sniffing and wiping her nose on her sleeve. "She says the man who attacked Dr. Don is in the play yard. She's very upset."

Katherine opened her purse and handed Maddie her rather damp handkerchief. "Dry your eyes, sweetie, and come out of there. See? Vincent's here. No one's going to hurt you. Now, tell us what you saw in the church."

"Come and sit over here with me." Vincent gently pulled Maddie to her feet and steered her to a chair across the hall.

Maddie dried her eyes. The color gradually returned to her face. Vincent's presence must have made her feel safe. "Dr. Don said mean things about me and I wished that something bad would happen to him. Grandma told me that Jesus doesn't want us to have hateful thoughts, so I went into the church to say I was sorry."

"So, then what happened?" Katherine said, pushing Maddie's bangs off her forehead.

"Dr. Don was up front by the flowers. I didn't want him to see me, so I hid behind the pews. Before I said my prayer, that man sneaked in the side door." She pointed back down the hall toward the play room. "He hit Dr. Don with a candlestick and threw him into the *babtizing* place." Tears filled her eyes again. "It was my fault that Dr. Don got hurt because I was mad at him. Will Jesus forgive me?"

"Of course. Jesus forgives us when we are truly sorry, no matter how naughty we are." Katherine hugged Maddie. "Everything will be all right, now."

Wrinkles creased Vincent's forehead. "What do you think? Do you think she's right? About her identification, I mean."

"She started to cry as soon as she saw Joe Hawkins entering the play yard. Maddie recognized him right away. I just talked to his wife. Don and I had a little trouble at Joe's Diner a few days ago when we stopped for lunch.

"I doubt Sally knows about the attack, or she would never have told me that Joe was crazy jealous of Don." Katherine pointed toward the play room. They're still over there."

"Why don't you take Maddie home? I'll have a little talk with Mr. Hawkins. I'll call you later if anything comes of it."

Katherine grinned. Thank goodness, something was starting to go right for a change. "She may have just solved Don's assault. Maybe that will get you off the hook with Chief Waddlemucker."

As Katherine turned the corner on their street, she looked for Grandmother's car in the driveway. Instead, she saw Godfrey's car parked at the curb. *Good. He'll know where she is.*

Godfrey opened his car door as Katherine pulled into the driveway. She gathered her things and turned off the engine. "Hurry, Maddie. Let's get out of the rain." She waved as she stepped out the door and called to Godfrey. "Have you heard from Grandmother?"

"Not since this morning. We made dinner plans. Why? Where is she?"

"I don't know. She didn't pick up Maddie from school. That's not like her." Katherine glanced at her wristwatch. "It's almost seven o'clock. I'm worried."

"Perhaps I should phone the hospital, and—"

"It's too soon to start calling in the troops. Come on in and I'll make some sandwiches. I need to feed this child." Katherine said, unlocking the front door. "You have no idea where she might be?"

"Actually, the last I heard this morning, she'd learned *Gently Used Clothes and Shoes* had Douglas's coat. She didn't say she was going there, but could that be what she did? Maybe I should—"

"What good would that do? That was hours ago and they'd be closed by now. Let's give it a little longer. If Grandma's not back within an hour, I'll call Chief Waddlemucker." *Even though I doubt he'll give a rip about her not showing up for dinner.*

Chapter Twenty-Nine

Agnes swallowed a lump in her throat as she gazed at Homer Blenkinsop. *Gadzooks!* Stumbling into a room full of printing presses cranking out counterfeit money, with a former friend and neighbor at the wheel certainly was disconcerting. *Counterfeiting! Federal offense! Prison time! Leavenworth! Think fast, Agnes, or your chances of getting out of here are diddly squat!*

"Homer Blenkinsop, you'd better surrender right now!" She jerked her head toward the back warehouse parking lot. "The place is surrounded by FBI agents and you haven't got a chance!" *That sounded pretty good.* Now, if she could stop shaking, and keep from soiling her bloomers, she might just get out of this alive. She started backing through the door into the clothing warehouse. So, Homer *was* Juanita's husband, and the *Gently Used Clothing and Shoes.* was a front for his counterfeiting ring. What were the odds of anything good coming of this?

"Not so fast, Agnes." Homer moved toward her with a menacing smirk. "You and I know there isn't an FBI agent within a mile. I don't know what you're doing here, but now that you've stumbled onto my little enterprise, we have a problem. Come on back in here and let's talk about it." His words sounded polite enough, but the tone of his voice was menacing, like a cobra, hypnotizing its victim with gentle swaying.

Agnes had backed up as far as the washing machines in the

warehouse. If Homer would just stay where he was… She turned, hoping to make a break for the back door…and bumped squack into Juanita.

Juanita grabbed Agnes's arm and spun her around. "What are you still doing here, Mrs. Burns? I thought you went home an hour ago."

Homer stepped through the door into the warehouse. "Mrs. Burns? This isn't Mrs. Burns. This is Agnes Odboddy, or should I say, Agnes Busyboddy! And, she's just blundered into the back room."

"What? She told me…" She glanced past Homer's shoulder toward the presses, still cranking out sheets of bills. *Ka-chunk…Ka-chunk.* "Well, that's a fine kettle of bull-Twinkies. What are we going to do with her, now that she's seen everything?"

Homer reached back through the door. He flipped a switch, and the machines stopped rumbling, and the room went dark. "Take her into the office. I need to think."

The clank of the printing presses still rang in Agnes's ears, almost drowning out her thumping heartbeat. *She's in on it, too.* She tried to free herself from Juanita's grip, but Homer grabbed her other arm. With one on each side of her, they propelled Agnes toward the office. She had no choice but to comply. *Isn't this enough to peel the shell off an Easter egg. Now, what am I going to do?*

Homer shoved her into a chair and leaned against the edge of his desk. "You've put me in a perplexing spot Agnes, and left me little choice."

Little choice? That didn't sound good. Could it all be a big mistake? Somehow, she doubted there was any mistake. She couldn't *un-see* the printing presses, and the bogus bills were real enough. Homer knew that as a hometown patriot, she wouldn't keep quiet about the counterfeiting operation. Her stomach lurched. *I've gotten into another fine pickle. This time I might not get out, but I'll give it my Christian best.*

"Homer. Everyone looks up to you. You're the Newbury Daily Gazette's editor. Don't make matters worse than they are. Of course, you have a choice. Let me call Chief Waddlemucker and—"

"Poppy-cock! Stop yammering. You're not calling Chief Waddlemucker or anyone else." He turned away. Was he afraid to look her in the face?

Juanita sat on a box in the corner, biting her bottom lip and twisting her hands. "What are we going to do? Counterfeiting is one thing, but I didn't sign up for mur—"

Homer lurched off the edge of the desk and stepped toward her with his hand raised. "Shut up if you know what's good for you!"

Juanita cringed, her eyes wide. Apparently, it wasn't the first time he'd raised his hand to her. Who would have thought nice old Homer Blenkinsop was a wife-beater? Not the character trait you want to learn about in a crook just threatened with exposure.

Homer dropped his hand. "Go home, Juanita. I'll handle this." He pulled her off the box and shoved her toward the exit. "Get going. I'll be along later."

Juanita's lip trembled. "What…what are you going to do with her?"

"Never you mind. I said I'd handle it. Don't worry. *I'm* not going to hurt her. There's apt to be a tragic accident, I'm afraid." He shoved her toward the door. "Now, scoot."

Juanita ran through the back door into the parking lot. An engine started, followed by the screech of tires. Juanita might have influenced Homer, but now that she was gone, there was no hope from that quarter. Agnes was on her own to outwit Homer.

Homer grabbed Agnes's arm and yanked her toward the back door. "We're going for a little ride. Someone can come back later and move your car. Wouldn't want them to connect your untimely demise with our little enterprise."

I can't let him put me in his car! It's now or never! Agnes pulled back. "Homer, this isn't necessary. Let's go back in the office and talk. I'm sure we can work this out." She twisted and kicked at his ankle. Her unexpected attack should allow her a few seconds head start.

Homer was too quick. He dodged her kick, pulled back his fist and struck Agnes's chin.

Flashing lights shot through her head. She was falling. She reached out her hand, clutching, grabbing at anything to break her fall. Her hand touched the cold enamel of the washing machine. As she fell, the squeal of her fingernails scraping down the side ushered her into a deep, dark pit of pain. Then, everything turned black.

The sound of distant carousel music grew louder as Agnes became more aware of her surroundings. *I'm not dead? Where am I?* She lifted her head and stabs of pain shot through her jaw and past her eyes. The faint scent of donuts drifted past. She blinked, trying to clear the fuzz from her brain. The pain gradually receded as she lifted her head. The room was too dark to make out any contents. Panic raced through her stomach. *I remember now. Homer hit me.* The ropes tied around her wrists and ankles cut into her flesh. Caught! Like a rat in a trap. She twisted and struggled to loosen the bonds from her hands.

Of all the times she had conjured up thoughts of Nazi spies and conspiracy theories, gotten into scrapes and ticklish situations, she'd never been knocked unconscious and taken prisoner. Getting out of this situation would require a bit of rumination. Trussed up like a Thanksgiving turkey and lying on a hard floor didn't leave a lot of options, but she wasn't about to lose heart. *I'm not a home front warrior for nothing. I need a plan!* The first thing to do was get free of the bindings. She rolled and struggled into a sitting position. Another wave of pain shot through her head. How long did she have before Homer returned and…

She wouldn't let herself think what he might do next. It was a miracle she was alive. Perhaps he was having second thoughts. No. If that were true, she wouldn't be lying here… Where, exactly was *here*?

She listened. Surely, that was carousel music from the carnival that had just left Newbury two days ago. That's it! *I'm in Boyles Springs, probably at the fairgrounds. That's not far from the military base.* If she could get free, she could make her way to the military base. They'd take care of these hooligans quicker than camel spit.

She wiggled her wrists back and forth and strained to loosen the rope. Voices! She leaned forward to listen. Was Homer coming back to finish the job? Perspiration trickled between her breasts as the voices moved past the building.

Oh my, if this wasn't the time to ask God for deliverance, there never was one. Did she dare appeal to His good graces again so soon after her last request? She'd only had a couple of Sundays to keep her promise of regular church attendance for His help with the Wilkey Market fiasco. How many times would He bail her out of the messes she got into, if she didn't hold up her end of the bargain?

She twisted, and gritted her teeth against the pain as the rope cut into her flesh. Was it just a little bit looser? She tried to keep up her spirits with thoughts of Maddie and Katherine. No, not Maddie. That just made her more depressed.

"So, God, it's me, again, Agnes Odboddy. I guess You're not surprised to hear from me. I'm in trouble and need Your help. If You could see Your way clear to lend a hand, I'd be ever so grateful. Homer says I'm a busybody, and he's right. I get myself into a lot of messes, and I promise…" She sighed. "I promise to stop sticking my nose into everyone's business if You'll help me out of this jam, just once more. And, I promise I'll stop asking for favors…well, at least I'll try to stop getting in trouble and having to ask for favors." She smiled. *There! That should do it!* Pastor Lickleiter said that faith the size of a mustard seed could move mountains. She didn't have a lot going for her at the moment, but she did have faith. He also said that God helped those who helped themselves. *I should at least be able to get these ropes off my wrist.*

With another twist, the rope loosened enough for her to pull her hands free! *Thanks, God!* She untied her feet and flexed her legs. Turning onto her knees, she gripped the wall, stood and stomped her feet to get the circulation flowing. Still a little dizzy, she felt her way around the room toward the crack of light coming from under the door. Along the wall, she touched the handles of gardening tools and stumbled over a lawn mower. *This must be a tool shed.* She reached the door. Locked. Of course! What did she expect?

Her hand moved across the door knob. There. A hole in the center. She reached for the silver chopsticks in her bun, now hanging somewhat sideways off the back of her head, and found only one chopstick. The other one must have fallen out in the scuffle with Homer back at the warehouse. Poking the chopstick into the keyhole, she wiggled it from side to side. Just a little bit more…With a final jiggle, hurray! The lock clicked and the door swung opened! *Thanks again, God! We're on a roll.*

Agnes stepped into the darkness and peeked around the corner. Not a soul in sight. She dashed around the shed and headed for the carousel. If she could make it to a crowd of people, even if Homer saw her, there wasn't much he could do about it.

As she turned the corner, calloused fingers seized her arm. Homer!

"Leaving us so soon? I think not. I'm not through with you yet."

Her stomach lurched. Free for exactly twenty seconds and caught again, before she could take three steps. "Let me go!"

Homer clasped his hand over her mouth. She struggled, but he was too strong.

Another man appeared from the shadows, pulled both her arms behind her back and shoved her forward. "Is this the one?" His gruff voice chilled her heart. "What are we going to do with her?"

Homer's handkerchief covered her mouth, muffling her screams. His vice-like grip pinched her cheeks. Weak-kneed, they practically dragged Agnes forward, though she struggled to break away. The men propelled her past several tents, away from the carousel and the safety that a crowd might have offered.

Homer chuckled. "I think tomorrow's Newbury Daily Gazette headlines will read, "Tragic Accident Befalls Newbury Octogenarian"

Octogenarian? Agnes shook her head and reared back. "*Mmmph!*" *If he's going to kill me, he could at least get my age right.*

The men seemed not to notice her dissent and dragged her forward. They stopped in front of a structure with a wooden door. "We'll just pop her inside and let nature take its course. Things should be pretty well straightened out by morning. Did you get rid of her car?"

"I sent Dimplewhite back for it," the hooligan muttered. "What about this one? Won't someone hear her scream?"

"Not when I get through with her." Homer's hand left Agnes's mouth for only a moment.

She jerked from side to side as Homer pressed a rag against her mouth and nose. A sickening odor assailed her nostrils. Strobing lights and a dizzying sensation filled her head. Her struggles ceased. Her body slumped forward. Her last thought was of Katherine. *Take care of*... and then she saw nothing.

Chapter Thirty

ing! Ring!

Katherine raced to the kitchen wall phone and snatched it from its cradle. "Hello? Grandma?"

"No. It's me. Chief Waddlemucker."

Katherine's stomach lurched. "Have you heard from her? Is she all right? Where is she?"

"Slow down. Are you talking about Agnes? Where is she supposed to be?"

"We haven't seen her since this morning. It's already…" Katherine glanced up at the clock. "…after seven o'clock. I was just getting ready to call and report her missing."

"*Humm.* That's not like her. I'll be right over. I have some news to share with you, anyway. See you in a few." The chief hung up the phone.

Katherine turned toward Godfrey and Maddie, sitting at the kitchen table. "He hasn't heard anything. I guess that's a good thing. At least she hasn't been arrested."

"Did you think she might be?" Godfrey carried the dishes to the sink, rinsed them under the faucet and placed them in the wooden drainer.

"With Grandma, you never know."

"So, if she's not in jail or in the hospital." Godfrey sent a wan smile toward Katherine. "I guess no news is good news…so to speak.

But, I can't understand…" He gave Maddie a quick smile. "Now, don't you worry, honey. She'll be along soon, I'm sure of it. Why don't you run into your room, and let us big folks have a talk."

"Okay. Should I put on my pajamas, Katherine?"

"That's a good idea, sweetheart. I'll be right there in a few minutes." Katherine sat back down at the table. "The chief is coming over. Maybe he'll have some ideas." Tears prickled her eyes. "I'm about at my wit's end."

Godfrey took her hand. "What if we went to the *Gently Used Clothing and Shoes* warehouse? That's who picked up the coat. I'm sure Agnes planned to go there this morning. Maybe that's a good place to start looking."

"What good would that do? I can't imagine anyone's there this time of night."

"Let's just say it's a hunch. I wasn't an FBI man for almost thirty-five years for nothing."

"Okay. If you say so. I'll take Maddie over to Mavis. We can go after the chief leaves."

Katherine returned from Mavis's house just as Chief Waddlemucker arrived. "Come back inside, Katherine. I have some important news you'll want to hear."

"Then, make it quick. We want to go down to the *Gently Used Clothing and Shoes* warehouse and look around. Grandmother was headed there this morning. Godfrey thinks…oh, I don't know what Godfrey thinks. Do you want to come with us?"

The chief nodded and sat on the sofa. "I can do that. But first, here's the scoop. We evaluated the fingerprints we took off the lock on the tiger cage at the carnival and found—"

"What has the tiger cage got to do with Grandmother being missing," Katherine said, grabbing her jacket off the coat rack. "Can't you see how worried I am? I thought you said this was important."

"Let me finish. We identified young George Wilkey's fingerprints. So, we questioned him, and he confessed not only to letting the tiger loose, but admitted he was responsible for leaving the rat on your front porch, and framing Agnes for the burglary at his mother's store!" The chief turned a smug grin toward Godfrey and then to Katherine. "So, was that important enough?"

Katherine closed her mouth and gulped. "Golly, gee." She turned from the front door and flopped into the sofa chair. "Why on earth would he do such a thing? What's he got against Grandma to go to such lengths?"

Chief Waddlemucker rubbed his thumb on the handle of his pistol. "Seems Agnes was on the Military Enlistment Committee a few months ago. She blocked George's enlistment. She thought since his brother died overseas, George should be exempt from serving. Not that it's a law or anything, but she convinced the committee that Mrs. Wilkey shouldn't risk losing her last remaining child.

"Hot-headed George didn't see it that way. He was furious. His shenanigans at your house were his way to pay back Agnes for blocking his request. Fool kid didn't realize that if he was that desperate to break his mother's heart, all he had to do was go over to Boyles Springs and sign up over there. Kids, these days! A lot dumber than in my day, that's for sure."

Katherine shook her head. "Grandma will be relieved to know it was just that goofy kid." She scooted forward on the sofa. "So, she's no longer suspected of the Wilkey Market break-in? What about the counterfeiting accusations?"

Chief Waddlemucker shrugged. "Guess there never was any real evidence against her, just gossip, because it appeared that she left the bogus bill at your carnival booth."

"Well, this is good news, but it doesn't help us find her." Katherine jumped up. "So, if you're coming with us to the warehouse, let's go." She grabbed Godfrey's arm and pulled him off the sofa.

Chief Waddlemucker struggled to his feet. Apparently, rationing of food stuffs had not altered his appetite and the girth of his belly was more prominent every day. "I'll follow you folks in the squad car. No speeding, now, or I'll be obliged to give you a ticket."

Driving across town with Godfrey, Katherine noticed the peaceful empty streets, shuttered businesses and quiet homes. Newbury appeared to be holding the woes of the world at bay—worry for loved ones overseas, and how the war in Europe might affect their future. *If only I could feel as confident about our future as our neighbors.*

Nearing the Crest Theater, she said. "I hear you bought the Crest Theater, Godfrey. I'm glad you've decided to settle down in Newbury." Would he propose to Grandma once he had something stable to offer her?

Godfrey pulled into the parking lot in front of *Gently Used Clothing and Shoes.* The rain had stopped and the moon hung low on the horizon. The light from the waning moon created ghostly figures of the mannequins in the front window.

"Drive around back," Katherine urged, scooting forward on the tan mohair seat cushions.

Chief Waddlemucker followed Godfrey around the back of the building.

"Oh, dear God! There's Grandma's Model A." Katherine grabbed the door handle and jumped from the car just as Godfrey pulled it to a stop. She peered through the windows and yanked open the door. "She's not here."

Godfrey and the chief hurried around the vehicle and opened the rumble seat. "Nothing." The chief scanned the rear of the building, and then walked to the back door. "Why, look at this. The door's ajar. Let's take a look." He drew his gun and stepped through the door. "Hello! Anyone here? Agnes?"

Katherine and Godfrey tiptoed behind him.

Godfrey groped around the door and found the light switch. "Perhaps a little light on the—" The room instantly filled with light.

"Look!" Katherine said, pointing toward the washing machines where Agnes's purse and one of her silver chopsticks lay on the floor. Katherine picked up the chopstick. "Something terrible has happened.

She'd never have…" Her gaze darted between the chief and Godfrey. She grabbed the side of the washing machine to steady herself against a wave of dizziness. *Oh, Grandma! What have you gotten into this time?*

"You're not going to keel over on me are you, princess?" Godfrey put a reassuring hand on her arm and squeezed. "Buck up. We'll find her or my name's not Godfrey Baumgarten."

The chief circled the warehouse and checked the office. He holstered his gun. "I've checked the whole building. Whatever happened, she's not here now." He moved to the door beside the washers. "Is this part of the warehouse or the next building," he asked, twisting the handle. "It's unlocked. Let's see what–" He shoved open the door and switched on the light. "I'll be a *monkey's uncle!* Will you look at this?"

"What is it?" Godfrey poked his head inside. "Katherine, take a look. If Agnes stumbled onto this, it's no wonder she's missing."

Katherine sucked in her breath at the sight of a printing press stacked six-inches high with printed bills. Each newspaper-sized printed sheet contained bills, four rows across and nine deep. After printing on both sides and cut apart, each sheet would produce thirty-six, realistic five-dollar bills.

Godfrey ran his hand over the sheet. "It's hardly productive, printing five-dollar bills, but, I guess, if they print enough of them…." He moved further into the room, gazing at the various machines. "I suppose a smaller denomination bill would be easier to pass," he mumbled.

Chief Waddlemucker moved to the other side of the room. "Not so fast. Come over here. Guess they weren't satisfied with small potatoes, after all. This machine is printing twenty-dollar bills."

"Well, that makes more sense." Godfrey hurried over and fingered the printed sheets, stacked three-inches deep on the machine. "There must be over $250,000 in this stack alone. Multiply that times how many sheets per day?" He whistled. "They probably have a *fence* buying the twenties at a discount. They could easily be peddled overseas. Quite a set-up."

He glanced at the surprised expression on Chief Waddlemucker's face. "What? It's not that difficult, Chief. I ran into a few counterfeiting operations such as this, during my years in the FBI. Once the bills are sold to the *fence*, it's practically impossible to trace anything back to the seller."

"I'm sure you're delighted to find this, Chief Waddlemucker," Katherine snapped. "You've solved your counterfeiting case, but what about Grandma?" Tears pooled in her eyes. "Whoever owns or rents this building is running this operation. Grandma must have stumbled onto the printing presses. For all we know, she could be dead."

The chief nodded. "Exactly what I was thinking. Not that she's dead," he hastened to add. "But, about the occupants of the building… We'll go back to the station and get right on this." He turned and headed for the exit, with Godfrey and Katherine following close behind.

Godfrey paused at the back door. "Hold it. I have a better plan. You take Katherine with you. I'll go find Vincent," he said, hurrying toward his car. "The Feds will want to confiscate the printing presses as quickly as possible." He yanked open his car door.

"*Uh*…okay. Sounds good." The chief nodded. "Do you know where Vincent is staying?"

Katherine raised her hand. "He was at the hospital a couple hours ago. He's probably back at his motel by now."

"I can't remember the name of his motel, but I know where it is," Godfrey called through the window as he revved the engine. "I'll meet you later at home, Katherine."

"I'll send some uniforms to guard the building, until the FBI gets here," Chief Waddlemucker yelled, as Godfrey's car tore out of the parking lot.

"I don't think he heard me." The chief opened the passenger door of his squad car. "Come on Katherine. Let's wake up the county clerk, figure out who owns this dump, and find Agnes."

Chapter Thirty-One

Twelve o'clock midnight. A stringent odor stirred Agnes to consciousness. It was the same odor she had smelled just before the world went *flooey*. *Chloroform!* She blinked to clear her vision. Another faint odor…wild, earthy. What was it? She touched her forehead. A slight headache and pain in her jaw, but nothing serious.

Where am I? A cloud passing in front of the moon obscured the details of her surroundings. She moved her head. Straw tickled her cheek and found its way into her mouth. She spit. *I must be in a barn. No, wait!* She could hear the faint shouts of workmen and music. From the carousel? She was still near the carnival. She flexed her arms and legs. *That feels better.*

Homer hadn't tied her up this time. Why was that? First, he knocked her unconscious in the shed, and this time, he'd used chloroform. How terribly unsporting of him! Once she got out of this mess, wouldn't she give him a piece of her mind? That is, if she got out.

Homer couldn't allow her to blab about his counterfeit operation. He said he had a plan to keep her quiet. The question was, just exactly how did he plan to *rub her out*, as they said on the Ellery Queen show? The fact that she had already survived two of his attacks suggested… what? Hesitation on his part to commit murder? Or just a matter of timing?

She would have to rely on her brilliant crime-fighting faculties if she was to get out of this alive. Such faculties were somewhat in question at the moment. However, as a home front warrior and a self-appointed scourge of the underworld, she was up to the challenge. She could match wits with the scoundrel any day with a *'d'* in it.

Renewed confidence surged through her chest as she struggled to sit up. She put her hand to her head. *Still dizzy, but clearing. God helps him who helps himself.* "Don't get me wrong, God," she whispered in the darkness, remembering her former prayer. "I still need Your help… to help myself."

Poor Katherine and Maddie must be half mad, wondering what had happened to her. Well, she'd be home soon, and wouldn't they be amazed to hear how she had escaped?

Brrrumm… Brrrumm

A sound in the far corner… *What was that?* She shivered in the chill air. Was there another prisoner in this room? She tilted her head to listen. It sounded almost like something scratching in the corner, like someone…or something… moving around in the darkness. Again, she was aware of the faint, unidentified odor…almost like… She sniffed again. Was she in an outhouse?

The clouds moved away from the moon revealing the faintest outline of something vertical near her face… She moved and her hand collided with cold metal. She closed her fingers around a steel bar. A quick movement seven inches to the left and her hand smacked into another steel bar. *Lord God and little fishes!* She was in a cage. An animal cage? A stab of panic, almost painful, shot through her chest. So that's what Homer meant by 'reporting a tragic accident' in the morning paper.

She could almost see the front page of the Newbury Daily Gazette now. *It is with a heavy heart that we announce that our dear friend and neighbor, Agnes Odboddy, almost regular attendee at The First Church of the Evening Star and Everlasting Light, exemplary citizen and unparalleled volunteer for causes both large and small, was eaten alive by a wild animal. Authorities were not surprised, knowing the brave and daring woman that she was, and likely for a pretty darn good reason, she entered a wild animal cage. She will long be remembered for her unfailing wit and charm...*

No one would think that she was kidnapped, chloroformed and foully murdered. Maybe Katherine and Godfrey would wonder why she had willingly entered an animal cage, but knowing the daft stunts she had pulled in the past, they would not wonder long.

If Homer parked her car in the carnival lot, everyone would assume she came under her own steam and foolishly entered the cage.

Now, how could she defend herself against a wild animal? She pulled the one remaining chopstick from her hair. Stainless steel and sharp, used correctly, it would be a lethal weapon against a human, but wasn't very effective against a wild beast.

Brrrumm... Brrrumm...

That noise again from the corner. This time it sounded less threatening and more like… She shook her head. *Oww!* But, the thought was just too crazy, more likely pure fantasy on her part—the last thought of a frantic, desperate mind immediately before death...

She scrambled to her feet, holding the chopstick out in front of her. Scenes from her past raced through her mind. Isn't that what happened just before death? Regrets for past sins... Thoughts of loved ones come and gone… Her breath came in ragged gasps. Waves of dizziness threatened to send her spinning again. No. She couldn't faint. *Not now. Stay strong, Agnes. Don't give up! Lord, I need you now!*

She took a step forward, ready and willing to fight to the death, but her wretched body defied her best intentions. Still off balance from the effects of the chloroform, everything spun around as a sense of her surroundings crumbled. Which way was up and which down? The last thing she knew, her legs felt like noodles. *Not now! Not now!* The strong smell of animal urine assailed her nostrils. And then, the edges of her consciousness turned inward to black.

Slurp... Slurp...

The ringing in her ears subsided. She felt as though she was rising from a deep hole. The blackness faded and consciousness returned...

and then panic as she became aware of a sharp sandpaper-like sensation rasping across her neck…her cheek…her mouth. Instantly awake, her hand flew to her wet face. She jerked back and yelped.

The clouds had thinned overhead and in the ensuing moonlight–the faint outline of a giant cat, not six inches from her face. He reached a paw toward her. The knot in her throat threatened to strangle her. Sure that her life was measured in seconds, as an almost regular church-goer, the prayer of every Christian given the opportunity to think at the moment of death, came to mind. *Lord, forgive this sinner and open the pearly gates.*

An image of Katherine and Maddie flashed into her mind. She couldn't give up. She just couldn't. *A weapon. I need a weapon!* She scrabbled through the straw, searching for the chopstick she had dropped when she fainted. *Where is it? Where is it?* Unable to locate the only protection she might have against the animal, she scrambled to her feet. What good would the tiny scrap of metal do, anyway? If she was destined to be the beast's dinner, no doubt he'd accomplish the deed whether she was standing with a chopstick in her hand or on her knees, mumbling in prayer.

Brrrumm… Brrrumm…

Wait. Was the beast actually purring? Or just tickled at the prospect of chasing down his breakfast, instead of finding it on the end of a stick?

I've got to get out of here! Agnes wiped the perspiration off her forehead, backed to the end of the cage and felt around the edges of the wooden door. Locked. Probably had a padlock on the outside. She'd have to put up a fight as best she could, bare-handed.

The creature moved forward and flopped into the straw in the approximate area where the chopstick must have fallen. He threw back his head. *RRROWWW!!*

The final cloud passed in front of the moon, illuminating dark stripes on the animal's pale body. A tiger! A glimmer of hope swept through her chest. Was it possible? Either the carnival had two tigers or… Could it be Shere Khan–the precious, tame tiger that had won Maddie's heart?

"Shere Kahn? Is that you?" Agnes whispered. *Please, let it be you. Oh, please, please, let it be you.*

The giant cat opened his mouth in a yawn, exposing three-inch long teeth. His yawn reminded Agnes of Ling-Ling, when she expressed pleasure in herself. Almost like a human yawn; it was a housecat's way of saying, "So, what do you think? Pretty cute, aren't I?"

Agnes chuckled as she recognized the tiger's gentle eyes. "Yes, you are Shere Khan, and you're a lovely boy, aren't you?" Agnes stooped, and stroked the tiger's head. He rubbed his ear against her hand. She let out her breath, knelt in the straw and patted his back. Her heart swelled in gratitude for her deliverance. No surprise. God was up to his usual tricks, but still on the job.

Homer had no idea that Shere Khan was just an over-sized striped pussycat. Although Shere Khan had momentarily put a *kibosh* on the morning headlines, no doubt, Homer would be back to check on the progress of things before long.

She shoved the tiger's belly. He stood and waddled into the corner.

Another search through the straw revealed her chopstick. She raised it over her head.

When Homer returned, she'd be ready for him. This time, one of them would bleed, though, according to the score so far; *Homer two, Agnes zero*, the odds were not in her favor.

Katherine put the tea kettle on the stove and lit the burner. She plopped into a kitchen chair and put her head in her hands. Was Grandma even still alive? Did Chief Waddlemucker have any luck at all finding information on the building's owner after he dropped her at home?

Ring... Ring...

"Thank God! It's about time." She grabbed the phone. "Hello, Grandma?"

"No. Sorry, it's Vincent. You were expecting Agnes to call? At this hour?"

How could he not know she's missing? She glanced at the clock. She'd been home about an hour, plenty of time for Godfrey to drive across town, find Vincent and bring him up to speed on the details of the counterfeit money and Grandmother's disappearance. "Isn't Godfrey with you?"

"I haven't seen him."

"Where could he be? He was on his way to your motel over an hour ago."

"I don't understand. What's going on?"

"Then you don't know that grandmother is missing? We found her car at the *Gently Used Clothing and Shoes* warehouse. We also found the back room full of counterfeit printing presses!"

"No! You're serious?" Vincent coughed into the phone.

"Serious as a heart attack. Godfrey and the chief and I went down to the *Gently Used Clothing and Shoes* to look for Grandmother."

"Wait. Why would she be at the *Gently Used Whatever* this time of night?"

"It's a long story. Anyway, we found her car in the lot and there were signs of a struggle inside. They've taken her, Vincent. I don't know where." Katherine gulped back a sob. "Like I said, the printing presses were in the back room. Godfrey went to find you so you could notify the FBI. I can't imagine why he never showed up. Where could he be?"

"Does he even know where I'm staying?"

"He said he did. Maybe he got lost or confused about which motel you're in."

"That would be rather difficult, since there's only one motel in town, but...maybe. I'd better notify headquarters and get down to the warehouse. I'll leave a note on my door, in case Godfrey shows up later. Why don't you try to get some rest? I'm sure Chief Waddlemucker will find Agnes safe and sound. Try not to worry."

"Easier said than done, but I'll try. Call me later?"

"I will."

Agnes awoke, shivering, curled in the fetal position, her head against Shere Khan's body. She had dozed only a little, thinking at any moment Homer would return to make sure the tiger had done his dirty work. She had dreamed of Godfrey, replaying all the poor decisions she had made about him. Her first mistake–Paris in 1918–having an affair with him when she was still married to Douglas…

Bigger mistake–allowing Godfrey back into her life last year, only to have their relationship end badly. What about now? A man can't change his wandering ways any more than Shere Khan could change his stripes. Godfrey claimed to care for her, but could she trust him again? She rubbed the sleep from her eyes, sat up and smoothed her hair over her ears. This was probably not the time or place to dwell on her love life.

Her hand tightened around the one silver chopstick clutched in her hand. Her gaze moved over the hump of Shere Khan's belly, softly rising and falling. She scooted away a safe distance from the sleeping cat and picked a strand of straw from her hair. She was safe enough last night, but what about this morning? Nor was the hungry beast the least of her worries. Wouldn't someone come soon to feed the tiger? Perhaps one of Homer's henchmen, sent to report the dreadful accident that had befallen the befuddled old lady who had unfortunately stumbled into the tiger's cage and become a victim of the savage beast?

Though Shere Khan's caravan was set apart from the other tents and caravans, she could still see movement and hear faint voices across the carnival yard. Would someone come and free her if she screamed? Or were they all part of the counterfeit gang, using the carnival to spread the bills across the state and amenable to her murder to cover their evil deeds?

Anyone walking up to the cage could see through the bars that she was inside. If they were all Homer's cronies, they'd report to him right away. If he would throw an old woman into a tiger's cage, he'd surely have an alternate plan if his first plan failed.

How would he do it? As close to the ocean cliffs as they were… She could almost hear the crash of waves against the rocks, as he pushed her over the edge. No! She shook her head, refusing to allow her imagination to go there. She took a deep breath to calm her quaking stomach.

Voices. Someone was coming!

With bars on three sides, only the wooden wall with the door provided any protection from view of someone approaching the cage. *It's now or never, Lord.*

She dashed to the door and flattened herself against the wall, her head woozy with fright as she clutched the chopstick over her head. What chance did she have with such a pitiful weapon?

Seconds ticked by.

Footsteps in the gravel.

A tread onto the wooden step.

A key clicked in the padlock.

Agnes held her breath. Two beads of perspiration trickled between her breasts.

The door creaked.

A hand appeared as the door opened… "Hey, Shere Khan? How's our boy this–" A young man stepped into the cage. His mouth dropped open.

Agnes leaped forward, her silver chopstick raised. "Don't take another step or I'll plunge this through your heart!" Her voice cracked. Her hand trembled. How would an old lady with a silver chopstick ever appear anything but ridiculous to a hardened killer?

"What the…" A freshly plucked chicken fell from the young man's hand and splatted soundlessly into the straw.

Shere Khan leaped forward, snatched the chicken in his powerful jaws and slunk to the farthest corner of the cage where he snarled and grumbled as he tore the legs from its pale denuded body.

Agnes's heart seized.

"Wha…" A young man stepped inside the cage and pushed the door closed behind him. "What the Sam Hill are you doin' in here, lady?"

Not Homer, nor one of the henchmen from last night–just a pimple-faced kid. Was there a chance she might escape, after all?

His eyes fixed on the silver chopstick over Agnes's head, the boy threw up his shaking hands. "Hold on, lady. What...?" He gazed past her head to Shere Khan. The crunch of chicken bones snapped from the corner. "We've got to get out of here. He's eating…" He reached behind him, pushed the door open and backed out. "Quick. Come out."

Agnes hurried out the door and down the steps.

The door slammed and the padlock clicked. "What's going on here? How…?"

Who'd believe she accidently got locked in a tiger cage? If he was part of the gang, she could be going from the fat into the fire. The truth tumbled out, about the printing presses and Homer tossing her into the tiger cage, obviously hoping the tiger would finish her off.

The boy appeared sympathetic. Possibly fearing how he would fare when Homer found her gone, he fought to hold his trembling hand steady. "I don't know nothin' about counterfeit money, lady, but we gotta' get out a' here. When Homer finds you gone, he'll know it was me let you out." The color drained from his cheeks. "What am I going to do?"

"Maybe you better skedaddle, too. Get to a phone and call the Newbury Police Station. Tell the chief how you found me and that I'm on my way back to town. I'll find a phone and call Colonel

Farthingworth. He and I go way back. We..." Voices coming nearer cut her soliloquy short. "Run!"

She took off one direction and the kid's pony tail flopped on his back as he ran the opposite way. Best get as far away from the tiger cage as possible. Maybe she could hitch a ride before Homer learned that she was gone and sent his henchmen to bring her back. Thoughts of the crashing surf at the ocean crept back into her mind and put wings to her feet as she headed for the main road.

Chapter Thirty-Two

Agnes crouched behind an oleander bush at the edge of the parking lot, out of sight from the carnival tents and the caravans. The faint sound of the carousel still cranked out its monotonous tune in the distance. Perhaps the early shift had arrived to work on the mechanics. It wouldn't be long before Homer or his henchmen discovered her missing and started searching.

There! Coming down the road, headed for town–a milk truck.

Agnes waited until the truck was fairly near and then leaped into the road, waving her hands.

The truck screeched to a stop, just feet from her knees. If she was a cat, she would have just used up one of her nine lives. She hurried to the driver's side window. "Can you give me a ride into town? There's a gang of killers after me and I…"

The driver's mouth dropped open.

What did I just say? Who would want to give a ride to a crazy old woman with straw in her hair, claiming she was being chased by a gang of killers? She patted her one silver chopstick, pulled a strand of straw from her tumble-down bun and tossed it to the ground. "*Um…* fooled you, didn't I? *Hee! Hee!* Actually, my car broke down and I had to sleep in the field. Would you be so kind as to drive me into town? Or, perhaps to the nearest telephone?" She placed her hand on the truck window and smiled, trying to look like a harmless old grandmother who baked cookies for the U.S.O., which, indeed, she did, and knitted socks for the troops…which, in fact, she also did…just not today.

The driver looked her up and down. "I only got one seat up front, but if you want, you can sit in the back with the milk jugs. The door's unlocked." He jerked his head toward the rear of the truck.

"Oh, thank you, sir. You're very kind." Agnes hurried around the back, climbed into the truck and slammed the door. Safe at last, and out of sight from Homer. *Thanks, God!*

Rows of metal racks were fastened from floor to ceiling along both walls. Some held empty quart-sized milk bottles; others held full bottles of milk. Smaller bottles held cream. Agnes's stomach gurgled. She'd had nothing to eat or drink since breakfast yesterday.

She scooted an empty rack forward and sat. Diffuse light streamed through the window in the back door. She grabbed the side of the rack to steady herself as the truck lurched forward, rattling the milk bottles.

Surely, the kind driver wouldn't mind if she drank one little bottle of cream. She balanced her feet against the swaying truck and plucked a jar of cream from the rack beside her. Gripping the little tab on top with her fingernail, she pulled off the cylindrical cardboard lid from the bottle and drank. Rich and smooth, the liquid slid down her dry throat, quenching her thirst. Almost immediately, she felt stronger.

Perusing the situation as the truck bumped along the country road, Agnes determined that the best plan would be to call Chief Waddlemucker. The chief should know of Homer's role in the counterfeiting ring as soon as possible. She nodded. *Yes. A much better plan than calling Colonel Farthingworth at the military base.*

The truck slowed and then came to a stop.

Agnes stood and peeked out the back window. They were near the edge of town at The Flying Red Horse gas station. She unlatched the door, hopped down and strode around to the driver's side of the truck.

The milkman leaned out the window. "Is this okay, lady? I got deliveries to make. Don't have time to drive you all the way home." He nodded toward the office. "Maybe you can use their telephone."

"Thanks ever so much. I drank one of your bottles of cream. I'm sorry I don't have my purse with me to pay—"

"What? You don't have…" He gazed up and down her disheveled appearance. "If your car broke down like you said… Say. Why were you hiding in them bushes, anyway? Why didn't you just walk into the carnival and use their phone?" The driver's face blanched. He jerked his head back through the window. Had he just recalled her first statement about being chased by killers? "You in trouble with the law or somethin'? I'm on parole. I can't be involved…!" He shoved the truck into gear and roared out of the gas station. The clank of milk bottles grew fainter as his van disappeared down the road.

"Thanks again," Agnes yelled after the retreating truck. She smoothed back her hair and straightened her belted dress. She turned and spotted the station attendant. "Excuse me. Do you have a telephone I can use? I need to call the police and report a kidnapping."

The attendant raised an eyebrow and pointed toward a telephone booth beside the office.

Agnes opened the door into the phone booth. "Oh, dear." She backed out of the phone booth and called after the retreating attendant. "My purse is still at the warehouse where the kidnappers tried to murder me. Of course, I managed to escape when they threw me in with a man-eating tiger... I don't suppose you'd lend me a nickel…"

The attendant's face paled. He dug in his pocket, handed her a nickel, and then dashed into the office and slammed the door. The lock in the door clicked.

"Poor kid. Must be the nervous type."

The nickel clinked into the telephone as she dialed the operator. "Give me the Newbury Police Department. Chief Waddlemucker, please. I need to report an attempted murder."

Less than three minutes later, the chief was on the line. "Where in blue blazes are you, Agnes? We found your car and signs of a struggle at the clothing warehouse. Poor Katherine is fit to be tied. Where are you?"

Agnes sighed. Should she go into details about her kidnapping or wait until she had a bigger audience to impress with her story? She decided on the latter. "I'm fine. I'm at the Flying Red Horse gas station at the edge of town. Can you send someone to pick me up? I'm dirty and hungry and in no mood to go into the sordid details of my kidnapping on the phone."

"But, are you hurt? I could send an ambulance." Chief Waddlemucker actually sounded concerned. That would be a first. Most of their conversations ended with her being annoyed, and him, exasperated.

"I'm fine, I told you. I'm not the least bit hurt, except for my pride. I should never have let that hooligan get the better of me."

"And, which hooligan would that be, pray tell? I suppose you mean Homer Blenkinsop?" The usual sarcastic tone in the chief's voice had returned.

"Didn't I say? Of course, Homer Blenkinsop. And, he could be about a half a block behind me." She glanced over her shoulder, "so if you don't mind sending someone out here to pick me up…the sooner the better. If you searched the warehouse, you must know Homer is behind the counterfeiting."

"We found the presses at the warehouse and figured he was the mastermind. We picked him up at his house early this morning, but when we questioned him about your disappearance, he denied knowing anything about it."

"That lying rat. Wait until I tell you… Will you just send someone? I'll tell you the whole story when I get home. Oh, and by the way, in case you haven't figured it out, Homer's wife, Juanita, is in cahoots with him, too. Her charity clothing program is a front for their counterfeiting scheme."

"Really? We didn't have any evidence against her. Agnes, after you've rested, we'll take your statement. I'll send Officer Pettigrew to pick you up and, don't worry. I'll notify Katherine that you're on your way home."

"Tell him to bring me a sandwich. I'm about to starve to death."

Chapter Thirty-Three

gnes opened the front door, tiptoed through the living room, and peeked into the kitchen. *Won't Katherine be happy to see me?* There she was, bending over the oven, shoving in a batch of bran muffins. "Surprise! I'm home!"

Katherine jumped and shrieked. The muffin pan clunked onto the metal oven rack. She slammed the oven door and turned. "Finally! Chief Waddlemucker said someone was bringing you home." She clutched Agnes around her waist. I'm so happy you're here."

"No more than I–"

"You shouldn't have sneaked up on me like that, though. You nearly scared the be-Jesus out of me. Are you hungry?"

"Well, as a matter of–"

"Now, sit down and tell me everything. Where have you been? What happened?"

"What didn't? I had barely–"

"Maddie's at school. Sit here and I'll fix you some breakfast. I suppose you're hungry. Oh, I already asked, didn't I?" She poured coffee into two mugs and set them on the table. "So, tell me everything. I can't wait to hear how–"

"Then, stop talking and let me get a word in edgewise." Agnes sat.

"Sorry. I'm just so happy to see you. There's still some Cream of Wheat left from breakfast. Can I fix you a bowl?"

"Gracious, yes. A limp tuna sandwich just didn't cut the mustard.

I've been fantasizing about coffee for hours." She grabbed the mug and took a sip. "*Ahh*. Wonderful."

When the bowl of hot cereal was empty, Agnes leaned back in her chair and recounted in gristly detail, the story of her capture and escape. Egged on by Katherine's '*oohs*' and '*ahs*,' Agnes added embellishments to her tale, using such words as *ingenuity, valor, gallantry, daring-do, pluck and knack* to describe her uncanny ability to escape from her kidnapper and attempted killer.

Katherine's eyes widened. "You spent the night in Shere Khan's cage?" She sniffed. "No wonder you smell… Well, no matter. I'm glad Maddie's not here. I wouldn't want her to hear about this."

"Oh yes, actually, I slept with my head on his stomach. He was very agreeable to my company. We're great pals."

Katherine wrinkled her nose. "That explains why you don't smell so good."

"No doubt I need a good wash-up." Agnes said with a chuckle.

Katherine refilled Agnes's coffee cup. "Grandma, you're a caution! What am I going to do with you? Maybe you should write a book."

Agnes looked into Katherine's eyes, shining with admiration and love. The lies and embellishments she had just recounted echoed in her ears and stabbed her heart. *What kind of example am I, spinning such tall tales to someone who loves me so much?* She lowered her head.

"Actually, I've greatly exaggerated much of what I've said for the past fifteen minutes. Homer knocked me upside the head before I even knew what hit me, dragged me to the carnival, and tossed me into the tiger's cage. I didn't even fight back." Agnes's face tingled.

"Then, how did you actually get away from him?"

"I was scared out of my britches when I woke up in Shere Khan's cage. I thought I was a goner for sure. If the young man hadn't come to feed him early this morning and unlock the door, I'd probably be… be…well, maybe not, but who knows what a tiger will do when he's hungry?

"I was headstrong and foolish not to tell anyone where I was going yesterday. Homer got the better of me, and it was just plain luck that I got away alive, thanks to Shere Khan's keeper." She laid her head on the table. The reality of her narrow escape sent shivers up her spine.

Katherine patted her arm. "Don't be so hard on yourself. You're… you're eccentric and somewhat fool-hardy for sure, but I love you. Now, let's see if those muffins are done." She stood and pulled the muffins from the oven.

"Why isn't Godfrey here? Didn't you let him know I was coming home?"

Katherine raised her eyebrows. "I haven't heard from him since last night when the chief and I left the warehouse, and he headed for Vincent's motel to tell him about the counterfeit money."

"Godfrey was with you and the chief at the *Gently Used* warehouse?"

"He's the reason we went there in the first place. When we found your car and your purse, we knew something terrible had happened. Godfrey left to find Vincent and tell him about the printing presses while the chief brought me home, but Vincent never saw him and the chief says he didn't show up at the station either, like they planned. I don't know where he is."

The pit of Agnes's stomach churned. "That's odd. That's not like him…" *Or, is it?*

Katherine spread margarine over the top of her muffin. "When Chief Waddlemucker called to tell me you were coming home this morning, I called Godfrey's motel room, but he didn't answer. The manager said Godfrey's car was gone." She took a bite.

Suspicion and trepidation clutched Agnes's heart. *No! I won't allow myself to think that way. I'll bet he's out to breakfast or…or still looking for me.*

She couldn't help but recall Godfrey's return to town last year, declaring his undying love, much like he had this past week, and then disappearing when a tempting, financial opportunity dropped in his lap.

She thought back over Godfrey's story of where he had been for eighteen months. Had a secret FBI mission really kept him in South America for over a year? As absurd as it sounded, she wanted to believe him. He said he was ready to settle down in Newbury. Hadn't he bought the Crest Theater with the apartment above it…or was that a lie too?

I won't believe that he's disappeared again. We'll laugh about this when he shows up later today, asking me to bake him another rhubarb pie.

Bing… Bong…

Agnes leaped from her chair with a sigh of relief. "See? There's Godfrey now. And me, smelling like a cat pan!" She hurried into the living room and threw open the door. "I'm back! I…"

Vincent stood at the door. "Agnes. I'm glad you're home." He sniffed and wrinkled his nose. "It must have been quite an…*umm*… adventure."

The crevice in Agnes's stomach turned into a canyon. "*Uhh*… Vincent. I thought you were Godfrey. Come on in." Agnes took Vincent's hat and coat and hung them on the coat rack. "I don't suppose you've heard from him?"

"'Fraid not." He sniffed again.

Agnes's face warmed. "Have a seat. Katherine! Vincent's here. If you'll excuse me…I need a bath." She turned and fled down the hall toward the bathroom.

"Vincent. I'm so glad you're here," Katherine said. "Can I get you something? I just pulled a batch of bran muffins from the oven."

"Sounds good. I love bran muffins."

Katherine returned in a couple of minutes with a mug of coffee, a platter of muffins and a dish of apple butter. She set the platter on the coffee table and handed the mug to Vincent. "Did you hear from Godfrey?"

"I haven't seen him. I wanted to come by and let you know what happened after you left the hospital yesterday. I confronted Joe Hawkins in the play yard."

"That's right. I remember now. I've been in such a dither over Grandma's disappearance, I'd forgotten all about Joe. So, tell me."

Vincent chuckled and spread apple butter on a muffin. "When I told him he was seen attacking Dr. Don in the church, he broke down and cried like a baby. Imagine. A big guy like that…just a big baby. Admitted he was jealous that his wife was flirting with the doctor. He was convinced Don and Sally were having an affair and planning to run away together. He lured Don to the church with that note accusing you of being involved with the counterfeit money. What an idiot."

"His wife said he was the jealous type," Katherine said. "That she flirted with all the guys to make him jealous, but it didn't mean anything,"

"Well, it meant something to Joe. He sneaked up behind Don in the church and whacked him with a candlestick, just like Maddie said. Says he's real sorry now and 'didn't mean to hurt him.' I don't know how you can whack someone with a candlestick and not mean to hurt them."

"Jealousy makes people do things they'd never think to do otherwise."

"I turned him over to hospital security. They escorted him downtown to turn himself in. Thought you'd want to know." He took a sip of coffee and a bite of muffin. "*Umm.*"

"So, what made Joe think I was involved with the counterfeiters, or did he make up that part?"

"I guess he overheard you and Chief Waddlemucker talking about the bill showing up in your dessert booth. He must have figured Don would stop romancing his wife in exchange for his silence that you were passing bad paper. Not that he *was* romancing Joe's wife…I guess. You'd know better than I do."

"He wasn't. But that's beside the point."

Bing... Bong....

Katherine opened the door for Chief Waddlemucker.

"Come on in. Have a seat. We're having coffee. Can I fix you a cup?" Katherine asked. "Grandma will be out in a minute. She's taking a much-needed bath."

"I should think. After such a night as she's had." The chief sat. "I'd love a cup of coffee. Good morning, Vincent. Everything straightened out down at the warehouse?"

"The guys from central are taking over. They didn't need me down there getting in the way." Vincent looked up. "Here's our girl now."

Wearing a red flannel bathrobe and a towel around her head, Agnes came in. "Oh. I thought I heard voices. I should get dressed."

"No need, Agnes. Sit down and relax," the chief said. "Godfrey's not here? He was supposed to meet me at the station last night after he talked to Vincent, but he never showed."

"He never showed up at my motel, either," Vincent said.

Katherine returned from the kitchen and handed a coffee mug to the chief.

"Help yourself to a muffin." Agnes said, settling into the sofa chair by the fireplace.

"Thanks. Don't mind if I do." The chief pulled out his notebook. "Before we begin…congratulations, Agnes. Thanks to you, we've cracked the counterfeiting ring. You can come down to the office tomorrow and claim Mayor Clinghammer's $500.00 reward." He sipped his coffee. "What are you going to do with all that money?"

"$500.00?" Katherine stood in the doorway with a plate holding more muffins. She glanced at Agnes. Were they both thinking the same thing? The chance of Grandma ever retrieving Grandpa Odboddy's coat with the money in the lining had likely vanished with the stringing of yellow crime tape around the warehouse. The reward money would more than cover the missing funds with some left over.

"She gets the whole she-bang. Now, Agnes," the chief licked the end of his pencil. "If you'll just start at the beginning, and tell me everything that transpired yesterday after you got to the *Gently Used What-Zit-Shop*, I'll take notes and have it typed up at the station. District Attorney Minglesauer was filing federal counterfeiting charges against Homer when I left the station. Your testimony will be useful at his trial."

"Be sure and add kidnapping and attempted murder to the counterfeiting charges." Agnes pulled her bathrobe closer to her neck. "Homer and his wife planned to kill me. I thought Juanita might intervene, but she seemed quite agreeable to my murder as long as she didn't have to know any of the details."

The chief stared wide-eyed at Agnes. He made notes on his tablet. "Go on."

"Homer tossed me into the tiger's cage like a breaded pork chop. Guess he was hoping Shere Khan would have me for breakfast. He said he would bring my car out to the carnival parking lot, so it would look like I'd stupidly gone into the cage for my own *whatever* reason."

"Into the tiger's cage? Well, I'll be hornswoggled." The chief whistled. "How would he explain that you'd gotten through the padlocked door without a key?"

"Apparently, my murder was a spur of the moment decision. I guess he didn't think about that. I don't know where he got the key to unlock it."

"And, I always figured Homer Blenkinsop for a stand-up guy. It's a good thing we got to the warehouse when we did. We wouldn't have searched inside if we hadn't seen your car in the parking lot. I'll admit though, I laid awake last night stewing over something that still puzzles me."

"What's that?"

"As soon as we got back to the station, I sent Officers' Pettigrew and Throckmorton to the warehouse to guard the printing presses until Vincent and Godfrey could get back with the FBI guys. It wasn't much more than thirty minutes from when Katherine and I left, and—"

Katherine shook her head. "It could have been a bit longer than that,

Chief. You drove me home before you went to the station, remember?"

"You're right. Maybe it was forty to fifty minutes. But, in any case, apparently before the officers got to the warehouse, Homer must have returned and taken the sheets of twenty-dollar bills off the printing press. Remember all those twenties? I can't figure it out. If Homer was planning to move your car and get rid of you, Agnes, why did he take the money and then leave your car behind? It doesn't make sense."

Chapter Thirty-Four

hief Waddlemucker's question rang in her ears. An ache assailed her chest. *Oh, dear God, not again. Don't let it be true. I'm going to be sick!*

The chief was right. There was no explanation why Homer took the money and left her car at the warehouse, when he planned just the opposite.

Who else could have stolen the counterfeit bills between the time the chief and Katherine left the warehouse and the detectives arrived? Within forty minutes? Who else knew about the printing presses? Who else knew how to fence counterfeit bills? Who never showed up at the station to meet with the chief later that night as he said he would?

Oh, Godfrey! Heart of my heart. Love of my life, what have you done? Agnes laid her head on the arm of the sofa chair and sobbed.

"Grandmother. What's wrong?" Katherine rushed over and put her arm around Agnes's shoulders. "Everything's okay. I know it's been terrible, but it's all over now. You're safe at home. Don't cry." She patted Agnes's arm. "Here, let me get you another handkerchief."

Agnes's head filled with images of ocean waves crashing against a rock wall, and disappearing into a spray of foam that melted into the sea–like her trust in the man she loved. There. She said it. The man she…loved.

Should she tell the chief what she suspected? Or should she hold her tongue? If Godfrey hadn't been seen since late last night, he could be hundreds of miles away with the counterfeit twenties by now. A single word from her and he'd be on the FBI's Most Wanted list and likely brought to justice within days. It was a pretty safe bet, the next time she saw him he'd be wearing black and white stripes.

Of all his traits–kind, considerate, loving, caring, generous Godfrey, his only character flaw was mind-boggling greed. Never able to pass up an opportunistic get-rich scheme, *Gandhi Godfrey* turned into *Al Capone Godfrey.*

How had she allowed this man back into her life? Never again. She would never give her heart to any man, only to have him weave his web of lies, make her love him, and then break her heart. She did that twice. Never again.

Hot tears trickled down her cheeks and into the grooves around her mouth. She wiped them away with the back of her hand. She couldn't keep silent. She had to speak. "I…I…think when you locate Godfrey, you'll find the counterfeit bills. I suspect he doubled back to the warehouse after you and Katherine left last night, stole the money, and lit out."

Chief Waddlemucker's cheeks paled. "No! What on God's green earth would make you suspect that?"

Tears sprang to Katherine's eyes. "You can't mean it, Grandma. Our Godfrey? You're suggesting that he—"

"Never mind how I know. I just know." Agnes said, crossing her arms over her chest. "You'll have to figure out the rest on your own. I'm going to my room. I'll come down to the station tomorrow and sign my statement and collect my reward. Right now, I want to be alone."

Oh, Godfrey. Her head throbbed. Her heart ached with disillusionment. Agnes stumbled down the hall toward her room, almost feeling the needle pricks of Katherine, Vincent and Chief Waddlemucker's eyes boring into the back of her head.

Chapter Thirty-Five

Katherine chopped carrots, celery, onions and potatoes and added beef trimmings into a large pot of boiling water. *There must be something I can do to cheer us up. Maybe I'll make some yeast rising bread, too. That's one of Grandma's favorite.*

For the third time since Chief Waddlemucker and Vincent left the house, she knocked on Grandma's bedroom door.

No answer.

It was almost impossible to believe the news about Godfrey, and Grandma was devastated. She knocked again. "Do you want something to eat, Grandma? I can make you a liverwurst sandwich. I'm making soup."

"Go away. I don't want anything. Just leave me alone." Grandma's voice broke.

Katherine turned back toward the kitchen. Best to let her work out her grief in her own way. *I have enough trouble working out my own grief.*

Ring... Ring...

She rushed to the phone. *Maybe it's Godfrey. Maybe it's all a mistake!* "Hello?"

"It's me. Chief Waddlemucker. How's she doing?"

"Grandma's locked herself in the bedroom. She won't even let me in to talk to her."

"Well, listen. Vincent just called and said the FBI agents are packing up the counterfeit presses this afternoon. I'm so sorry about this, Katherine. Tell Agnes we have an All-Points-Bulletin across California describing Godfrey's car. He won't get far. I know how much your grandma thought of him. We all did. Wish I could make this go away."

For the next fifteen minutes, the chief brought her up to date on several events he had discovered earlier that morning. "Let me know if there's anything I can do."

"I will. Thanks for the updates." She hung up the phone. It rang again as she turned away. Katherine grabbed the receiver. *Godfrey?* "Hello? Odboddy residence." She held her breath.

"This is the long-distance operator." The lady said, in a distinct Eastern accent. "I have a Mrs. Roosevelt on the line from Washington. D.C. May I speak to Agnes Odboddy?" The telephone line crackled.

Mrs. Roosevelt? Oh, my stars. This will get Grandma out of her room quicker than spit. "Just a moment. I'll call her." The receiver swung back and forth on its long black cord as she hastened down the hall and knocked on Grandma's door. "Grandma. Mrs. Roosevelt's on the phone. Long distance from Washington."

Grandma's muffled voice came through the closed door. "Sure she is. She's probably calling to invite me to tea next Thursday."

Katherine knocked again. "Grandma. It's really her. You've pouted long enough. If you don't get out here this instant, I'm telling the First Lady you refuse to talk to her. How do you like that?"

There was no reply. *Now what am I supposed to do?* Katherine returned to the phone. "I'm sorry. Agnes Odboddy isn't available. This is her granddaughter. I'll take the call."

She waited on the phone for a few minutes until Mrs. Roosevelt came on the line. "Katherine? It's Eleanor. How are you, my dear? And, Agnes? I was hoping to speak to her."

"Oh, Mrs. Roosevelt. I'm so sorry. Grandma isn't feeling well. She can't come to the phone. Can I take a message?"

"I received Agnes's letter about her friend, Lilly. The one in the

Japanese internment camp in Texas? You must understand that I can't get her released, but I'm sending a representative to the Crystal City camp to check on their housing, schools, and medical facilities. He'll report directly back to me. If he finds any deficiencies, I'll make sure they are remedied immediately. I'm sorry I can't do more. Can you tell Agnes I called?"

"Oh, thank you so much, Mrs. Roosevelt. Grandma will be so pleased."

"Not at all, my dear. Please give Agnes my best regards. If you're ever in Washington again, let me know. I so enjoyed meeting both of you this summer."

"I will. Thank you. Good-bye." Katherine replaced the receiver on the wall phone.

She returned to Grandma's bedroom door and knocked again. "Grandma? I really need to talk to you. It's important. Please open the door."

She cocked her head and listened. "Grandma? Are you all right? If you don't come out right now, I'll call Chief Waddlemucker and have him break down the door." *When she realizes she missed Mrs. Roosevelt's call, she'll have a cat-fit. Serves her right.*

The door cracked and Grandma put her head out. "Can't you see how humiliated I am? Do you think I need someone to rub it in? I should never have let Godfrey wheedle his way back into my life. Fool me once, shame on him. Fool me twice, shame on me." Tears sparkled in her eyes. "Now, what's so gol-darned important?" She threw back her shoulders and jutted her chin.

Katherine reached for Grandmother's hand. "Godfrey fooled everyone. I was just as willing to let him into my life. So did Maddie and Mildred and everyone else in Newbury. It's terrible to learn that someone you love has feet of clay. Nothing I say will change that, but no one's laughing at you. We're all hurting.

"Now, come into the kitchen and talk to me. I've got a lot to tell you." Katherine led her into the kitchen and pulled out a chair. "I'll make you some lunch."

Katherine bustled around the kitchen making sandwiches. "I have some very good news and bad news. Which do you want first?" She sliced the sandwiches in half and laid one on a plate.

"I've heard all the bad news I can handle for one day. Start with the good news."

"That really was Mrs. Roosevelt on the phone…You missed her call—"

"You call that the good news? Good grief." Grandmother's face flushed.

"I told you it was." As briefly as possible while they ate, Katherine recounted the gist of Mrs. Roosevelt's call regarding Lilly's internment camp, and the information Chief Waddlemucker had shared.

She explained how young George Wilkey had confessed that he put the rat on the porch, broke into their house, and left Agnes's handkerchief at the Wilkey Market, intending to frame her for the burglary.

"Young George? For the love of Pete, why would he do a thing like that?"

"Seems he heard it was your idea to keep him from joining the Navy. He was mad and wanted revenge." Katherine took another bite of her sandwich.

"The very idea. What is this world coming to? All I was trying to do was save his mother from losing another son." Grandmother shook her head. Not even the news of her exoneration of the burglary charges overcame her mounting grief over Godfrey's betrayal.

Upon hearing that Dr. Don had accepted the job in Sacramento and he and Katherine had mutually agreed to call it quits, Grandmother said, "There's not a man in this town worth the powder to blow him up! You're well rid of him, that's what I say."

"That's downright nasty, Grandma. Surely you can't mean that. There must be–"

"Maybe I'll feel different tomorrow, but today, that's how I feel."

Agnes popped the last bite of her sandwich in her mouth. "So, this all happened in less than twenty-four hours? If I got kidnapped more often, maybe we could solve more of our insurmountable problems. Is there anything else?"

Katherine grinned. "I guess that about covers it. Oh, wait! I almost forgot. The man who attacked Don in the church confessed. He's probably napping in the bunk next to Homer's in the county jail as we speak." Katherine snickered as she stacked cups and dishes in the sink.

"*Uh-huh*. Good to know." With a quivering smile, Agnes added, "What a difference a day makes. And, let's not forget that the love of my life just absconded with hundreds of thousands of dollars in counterfeit bills. That pretty much puts the ring in the pig's nose, doesn't it?" Agnes stood, dusted crumbs from her dress and went back to her room. Her bedroom door clicked behind her.

Katherine turned on the faucet to rinse the cups and saucers. It was going to take longer than she thought. She glanced at the clock. It was almost time to pick up Maddie from school. How she dreaded facing Maddie. How could they make her understand when she asked about Godfrey, and why Grandmother was so sad?

Chapter Thirty-Six

A crash of thunder shook the house and the wind rattled the windows. Rain filled the gutters to overflowing and ran down the driveway in sheets. Clouds blackened the sky and darkness enveloped the neighborhood.

Katherine sat beside the fireplace reading a Hollywood fashion magazine, while Benny Goodman led his band in a rousing rendition of *Goodnight My Love* on her record player.

Shortly after eight o'clock, Katherine hurried to answer the phone. "Hello?"

"Hi, it's Vincent. I wanted to call before I left town. I'm escorting Homer Blenkinsop to San Francisco in the morning. He'll be arraigned in a federal court. I'll have to stay in the city long enough to see him properly charged, and give my report to my superiors."

"Oh? How long will you be gone?" The disappointment she felt at him leaving town surprised her compared to the few thoughts she'd given Don over the past twenty-four hours. How would one reconcile that?

Katherine gripped the phone a bit tighter. Lightning lit up the back yard outside the kitchen window. She jumped when a clash of thunder shook the windows. "I mean, will you be coming back to Newbury?"

"I won't know until later. It depends…" Vincent hesitated. "Would it matter if I couldn't come back?"

"Well, of course it matters. We're friends, aren't we?" She bit her bottom lip.

"Before I go…I have to ask… Are you still going to marry that doctor guy?"

"Actually," Katherine paused as she glanced toward the window where rivulets of rain streaked down the glass. "Dr. Don and I have called off the wedding."

"Oh, I say… I hope it wasn't because of me. I mean, I…I…did pop off when I shouldn't have. I had no idea you were engaged when I asked–"

"No, you were quite chivalrous about your intentions. Our decision to call it quits wasn't because of you." *Not exactly. That was only part of it.*

"Well, that's good. So, if you're not engaged… Is there any chance we could ever be more than just friends?" Vincent sucked in his breath. Was he hoping to press an unexpected advantage?

"Let's take it a step at a time. For now, being friends is all I can promise. But, when you come back… Who knows where things might go, okay?"

By ten o'clock, the storm intensified with thunder and lightning every few minutes. Agnes pulled Maddie's bedroom door shut and peeked into the living room. Katherine had just placed another Glenn Miller record on the phonograph.

Agnes's eyes burned and her head throbbed. Tea! That's what she needed. She set the tea kettle on the stove and lit the burner. A clap of thunder crashed. The kitchen lights flickered.

The phone rang. Agnes called to Katherine in the living room. "I'll get it! Hello? Odboddy residence. If you're collecting for the needy, I've done my share…" *Like Douglas's coat, most likely gone forever, now that the warehouse is a crime scene.* She scowled into the telephone receiver.

"Mrs. Odboddy? This is Miss Magillicutty from the Newbury Police Department. I'm calling for Chief Waddlemucker. He wants you to meet him at the Newbury County Hospital as soon as possible."

Agnes raised an eyebrow, her curiosity peaked. "Tonight? Whatever for? Is someone sick?" She glanced toward the living room. *Katherine's here. Maddie's in bed, fast asleep.*

Mildred? Her heart rebelled. *Not again!* Was this another ruse to get her out on another wretched night and frame her for another crime? "What's this all about?"

"Sorry, Mrs. Odboddy. I don't have any details. Just passing along the message that you should come down to the hospital. It seems there's been an accident and..." *Buzzzz.* The phone went dead.

Agnes clicked the receiver. "Hello? Hello? *Uhh...* Thanks for nothing!" She slammed down the receiver. "Katherine? Did you hear that?"

Katherine appeared in the kitchen doorway. "How could I? Who was it?"

"Some lady said she was calling from the police department. Chief Waddlemucker wants me to come to the hospital. Then the phone went dead. What do you think? If you ask me, it sounds kind of fishy. Haven't we been down this road before?"

"What are you going to do?"

Agnes held the receiver to her ear. "I'd call the police station back if I could, but the storm must have knocked down a telephone line. Should I go down or not? I don't know what to do. I'll call Godfrey. He'll know..." Her face warmed. For a moment, she'd forgotten... She'd never seek his advice again... She cleared her throat. "Well, that dog won't hunt, will it? Can't call him if the phone is dead." *And he isn't there, anyway.*

"If you're going out on a night like this, I'm going with you," Katherine said. "I'll run over and ask Mavis to come sit with Maddie. I'll not have you running into the storm by yourself, again." Katherine grabbed an umbrella and headed out the door.

Within thirty minutes, Mavis sat by the fireplace with a cup of tea and Katherine's movie magazine while she and Agnes drove across down through the pelting rain.

Agnes pulled Ole' Nelly into the Newbury County Hospital parking lot. She held the umbrella over Katherine's head as they hurried through the glass doors of the emergency department. "I don't even know who we're supposed to ask for, once we get inside."

Agnes shook the rain from the umbrella and stamped the water off her feet while Katherine stood in the reception desk line. "Excuse me. We got a call from Chief Waddlemucker to come to the hospital. Do you have any idea where he is?"

The receptionist flipped through several papers. "You must be Agnes Odboddy. Chief Waddlemucker left a message to call him as soon as you arrived."

"No. I'm Katherine." She pointed to Agnes. "Agnes is my grandmother."

"Fine. If you'll have a seat, I'll page the chief. He's probably up on the ward with the victim."

"Who, exactly, is the victim?"

The receptionist gave her a smug smile. "We can't give out patient names unless you're a relative."

Agnes stepped up to the reception window. "Horse feathers! How are we supposed to know if we're relatives if we don't know who the victim is? *Humph!* Just let Chief Waddlemucker know we're here."

Katherine clutched Agnes's arm. "Oh, Grandma! You don't think it's Vincent or Don?"

Agnes's heart seized. *Or my friend, Mildred...* There was no point thinking the worst. They'd know soon enough. "There, there. Let's not jump to conclusions. The chief will be here any minute and explain everything." She took a deep breath to calm her quaking stomach.

Agnes took Katherine's hand and guided her to the chairs. All the while her stomach churned. Surely, Katherine was not going to lose another person close to her? Hadn't she lost enough, growing up without a father, and then losing her fiancé at Pearl Harbor? Agnes shoved the one remaining chopstick back into her bun and reflected on the words of the twenty-third Psalms. *Our Father, which art in Heaven, hallowed by thy name…*

Chief Waddlemucker ambled into the emergency room, raised his hand and waved. "You got my message. Good. Come with me."

Agnes jumped up. "Why did you bring us out on this terrible night? Who's been hurt?" Her gaze searched the chief's face for some indication. *Good news or bad?* How could being summoned to the hospital in a thunderstorm be anything but bad?

Chapter Thirty-Seven

Agnes took Katherine's hand and braced herself for what seemed like minutes, but was likely only seconds before the chief answered. "It's Godfrey. His car was found down a cliff by the ocean… I thought you'd want to know, Agnes."

Godfrey? Her head reeled. It hadn't occurred to her that it might be Godfrey. She figured he'd be hundreds of miles away by now, passing phony twenty-dollar bills left and right, headed back to a bevy of sultry senoritas in South America and gloating over his ill-gotten gains.

"So, why call me? What makes you think I give a crud muffin if that son of a biscuit-eater dies or not, after what he's done?" Her heart seized again. *Oh, please, God. I may hate his guts, but I don't want him to die!*

The chief shoved his hands in his pockets. "He's not going to die. He's been in surgery all evening. They had to set a broken collar bone and treat a head wound. He's awake now. He's refusing to answer any of my questions until he talks to you. Can you please come and see if you can get him to talk?"

Agnes closed her eyes. Never again would she allow a man to twist her heart into a pretzel and then snap it in two. This was her opportunity to tell him exactly how she felt about his lies and treachery and…and… "I'll see him." She straightened her shoulders. "I have a few things I want to say to Mr. Baumgarten. Do you want to come, or wait here, dear?"

"I'll come with you." Katherine dabbed her eyes with a hankie.

The chief, Katherine, and Agnes rode the elevator to the second floor. At room 211, Agnes tapped on the door and pushed it open.

Agnes took a deep breath and peeked inside. Godfrey lay propped against a pillow, his face pale, his eyes closed. A bandage covered his left shoulder, wrapped across his bare chest and under his right arm. Another bandage wound around his head. His cheeks were sunken with purple bruises from his left jaw to his forehead.

Agnes gasped. As angry as she was, it was hard to see him so battered and broken. She hardened her heart. Served him right, running off the ocean cliff road in the dark, the back seat of his car probably stacked high with sheets of counterfeit money. Why he had gone toward the ocean in the first place was anyone's guess. It would have made more sense to flee south, toward Santa Rosa and San Francisco. She shrugged and moved closer to the bed. "Godfrey, it's me," she whispered.

Godfrey's eyes flew open. "Agnes. My dear. Thank God. We thought we'd lost you for good. What happened? Where have you been?"

Agnes crinkled her eyebrows. *Where have I been?* Perhaps the chief hadn't told him about her escape from Homer's clutches.

Apparently, when Godfrey saw an opportunity to steal the counterfeit sheets, he lost all interest in Agnes's well-being. Now that he was caught, he had a moment to think about her welfare. She scowled and tossed her head. "*Humph!* Where have I been? Just conked in the head and tossed into a tiger cage, that's all. A better question is, where have you been, and how did you think you could get away with all that money?"

"Tiger cage? Money?" Godfrey gazed from Agnes to Chief Waddlemucker. "I don't… What is she talking about?"

The chief cleared his throat. "Okay. I've been patient enough with you, seein' as how you were hurt and all. But, it's time to answer a few questions now, bucko. What did you do with it? It wasn't in your car when we towed it off the rocks out at the ocean. You'd best come clean, Godfrey. Do you have an accomplice here in town?"

"Accomplice? Why would I…" He stared at Agnes, his face even paler than before, which hardly seemed possible. His gaze moved to Katherine. "I don't understand any of this. What is he talking about, Katherine? What does he think I've done?"

Katherine smoothed a wrinkle from his blanket. "Grandma and Chief Waddlemucker want to know where you put the counterfeit twenties you took when you went back to the warehouse."

"I didn't take…" He paused. "You mean the money's gone?" He started to chuckle and then winced as he turned to Agnes. "Oh, I get it now. And, of course, *your* first thought was that I must have gone back and then skipped town with the money." His bruised jaw twitched. He grimaced. "I suppose I can understand how you'd come to that conclusion, considering our history but…it would have been nice to think you were more concerned about me, than you were about the counterfeit bills."

He turned his head to the wall. "That was *my* first concern when you didn't come home, Agnes, but I guess it's too much to think that you'd give me the same benefit of the doubt… Why wouldn't you wonder if something bad happened to me when I didn't show up at the police station or contact you this morning?"

Agnes moved closer to the bed. "Whatever do you mean… *something bad*?"

Godfrey didn't answer. He closed his eyes, as though tuning out his visitors.

Chief Waddlemucker coughed. His face turned red as a stoplight. "We *were* looking for you. We put out an APB this morning, Godfrey. But, in all honesty, with you disappearing right after we discovered the counterfeit money gone, I'll admit I thought…I mean, we all thought… Well, you can't blame us for thinking–"

"Why don't you tell us what happened," Katherine said. "Take your time. Just tell it the way it happened."

"Yes, please do. Pray tell us, just the way it happened." Agnes could not keep the teeniest tone of *snipe* from her voice.

Godfrey leaned forward. "Would you crank up my bed a little higher, Agnes?"

The chief moved to the foot of the bed before Agnes could react. He turned the crank, as though complying with the request might in some way exonerate his behavior.

"That's far enough. Thanks, Chief." Godfrey sighed. "After we found the printing presses and you left with Katherine, I started toward Vincent's motel, like I said…"

Agnes took a deep breath. As Godfrey began to weave his tale, she became an invisible witness to the events he shared. She could see and feel each emotion, every element, hear every conversation. She sensed his fear, heard the conversations, and experienced every detail as though she was inside his head, looking out through his eyes...

Chapter Thirty-Eight

Godfrey pulled away from the warehouse, headed for Vincent's motel. By the time Chief Waddlemucker drove Katherine home, he and Vincent could inform the FBI about the warehouse with the printing presses. They'd probably get back to the police station about the same time as the chief.

But, what about Agnes? Something terrible had happened. Finding her personal belongings on the floor was a sure sign that she had been there, put up a struggle, and was taken prisoner!

He had to find her. He pressed the gas pedal and blew through a stop sign, headed for Vincent's motel. The sooner the chief got back to the station and learned who occupied the warehouse, the sooner they'd know who was responsible for snatching Agnes. His stomach wrenched at the thought of his darling in the clutches of the low-life. What would they do to keep their secret? The inevitable was almost enough to bring him to tears. Was it already too late? His fist struck the steering wheel. "I can't let it happen." His words echoed through the empty car. There must be something he could do that would be quicker than the chief searching through the county records to identify the occupant of the warehouse.

He hit the brakes. Maybe there was a phone bill or a rental agreement at the warehouse with a name on it. It would take too much time for the chief to open the Newbury City Clerk's office, locate the owner's name in the county records, and then track down the person who had Agnes.

Godfrey spun his car in a U-turn, headed back across town. As the warehouse came into view, he spotted another car and two men standing alongside Agnes's car. "What the heck?" He slammed on the brakes and flipped off the headlights. Could it be the kidnappers? Two to one…not such good odds.

He stopped at the curb and pulled his service revolver from the glovebox. Locked and loaded. Who knew how many more kidnappers were inside, but justice was on his side, and he couldn't wait for reinforcements. Agnes's life might hang in the balance. He gently eased the car door closed. Keeping to the shadows, he crept around the perimeter of the parking lot. Drops of perspiration dotted his forehead.

The thought of Agnes being tortured and murdered strengthened his resolve as he crept closer to her car. He flexed his fingers and gripped his gun.

One crook had his head under the dashboard of Agnes's Model A, tinkering with the wires, trying to hotwire the ignition, no doubt. Moving Agnes's car was a dead giveaway they were responsible for her disappearance.

The second man had entered the warehouse. Better odds. Now, one to one.

Godfrey crept closer, still without a specific plan. If he shot the man in Agnes's car, it would warn the one inside. How to proceed?

Godfrey ran the last few yards and stopped several feet from the driver's side door. "Come out of there with your hands up. FBI. You're under arrest," he muttered, keeping his voice low, lest he alert the second villain inside the warehouse.

The thug backed out of the car, started to raise his hands, and then leaned over and rammed his head into Godfrey's belly. "Flynn! Get out here, quick!" The ruffian grabbed Godfrey's arm and twisted. Surprised by the unexpected attack, Godfrey struggled, but the younger, heavier man grabbed his gun and now, had an arm around his neck in a vice grip.

The second scoundrel burst out of the warehouse.

Out-numbered, Godfrey twisted and kicked, but a well-placed fist to the side of his head dropped him to the ground. Was this why guys over sixty were retired from the FBI? Not as agile or quick-witted as he once was, he was now their captive. What a fine mess of things he'd made.

Within minutes, Godfrey's hands were bound with a light rope found by the side of the warehouse, and a rag stuffed in his mouth. "Now, what's the plan?" The young man whispered.

"I'm thinking. I just found something interesting inside. Homer's printing twenties. Wadda ya' think a' that?"

"Twenties? *Nah!* We agreed to stick to fivers. Do ya' think the old coot was double-crossing us? Printing them for hisself?"

"That's what I figger'. While we do all the dirty work for peanuts."

The man loosed his grasp on Godfrey. He slumped against the wheel of Agnes's car.

"Here's how I see it, dag-nabbit," says the older thief. "I'm passin' his bills and runnin' a merry-go-round for a bunch a' snot-nosed brats and he's settin' hisself up for life. I don't know about you, but I'm for grabbin' the twenties and skippin' this jerk-water town."

The young crook jabbed a finger toward Godfrey. "What about this one?"

The older guy gazed across the parking lot. "Go fetch his car and bring it here. We'll stash him in the trunk and dump it out at the ocean. Not likely he'll be found for a while. We'll skedaddle and be outta' the county before anyone finds his car."

"Or, before Homer finds out we've taken his money."

"Bingo!"

The two ruffians disappeared into the warehouse for a few minutes and came out with two boxes filled with counterfeit twenties.

Godfrey was tossed into the trunk of his car. He could only kick the sides of the trunk in exasperation as the crooks drove his car along the ocean, toward Boyles Springs. Frustrated by his capture and distraught that he had failed to rescue Agnes, Godfrey was near tears by the time the car pulled to the side of the cliff road and stopped.

The engine rumbled and the trunk trembled. It wasn't likely that he would live to see another day, or another hour for that matter. *I'll be standing at the pearly gates any minute now. Lord, remember me.*

Godfrey's car lurched forward, throwing him against the trunk's sidewall. He tumbled from side to side as it plunged over the cliff. It was true! Scenes from your life did flash before your eyes before you die.

First, he saw his college graduating class. In the next instant, he was at the Eiffel Tower, the weekend he and Mildred and Agnes met in 1918, while on a secret mission. Next, Agnes's frustrated face came into his thoughts, distraught over losing Douglas's coat. *Oh, Agnes. I love you!* Regrets! Regrets for things done and not done. Things said and not said.

In the next moment, pain shot through his body as the car hit the rocks and then he saw nothing…

"And, that's about it, kitten-lips. The next thing I knew, I was waking up in the hospital." Godfrey reached across the hospital bed and took Agnes's hand. "That's just how it happened."

"What?" Agnes shook her head, so engrossed in his tale, she was somewhat surprised to find herself in his hospital room and not somewhere out by the ocean in the trunk of Godfrey's car. "Oh, Godfrey. I'm so sorry." Agnes threw herself onto his bed. "I've misjudged you. I'm so sorry!"

Godfrey chuckled. "Don't worry, my dear. All's well that ends well, or I wouldn't be here telling about it now, would I?"

Agnes dabbed her eyes and gave him a wan smile. "So how did you get out of the trunk?"

Godfrey raised an eyebrow. "I'm not sure. I can't remember

a thing."

Chief Waddlemucker spoke up. "I can tell you that part. We got a call from a couple out at the beach. They were rock climbing, or bird watching or something. Since the fellow drove that road daily, he knew Godfrey's car hadn't been there the day before, so they climbed down the rocks to take a look. The trunk had sprung open a little and when the guy opened it, there was Godfrey, trussed up like a Christmas goose.

"He sent the girl back to town to call the police while he untied Godfrey and tried to make him comfortable. Long story short, we sent an ambulance and fetched him along to the hospital. He's been here most of the afternoon, having his bones put back in their sockets, getting rehydrated and regathering his wits about him."

"Why didn't you call me sooner, Chief?" Agnes squeezed Godfrey's hand.

"I called as soon as the doctor gave the all-clear for visitors. Godfrey refused to answer any of my questions until he spoke to you."

Agnes's lip trembled. "How can you ever forgive me for doubting you? I'm so sorry. I thought you'd stolen the money and abandoned me…again."

"There's nothing to forgive, lambkins. We all make mistakes, me included. What made me think I could take on those crooks alone? Trust me, from now on, I'm hanging up my six-shooter and leaving the hooligans to the police."

"We'll take care of things, don't you worry." The chief headed for the door. "Homer and his wife are already in custody. We're on the look-out for the two thugs that took the money and 'skedaddled', as you so aptly phrased it, Godfrey. I suspect we'll have rounded up everyone who had a hand in the counterfeiting ring by morning"

Agnes planted a kiss square on Godfrey's mouth. "And, I'll take care of my man until he's better."

"Your man?" Katherine snickered.

"That's what I said. And mark my words. I'm not letting him out of my sight again."

Chapter Thirty-Nine

Agnes gazed at her family, seated at the kitchen table. Her heart warmed at the sight of Katherine, her hair rolled up in curlers, flipping a pancake and Maddie, pouring honey over her short stack.

It was good to be home again and have everything back to normal. The icebox hummed. The coffee pot gurgled. Ling-Ling's little pink tongue made clicking sounds as it shot in and out of her bowl of milk. All the comfortable sounds of home.

Katherine scooped another pancake from the frying pan. "I'll have your breakfast in a minute."

Everything was right with the world once more. Last night's storm had cleared and the sun blazed through the kitchen window, symbolic of last night's events, starting off so woefully and ending in the joyous realization that Godfrey was innocent and would soon be out of the hospital and back in their midst.

Agnes sighed. Then, what explained the hollow feeling in the pit of her stomach? When had it become more desirable to start the day with worry rather than in thanksgiving? She was just being a silly old woman. She could bake some cookies and take them to Godfrey. Maybe she'd call and see if Mildred wanted to play cards. "Who was on the phone before, while I was getting dressed?"

Katherine turned to Agnes. "It was Chief Waddlemucker. He said they arrested the carnival owner. Seems he was working with Homer, passing the counterfeit money through all the towns where they performed. The chief says the state has yanked their license and the carnival has closed for good."

Maddie set her glass of milk down with a bang, and glanced anxiously toward Agnes. Her lips quivered. "What will happen to Shere Khan if the carnival is closed?"

Agnes bit her lip. "I…I don't know." What do you do with a full-grown tiger when the country's at war, meat is scare and zoos were hard pressed to care for the tigers they had, much less inclined to take on another one displaced from a carnival? Wasn't it more likely the animal would be destroyed for lack of a suitable placement? She stared at her plate, hoping Maddie would not realize the extent of the threat to her feline friend. Now, it seemed, the tentacles of war had touched even innocent animals.

Katherine turned off the stove burner and pulled out a chair. "I've read that zoos are shutting down all over the United States." She glanced at Maddie. "This is terrible. We can't let anything happen to Shere Khan. Not after what you've been through."

Tears welled in Maddie's eyes. "Can't you save him, Grandma?"

What could I do? Who wants a tiger? Agnes closed her eyes for a moment, and then she smiled, as though she had solved a ten-letter word in a crossword puzzle. "Don't worry your pretty head about it, Maddie. Grandma has a plan." She stood and paced the kitchen, waving her hands as she spoke.

"Suppose we call the ladies at The First Church of the Evening Star and Everlasting Light and let them know how much the tiger means to us. We'll make him the church mascot and start a community project to *Save the Tiger*. Yes, that's what we'll do. Considering my history with Shere Khan, I'm the best person to lead such a campaign, right?"

Katherine raised her eyebrows. "But, Grandma. Don't you think–"

Agnes turned at the icebox and paced back. "First, we need a place to park his wagon, and—"

Maddie clapped in delight. "Would Mr. Higgenbottom take him?

With our chickens."

"That's a grand idea," Agnes said. "I'm sure Mildred could convince her brother. His wagon wouldn't take up much room."

"Wait a minute." Katherine tapped the table. "I don't think that Mrs. Higgenbottom wants—"

"And, we'll need enough money to feed him until—"

"Could you use the money the mayor gave you?" Maddie said.

"The reward for locating the counterfeiters! Even after I replace the war bond money, there should be some left. Maybe we'll even find Douglas's coat… There should be enough to feed the tiger for a while–until we can find him a permanent home."

Katherine shook her head. "Someone has to feed him and clean his cage."

Agnes snapped her fingers. "If the young man who let me out of the cage wasn't involved with the counterfeiting, maybe Mr. Higgenbottom would agree to let him work at the farm for room and board. He could take care of Shere Khan."

"Oh, Grandma. I doubt if–"

"I'm sure the church ladies will help me start a letter campaign to all the zoos in the country until we locate one that agrees to take Shere Khan."

Katherine wrung her hands. "I should think that you've had enough of that tiger. Wouldn't it be nice to just relax for a while? Do you really need to jump into another big project like this?"

"Now, Katherine. You know me better than that. Godfrey is getting better, and he'll be home soon, bless his heart. I'm off the hook for the Wilkey's Market burglary. Homer and his cohorts are behind bars. With everything resolved, what would I do to keep busy? I can't bake cookies or collect cans every day." A grin lit up her face.

"Don't you see? The world is at war, and I can't do one thing to change that. I can't feed and clothe every refugee. I can't stop Hitler's insane march across Europe. I could knit socks for 365 days a year, and it wouldn't make a bit of difference."

"But, Grandma–

"Oh, Katherine! Think about it. We've done everything in our power to be hometown patriots, to fight the war from the home front and nothing we did changed a thing…and then there was a tiger."

More information regarding WWII issues discussed in this novel

Presidential Order re Japanese Internment Camps:

On March 21, 1942, Roosevelt signed Public Law 503 (approved after only an hour of discussion in the Senate and thirty minutes in the House) in order to provide for the enforcement of his executive order. It implemented the incarceration of Japanese Americans along the West Coast of California and Washington.

As a result, approximately 120,000 Japanese-Americans, men, women, and children of Japanese ancestry were evicted from the West Coast and held in American internment camps and other confinement sites across the country. *For more information, see below.*

https://en.wikipedia.org/wiki/Executive_Order_9066

Rationing in the USA:

Food was in short supply because much of the processed and canned foods was reserved for our military and our Allies. Because of these shortages, the government's Office of Price Administration established a system of rationing foods and goods in short supply. Every American was issued a series of ration books. A person could not buy a rationed item without also providing a ration stamp. Ration books contained stamps good for certain rationed items, like sugar, meat, cooking oil, and canned goods.

Due to gasoline and tire rationing, the transportation of fresh foods was limited. Priority was given to transporting soldiers and war supplies instead of food.

Some products such as coffee and sugar were limited due to restrictions on importing as well as difficulties transporting goods from other countries. *For more information, see below.*

https://www.nationalww2museum.org/students-teachers/student-resources/research-starters/take-closer-look-ration-books

Savings Bonds and stamps

Savings bonds were sold to finance the war effort and sold for $18.75. Upon maturity in ten years, it paid $25. The $6.25 difference was interest. Various other denomination stamps were also available. Low income Americans rarely had $18.75 in their pockets with which to purchase a government bond. But they often had loose change and could purchase a 10 cent or 25 cent stamp which could be pasted into a book. Buying 75 such 25 cent stamps entitled them to a $25 savings bond. ($18.75) *For more information, see below.*

http://www.moaf.org/exhibits/checks_balances/Franklin-roosevelt/war-bond-stamp-book

About the Author

Elaine Faber is a member of Sisters in Crime, Cat Writers Association, and Northern California Publishers and Authors. She lives in Northern California with her husband and two housecats. She volunteers at the American Cancer Society Discovery Shop in Elk Grove, CA.

Elaine has written poetry and short stories since childhood. She has published six novels and a book of short 'cat' stories. Multiple short stories are published in magazines, on-line weekly magazines and in thirteen short story collections (anthologies). She writes a series of cozy cat mysteries, and humorous WWII mystery/adventures.

Black Cat Mysteries: The three Black Cat Mysteries noted below, feature Thumper, (Black Cat). With the aid of his ancestors' memories, he helps solve mysteries and crimes.

Mrs. Odboddy Mystery/Adventures: Elderly, eccentric Mrs. Odboddy fights WWII from the home front. She believes war-time conspiracies and spies abound in her home town. Follow her antics as a self-appointed hometown warrior, she roots out and exposes malcontents, dissidents and Nazi spies.

Black Cat's Legacy ~ http://tinyurl.com/lrvevgm
Black Cat and the Lethal Lawyer ~ http://tinyurl.com/q3qrgyu
Black Cat and the Accidental Angel ~ http://tinyurl.com/07zscm2
Black Cat and the Keys to the Treasure ~ (work in progress)
All Things Cat (short stories) ~ http://tinyurl.com/y9p9htak
Mrs. Odboddy – Hometown Patriot ~ http://tinyurl.com/hdbvzsv
Mrs. Odboddy – Undercover Courier ~ http://tinyurl/com/jn5bzwb
Mrs. Odboddy – And Then There Was a Tiger
Elaine's Website – http://www.mindcandymysteries.com
Email your questions or comments to:
Elaine.Faber@mindcandymysteries.com.
Amazon reviews are welcomed and encouraged.

Also by Elaine Faber

Mrs. Odboddy: Hometown Patriot

A WWII tale of chicks and chicanery, suspicion and spies.

Since the onset of WWII, Agnes Agatha Odboddy, hometown patriot and self-appointed scourge of the underworld, suspects conspiracies around every corner…stolen ration books, German spies running amuck, and a possible Japanese invasion off the California coast. This seventy-year-old, model citizen would set the world aright if she could get Chief Waddlemucker to pay attention to the town's nefarious deeds on any given Meatless Monday.

Mrs. Odboddy vows to bring the villains, both foreign and domestic, to justice, all while keeping chickens in her bathroom, working at the Ration Stamp Office, and knitting argyles for the boys on the front lines.

Imagine the chaos when Agnes's long-lost WWI lover returns, hoping to find a million dollars in missing Hawaiian money and rekindle their ancient romance. In the thrilling conclusion, Agnes's predictions become all too real when Mrs. Roosevelt unexpectedly comes to town to attend a funeral and Agnes must prove that she is, indeed, a warrior on the home front.

Mrs. Odboddy: Undercover Courier

Asked to accompany Mrs. Roosevelt on her Pacific Island tour, Agnes and Katherine travel by train to Washington, D.C. Agnes carries a package for Colonel Farthingworth to President Roosevelt.

Convinced the package contains secret war documents, Agnes expects Nazi spies to try and derail her mission.

She meets Irving, whose wife mysteriously disappears from the train; Nanny, the unfeeling caregiver to little Madeline; two soldiers bound for training as Tuskegee airmen; and Charles, the shell-shocked veteran, who lends an unexpected helping hand. Who will Agnes trust? Who is the Nazi spy?

When enemy forces make a final attempt to steal the package in Washington, D.C., Agnes must accept her own vulnerability as a warrior on the home front.

Can Agnes overcome multiple obstacles, deliver the package to the President, and still meet Mrs. Roosevelt's plane before she leaves for the Pacific Islands?

Mrs. Odboddy: Undercover Courier is a hysterical frolic on a train across the United States during WWII, as Agnes embarks on this critical mission.

A WWII tale of mystery, mischief, and mishaps.

Black Cat's Legacy

Thumper, the resident Fern Lake black cat, knows where the bodies are buried and it's up to Kimberlee to decode the clues.

Kimberlee's arrival at the Fern Lake lodge triggers the Black Cat's Legacy. With the aid of his ancestors' memories, it's Thumper's duty to guide Kimberlee to clues that can help solve her father's cold case murder. She joins forces with a local homicide detective and an author, also researching the murder for his next thriller novel. As the investigation ensues, Kimberlee learns more than she wants to know about her father. The murder suspects multiply, some dead and some still very much alive, but someone at the lodge will stop at nothing to hide the Fern Lake mysteries.

Cover photo *Boot's Eyes*: © Elaine Faber

Black Cat and the Lethal Lawyer

With the promise to name a beneficiary to her multi-million dollar horse ranch, Kimberlee's grandmother entices her and her family to Texas. But things are not as they appear and Thumper, the black cat with superior intellect, uncovers the appalling reason for the invitation. Kimberlee and Brett discover a fake Children's Benefit Program and the possible false identity of the stable master. To make matters worse, Thumper overhears a murder plot, and he and his newly found soul-mate, Noe-Noe, must do battle with a killer to save Grandmother's life.

The further Kimberlee and her family delve into things, the deeper they are thrust into a web of embezzlement, greed, vicious lies and murder. With the aid of his ancestors' memories, Thumper unravels some dark mysteries. Is it best to reveal the past or should some secrets never be told?

Cover photo *lawyer with cat* © CURAphotography,shutterstock.com image 19277278

Black Cat and the Accidental Angel

When the family SUV flips and Kimberlee is rushed to the hospital, Black Cat (Thumper) and his soulmate are left behind. Black Cat loses all memory of his former life and the identity of the lovely feline companion by his side. "Call me Angel. I'm here to take care of you." Her words set them on a long journey toward home, and life brings them face to face with episodes of joy and sorrow.

The two cats are taken in by John and his young daughter, Cindy, facing foreclosure of the family vineyard and emu farm. In addition, someone is playing increasingly dangerous pranks that threaten Cindy's safety. Angel makes it her mission to help their new family. She puts her life at risk to protect the child, and Black Cat learns there are more important things than knowing your real name.

Elaine Faber's e-books are available on Amazon for $3.99. Print books. $16.00.

Cover photo *Black and White Cat*: © vivienstock, http://us.fotolia.com/id/46333972 (halo added)

All Things Cat

"A story isn't a story if there isn't a cat in it." Elaine Faber

All Things Cat is a selection of Elaine Faber's short stories about cats. Their stories take place both past and present in diverse surroundings: Salem, Massachusetts; a pirate ship off the coast of Maine; a haunted hotel in the Sierra Mountains; Roswell, New Mexico; the oval office in Washington, D.C., to name but a few locations.

The felines interact with extraordinary and remarkable characters including witches, leprechauns, a sewer truck driver, a hen-pecked husband driven to plot murder, and animal characters present at the birth of the Christ Child.

Some stories are self-narrated by a cat sharing most unusual circumstances—abandoned by his master, as the prize in an Old West poker game, routing a burglar in a WWII meat market, overcoming self-doubts about his hunting/stalking abilities, and adopting the First Family in the White House.

All Things Cat will delight the reader and provide a sneak peek into the heart and mind of cats from all walks of life. Elaine has brought both wit and tenderness to this charming collection of short cat stories. Several stories are excerpts from Elaine's full length cozy Black Cat Mysteries series and WWII novel, Mrs. Odboddy - Hometown Patriot.

Cover photo *Truffie* © Elaine Faber